THE SILENT GUARDIAN

Dylan Callens

Cosmic Teapot Publishing

Published by Cosmic Teapot Publishing
Hanmer, ON, Canada
www.cosmicteapot.net

Ordering Information:
Quantity sales. Special discounts are available on quantity purchases by corporations, associations, and others. For details, contact the publisher at the email address above.

In loving memory of my sister, Crystal Callens.

A hero is someone who, in spite of weakness, doubt, or not always knowing the answers, goes ahead and overcomes anyway.

CHRISTOPHER REEVE

CONTENTS

ONE

As a child, I didn't choose silence. My family and entire community lived by the oath. The Renegades wove it into the fabric of our lives: silence, obedience, and discipline. Before I turned thirteen, I doubt I had ever heard a voice from a living person. We were taught language through audio recordings. Among ourselves, we communicated using a unique sign language known only to handful of people around the world.

At the time, I believed we were the *real* Phylax. That the commune was the heart of our order. I didn't learn until later that we were an instrument for someone else's nefarious purpose.

One day, our priest signed to me, asking what I liked best about being a Phylax. I paused, fingers hovering mid-air before signing, *I like how it feels to be part of something special, something greater than myself.*

He nodded in agreement, a smile on his lips. Then he asked me how I felt about the silence.

I hesitated longer this time, fingers trembling. How could I explain it? Eventually, I signed, *Sometimes, I find it hard to understand why it's necessary.*

His reaction caught me off guard. He spoke to me in English, his voice shattering our oath. "Sometimes, I don't understand it either."

Blood flushed my cheeks. A priest of the order—one of the revered few—had spoken aloud. I had always assumed their vow was more profound than ours, that they were above such transgressions. Yet here he was, breaking the vow as quickly as one might break bread.

He must have noticed my surprise because he quickly added, "It's okay to speak to me in this building. It's different here." Still, I pressed my lips together, shaking my head. They etched the oath into my very being. It was too sacred to be broken so casually.

Over the next several weeks, the priest would seize any quiet moment to ask me questions aloud. Each time, I lowered my gaze, responding in signs. I clung to the rules drilled into me since childhood.

It was close to a month later when the priest asked, "Is your father good to you?"

The question made me tense up, my hands freezing mid-sign. Unbidden images of my father's clenched fists and the sting of his belt surged to the surface.

The priest's expression softened. "Oh. Is it

that bad?"

I could still feel the sting of new wounds along my back, raw from three nights earlier. The humiliation was fresher than the lacerations themselves. My vision blurred as tears welled up; for once, I couldn't hold them back.

The priest gasped as he noticed my wet cheeks. He stepped forward, wrapping me in a hug. "How bad is it, my son?" he whispered.

The word *son* hit me hardest. It was a word I had longed to know in a tone filled with love, not anger. I choked a sound that startled me as much as it did him. Through broken sobs, I croaked, "It's bad."

The priest glanced toward the two guards at the door, a crooked smile twisting his lips. "Not nearly as bad as it's about to get."

I didn't grasp what was happening until it was too late. The priest stepped aside. Suddenly, a punch connected with my stomach. The air rushed out of my lungs as I collapsed to my knees. Before I could catch my breath, the second guard's fist struck my temple. White-hot pain exploded behind my eyes. I sunk further to the ground. Instinctively, I clutched the branding scar on my arm.

Tears blurred my vision. "Please," I gasped, desperation gripping my throat. "Please stop," I whimpered.

Dazed, I saw my mother approaching. Relief flooded through me—surely she would stop this.

Wouldn't she?

"Help me," I pleaded, my voice cracking.

Except, I saw her share a laugh with the priest. My chest tightened; betrayal washed over me like icy water. She wasn't here to save me. She was part of this, a willing participant in my torment.

Another blow landed, this time against my ribs. I heard a sickening crack as sparks danced behind my eyelids. Through the haze of pain, I looked at my mother again, desperately hoping she would intervene. She didn't. She stood there, still laughing, while my world dissolved into betrayal.

A final strike to my head briefly plunged me into darkness. When I awakened, a blur of motion caught my attention—a man rushing toward us. Later, I learned that his name was Philip.

Philip swept a guard's legs out from under him, then swiftly snapped his neck. The other guard turned, but Philip was faster, striking before the man could react. The priest cowered in the corner as Philip advanced. My vision faded again before I could see what happened next.

My consciousness flickered in and out. I remember brief, disjointed images—the guards lying motionless on the floor, the sensation of being lifted, the cool air outside the church. Then, nothing.

Only later did I learn the truth: these were

Renegades, not the Phylax at all. Their so-called *Temptation* was meant to break me. Without Philip and the genuine Phylax's help, I would have perished at their hands.

That feels so long ago. Decades have passed. I am no longer that helpless little boy.

TWO

Tonight, my mission reaches its culmination. For the past two years I have waited, observed, and blended into the darkness. I finally have the opportunity to kill the Emperor of China, Qin Shi Huang.

The Phylax's information is infallible. Qin has been traveling across China for months, just as they said he would, inspecting his empire—but the inspections are only a pretense. Beneath the façade of governance, he pursues something far more elusive: immortality. His alchemists whisper of a substance that will grant him eternal life. He chases these promises like a dying man gasping for air. He has sent envoys to the mountains, seas, and the ends of the known world in search of it. They return with formulas laced with mercury, and still, he drinks.

Soon, he will rest in this yurt, far from the security of the imperial palace. The countryside hides him, his presence unnoticed by ordinary people; however, I know why he is here. Another rumor of alchemical wisdom has drawn him to this place. His scholars claim that the key to eternity lies hidden somewhere nearby.

Qin Shi Huang believes he can command the universe itself. He has reshaped China to suit his will. Yet, time is not a kingdom to be conquered. No matter how tightly one tries to grip it, it cannot be tamed. Not even the Phylax have the power to curb time to become immortal.

The yurt is modest for a man of his power. These journeys demand discretion, not grandeur. His usual contingent of guards is smaller than usual. I know that once he enters the yurt, the guards will be out of earshot. The stillness of the night has lulled them into complacency—a perfect opportunity. No one expects an assassin to strike here, in this forgotten corner of the empire.

It's strange how the years of planning feel like the tricky part. Killing the emperor is almost a relief after years spent in obscurity, mastering ancient China's culture, customs, and language.

I hold up the knife in my hands. It is a custom-forged jian dagger—my favorite weapon from this period. The firelight dances along the iron, and for a moment, I catch my reflection in the metal. Three asymmetrical scars cut across my cheek, each one a story I no longer bother to tell. My face in the blade looks older than I remember—hardened, worn thin by too many years of silence and violence. The firelight catches the hollows beneath my eyes, the tightness in my jaw, and the way my expression never quite lets its guard down. I think about how rare this used to be, to see yourself so clearly. For most of human history, a reflection was something caught in passing—glimpsed in still water, never fixed, never certain. Most people wouldn't have truly recognized their own face. What a strange feeling that must have been—to go through life only half-known to yourself.

Once Qin is dead, the real challenge begins. Five thousand miles. That's the distance between here and the Sanctum at the Acropolis, the Phylax headquarters. Five thousand miles of the most challenging terrain imaginable. I must make the journey alone.

If I can find horses or camels along the way, it will ease the burden—at least a little. However, horses are scarce, especially when crossing regions plagued by bandits, hostile tribes, and unforgiving deserts. The bureaucratic checkpoints and constant suspicion from local authorities make every move feel monitored.

Traveling with a caravan would be safer. Unfortunately, that's against Philip's rules. I'm sure he didn't create them, but in my mind, they've always been his. Following the rules is part of the discipline he instilled in me, even though I haven't seen him in over fifteen years.

Silence is a privilege; dealing with others is true loneliness. Regardless, what I do—what the Phylax does—is a calling far beyond the trivial need for companionship. Without us, there will be nothing left of humankind in the future.

The fabric of the yurt rustles as Qin steps inside, the heavy tent flap falling behind him with a muffled thud. A dim lantern glows, casting long shadows across the room—shadows where I remain concealed. His gait is uneven. From here, the potent stench of jiu—the rice wine flowing freely during his tours—reaches me. It's thick on his breath. His ordinarily sharp focus dulled by the haze of drink.

He moves with arrogant carelessness. He believes no one would dare cross him, even in this remote tent with only a few guards stationed elsewhere in his camp. That arrogance is his downfall. He doesn't see me crouched in the murk, tracking his every move.

The knife rests in my palm as I inch forward, stealthy as the night outside. My plan is simple: make it appear that one of Qin's guards betrayed him with a clean cut across his throat. No one will question the death of a man who ruled by fear.

I move with precision, angling my steps to position myself behind him. As I'm about to strike, my movement catches his awareness. He spins around faster than I can anticipate. His arm shoots up to block my blow at the last instant. The blade glances off his forearm, drawing blood—but not enough to stop him.

A primal yell tears from his throat as he

stumbles back, calling for his guards. "Dù wèi!" Fear strangles his voice.

Even as Qin's yell fills the small space, I remain calm. No panic, no fear—I know the guards are too far away to hear him. It's all in the operational synopsis. They're stationed farther down the encampment, well beyond where his voice can reach, at least for the next few moments. The Phylax always ensures these details—timing, distance, vulnerabilities. I trust their information with complete conviction, even more so when Qin stumbles backward, clutching his wounded arm.

I move swiftly, refusing to give him time to recover. A second knife slips into my fingers. It is a comforting weight. My movements are fluid, honed by years of training. I dart forward, closing the distance quickly.

I strike again before Qin can react. The first blade slashes into his other arm, cutting deep into muscle. He lets out a strangled gasp, fear spreading across his face. I don't stop. I drive the second knife into his chest. Circling him, I pull him tightly against me—one hand clamps over his mouth to muffle any further cries.

Before his strength fades, Qin musters one final act of defiance. His fingers claw desperately at the air, searching for something—anything—to aid him. His hand stretches outward, trembling as it finds a thin string hidden against the fabric of the tent. He grips it, pulling hard before I can grasp what he's doing. The realization hits me too late—the string must be connected to a bell in the guards' tent. A signal to bring them running.

I yank him back, away from the alarm, holding him as his body weakens. When he finally goes limp, I release him, letting him slump to the floor. I retrieve my knives and pause.

This cannot be happening. The Phylax never make mistakes. They are meticulous; their information is always precise. Every detail of the mission was laid out perfectly, down to the tiniest feature of Qin's encampment. The layout of the yurt, the guards' positions, and the weapons they carry—all ingrained in my mind during two years of preparation. There was no mention of a signal string. Not a word about hidden alarms.

I try to push the doubt away. *No one will come through the door*, I tell myself. *I'm safe.*

Even as I cling to the thought, I can hear the guards approaching.

I listen closely, relieved to hear only two sets of footsteps approaching. My muscles tense, and my awareness sharpens as I prepare for the fight.

As the first guard bursts through the entrance, I hurl a knife. It slices through the air, embedding itself deep into his eye. He collapses without a sound, dead before he hits the ground.

The second guard is quicker. He takes

in the scene instantly, charging at me with fierce determination. His speed catches me unprepared; his sword pierces my side before I can evade. Searing pain explodes through my body, much like the branding iron that scarred my arm so many years ago.

Instinct takes over. I lash out, my knife arcing upward in a desperate swing. By sheer luck—or perhaps fate—the blade slices into his neck, cutting deep. A sickening gurgle escapes his lips as blood spurts from the wound. He staggers, then crumbles to the floor.

I collapse beside him, the agony in my side making it impossible to stand. I lie there, struggling for oxygen. Darkness creeps in at the edges of my vision. The pain is overwhelming, each heartbeat sending a fresh wave of fire through my body. I press a trembling hand to my wound; the blood is warm, seeping between my fingers. Fortunately, my lungs are not punctured.

I ask myself, what would Philip do? Consumed by a vision in my mind's eye, I see his spirit hover over me. He aggressively signs, *Move! Move! Move!*

I know he's right. Gritting my teeth against the nausea threatening to overtake me, I force myself to my feet. Every movement is agony; I've never felt so terrible. I stagger out of the tent, each step a monumental effort.

The camp outside is eerily calm, drenched in the sanguine glow of moonlight. The tents are soundless sentinels, oblivious to the upheaval within. No one here yet knows that the man who unified this mighty nation is dead or that I have irrevocably altered the fate of their society. I did it without knowing why, except that it is for the betterment of all humankind. Without me, without the Phylax, everyone is doomed.

I fix my gaze westward. I've rehearsed this occasion countless times. It's a trip I must endure primarily by foot through harsh deserts filled with bandits. It will last several months. Thankfully, that preparation guides me now, cutting through the haze of pain. All I have to do is stay focused and avoid the patrols. It's a small sentry detail tonight—manageable if I remain cautious.

With what little strength I have left, I slip past the lone guard I spot. Clutching my side, I take the first few steps into the cold sand. I look back once. When I do, I am sure the soldier stares back at me. I wait to see if he alerts others. To my relief, he doesn't. He simply watches me. I think he gives a subtle wave. I don't question this unexpected mercy. Fire reflects off his eerily blackened armor before I turn and continue into the cold. The chill pierces my skin.

A small town lies a few miles away. *I can make it. I have to make it.* I repeat the mantra. Each step is a victory, each exhalation a defiance of the pain threatening to consume me. The expanse envelops me. I continue, one foot in front of the other.

With fidelity, we protect humankind.

THREE

I dream of a clearing at dusk, the sky above bruised with deep purples. The air carries a restless hush, as if the world is holding back before a violent war. In the center of the clearing, a boy stands beside a towering stone figure, his small arms wrapped tightly around it, clinging to its safety. A short distance away, a slender figure—child-sized—clutches the hand of a tall presence hidden in shifting shadows. Their features blur in the dim, flickering light.

Out of the swirling twilight, two violent gusts of wind tear into the stone figure. The boy reels backward. Fractures spider across the statue's surface. A roar rips through the silence. The statue explodes, stone fragments hurtling across the clearing. The boy stumbles, disoriented. At his feet, where the statue once stood, a deep crimson stain spreads into the soil, blooming outward.

Before the boy can reach out, one of the raging winds coils around him like a vine. He catches a glimpse of the shadow-cloaked figure and the child silhouette clinging to it—far away, safe from the storm. He is torn from the clearing. The wind howls in his ears, and the lamplight is lost beneath the swirling dark as he's carried off into oblivion.

This scene jolts me awake. It's the same dream every time, haunting me with its vivid detail. I can't escape it and don't know what it means.

Shaking off the nightmare, I awaken to an unfamiliar place. The room is dim, illuminated by gray light through a small window. Wooden beams crisscross above me. Uneven rammed-earth forms the walls. A fire crackles nearby.

A woven mat rests beneath me, and a thin blanket drapes over my aching body. I try to move. A sharp pain shoots through my side, making me wince. My hand moves to my ribs, feeling the rough bandages around my torso. My head feels heavy, with a dull throb at the base of my skull. I squeeze my eyelids shut. My body is forced into stillness, but my mind refuses to be.

Qin's scholars believed time moves in cycles. Life, death, war, peace—each one a season. The ancient Chinese see history as a wheel. Empires rise then crumble, only to rise again under different names. A farmer plants his crops, harvests them, and watches the fields wither, knowing the cycle will begin again. Even the stars above follow this pattern, shifting in predictable rhythms, like a breath the universe takes over centuries.

I am no different than the farmer or the stars. My life follows a cycle, too. Death and war—the part where I hunt and kill. Life and peace are the parts where I return to Athens, the only place that remains unchanged between missions. Over and over again, my purpose resets. Different enemies, different places, but always the same rhythm.

I have no choice but to wait, which isn't in my training. The last thing I remember is stumbling away from Qin's encampment. My body screamed in pain as I wandered into the barrens. I recall the agony of each step, the sand shifting beneath my feet as I pushed forward. Did I reach the nearby town? I must have, but my memory is no clearer than sand in a windstorm.

A woman approaches. She's slight and composed. Her size doesn't match the force with which she moves. Her long dark hair falls loosely over one shoulder. There's a faint scar below her left eye, shaped like an exclamation mark.

Her steps are purposeful. She kneels beside me, examining my wounded torso. "You're lucky," she says in Chinese. "If the blade had gone any deeper, it would have punctured your lung. You'd be dead right now. I had to stitch you up, so you'll need time to heal." She looks at me expectantly. "How do you feel?"

Lucky? The word mocks me. There is no luck

for me, especially not in this unknown place. I cannot move without pain flaring through my side.

I try to piece together who she might be. There's something off about how she speaks— the rhythm of her words or perhaps a faint accent that doesn't quite match this time or place. The answer is out of reach.

She tilts her head, studying me with a curious smile. "Not much of a talker, are you?" she asks, almost amused. I acknowledge her question with a simple motion.

"Maybe that's for the best," she says. "My name is Xia. Lucky for you, I'm a healer. It's why you're still breathing. You're welcome." Her tone carries a hint of sarcasm.

My nod is barely perceptible. I'm too exhausted to do more than that. When she leaves the room, it barely registers, just the fading sound of footsteps.

Philip would be disappointed. I can see him signing the relevant commandments to me:

Trust the silence.
Always work alone.
Trust no one outside the Phylax.
Always leave an escape route.
Get back to the Acropolis before the three-year window is over.
Eliminate witnesses when necessary.

Does Xia count as a witness? If so, the rules

are clear.

If Philip were here now, he'd remind me that survival is a solitary endeavor. My mission should never rely on anyone's hands but my own. He'd say I let my guard down and was foolish to allow this injury. Most of all, I should have planned for every possibility. His voice lingers in my head, even as I prepare for what's next.

I'm not excited to go to the Acropolis, where I will debrief with the Council of the Phylax. The Archon will likely be present. He deserves better than what I've done on this mission.

The Sanctum at the Acropolis is a hidden marvel. It is the greatest wonder of the world; however, very few people know it exists. Every time I see it, I can hardly process its grandeur. It is unlike the impressive temples or monuments people think of when discussing wonders. It's something more profound. The Phylax's history alone fills every stone with ancient secrets.

The entrance hides itself from all except those who know exactly where to look. At its heart is the central ceremonial room, a masterpiece that outshines any ancient temple. The perfectly circular room has braziers lining its edges, casting warm light across the ornate walls.

Gold and silver inlays form the Mark of the Phylax, a two-headed snake coiling toward the loop of infinity. The heads don't touch. Instead, a pathway reaches, connecting the serpent like a bridge through time. The Mark of the Phylax is a symbol of power. They sear it into our flesh as a lifelong reminder of our oath. It adorns our most sacred buildings. We carve simple versions into safe houses to signal that a location is secure. The Mark of the Phylax is our guiding light.

Elaborate murals depicting triumph, sacrifice, and the embodiment of time line the walls between the braziers. The floor is polished green marble with streaks of gold. I believe it holds secrets of its own. Stone steps engraved with ancient text, which translates to *With Fidelity, We Protect Humankind,* leads to a platform. The most sacred rituals take place there. The room is a beauty meant to impress upon those who enter that they are part of something far more significant than themselves.

After each mission, when I returned to the Sanctum, the Phylax expressed appreciation for my efficiency. They studied every detail of my work—every clean cut, every perfectly timed action. *Impressive*, they signed with approval. *You're doing a remarkable job, Adam.*

That praise fueled me. I have always wanted to be a legend and see my image immortalized on a mural in the Sanctum. This desire was an unending hunger I could not ignore. I trained harder, moved quicker, and followed their instructions to the letter. Rising through the ranks was all that mattered, so I sacrificed.

As I lie here, struggling to inhale, I think

about what will happen when I revisit the place I love. This time, there will be no praise. I'll have to beg for forgiveness. Even then, I'm not sure they'll let me live. They won't appreciate how sloppy my work was and how I failed in the most essential ways. The thought is a poison that churns my stomach. They hate mistakes, even if I did kill my target.

Yet something else creeps into my periphery, unsettling me more than the prospect of their judgment: the Phylax made their own mistake. The report they gave me on Qin was wrong. Why? They never slip up. They are supposed to research every detail meticulously. The fact that there was a vital error raises questions I can't afford to ignore. Did they overlook it? Or is there something more I'm not seeing?

I hear footsteps rustle outside the room. The door creaks open. Xia enters, carrying a bowl of water and a cloth.

"You're awake," she says, kneeling beside me. "Good. How are you feeling?"

I raise a thumb in response. Xia watches, a frown forming as she notices my gesture.

"Oh yes, you don't talk. Can you write?"

I hesitate. Do I want to communicate with this woman? She might have answers, or she could be a threat. I decide to nod.

"Good," she says. "I will find parchment and ink in a bit."

She places the bowl on a nearby stool. "You

are from the west," she remarks. "You'll scare people if you go outside looking this way." She gestures vaguely toward me. "Qin's soldiers execute anyone from the west. You'll need to do something about your appearance to blend in."

I acknowledge that she's right. I have spent two years here learning about their customs. Camouflage hasn't been easy. My pale skin betrays me in daylight. I cloak myself as much as possible, avoiding unwanted attention. Skirting the edges of towns, traveling at odd hours—yet curious glances follow me.

Xia watches me a moment longer. "It doesn't matter right now," she says dismissively. "You're too injured to travel." She gestures for me to sit up. "I need to check your wound."

Bracing myself, I sit up from the mat. My side throbs so much that my vision blurs for a second. She moves closer, waiting until I settle before she begins.

Her fingers are surprisingly gentle as she removes the old bandages, caked in dried blood. With expertise, she unwinds the layers in smooth, fluid motions. A furrow of concentration creases her brow, focused intently on the task.

She wrings out the cloth, water rhythmically dripping back into the bowl. "This might sting," she murmurs, her voice carrying a melodic tone uncommon in this region. The warning does little to prepare me. She dabs the damp cloth against the wound.

Pain shoots through me. I wheeze, muscles tensing involuntarily. The agony catapults me back to when I was ten—sprawled on the cold ground as my father's fists rained down, each blow carving a mark into my skin and soul. The memory surges forward: ribs cracking under his heel, skin splitting with sharp stings, hot tears welling but never spilling. His anger was a relentless storm in which the Renegades trapped me.

The room blurs as the present collides with the past. Xia's gentle touch anchors me, returning me to the moment. She might sense the turmoil swirling inside me.

"Sorry," she says softly, not pausing in her work. "It has to be done." She dips the cloth again, continuing with methodical care.

I clench my jaw, forcing myself to stay in the now. I don't enjoy revisiting that part of my past, though I've survived worse. Yet, the ghost of those beatings remains a phantom that refuses to fade.

Xia leans back, inspecting the stitches. "It's not my best work," she admits, lips drawn into a thin line. "It's holding. You're lucky you didn't tear it open, thrashing around in your sleep."

Lucky. There's that word again. I look down at the rows of thread running along the gash in my side. It's not pretty, but it is functional. The stitches are tight enough to keep the wound closed. I feel an odd mix of gratitude and frustration; I hate being dependent on anyone. I can't deny Xia has kept me alive. I might not be so fortunate when I reach the Sanctum.

She grabs a fresh roll of bandages, wrapping them around my torso. I watch her hands move steadily. When finished, she sits back on her heels, meeting my gaze.

She studies me as if trying to unearth a hidden truth. Finally, she sighs. "We can skip writing for now. You need to rest." She pauses while tidying up. "When I found you, you were lying outside town, half-buried in the dirt. You were barely alive. I had to fetch a cart to bring you here. If I hadn't come along—" She trails off, her eyes drifting to the bandages she just wrapped. "You were as good as dead." She adds, almost to herself. "Whatever happened, it must have been something brutal."

She steps away, gathering the soiled bandages and bowl. I settle back against the mat, feeling the strain of my injuries pulling at me. I know I can't stay here long. Philip would insist I leave as soon as I can stand. I should not linger where I'm vulnerable. The Phylax creed is clear—survive alone.

Sleep's grasp tightens around me, dragging me toward its inevitable abyss. I try to plan my next move, but the details slip away. Everything is a tangle of pain and half-formed ideas. The darkness is relentless, smothering me with its suffocating grip. It pulls me under. My thoughts scatter, leaving nothingness in its wake.

FOUR

A soft rustle pulls me from the fog of sleep. Xia must be moving about the house.

I blink, trying to clear the grit clinging to my vision as it adjusts to the pale shafts of morning light filtering through thin slats in the window. Each inhalation sends a sharp, fiery reminder through my side. The discomfort is a constant testament to my weakness, a state I loathe.

Confucius once said, "Our greatest glory is not in never falling, but in rising every time we fall." I do not feel glorious. I feel powerless. What does it mean to rise again when I am reminded of my failure every time I move?

This time, the shuffling is closer. I turn to see Xia by the window. She's arranging bundles of herbs on the narrow sill. Morning light spills across her profile, catching the curve of her cheekbone. Each placement is purposeful as if the arrangement itself were a ceremony.

Once she lays out the herbs, her attention shifts. She stares beyond the confines of the room. The muscles in her face tighten subtly.

She surveys the street with the intensity of a hawk, scanning for the slightest hint of movement below. She stands there, unmoving— a quiet sentinel at the window. Lines of worry etch deeper into her brow as her focus sharpens on something I cannot see.

A sense of unease ripples through me.

I watch her a second longer, noting the tension coiled in her shoulders, the way her fingers twitch, readying herself for action.

I close my eyes.

Memories of Florence seep into my vision— the narrow alleys bathed in the glow of lanterns, the hushed murmur of conspiratorial voices, and the scent of wet stone. The mission had succeeded. I swiftly dispatched Alessandro de' Medici. My journey after that was anything but simple.

Florence was a city of unexpected twists, each corner teeming with life, unpredictability, and danger. I had planned every step, mapping the labyrinthine streets. Yet, as I waded through the throngs, the city's fabric seemed to conspire against me. A troupe of street performers had been my downfall—a momentary lapse as I watched their acrobatics.

A gang of criminals struck with their crude knives. They left me with shallow, jagged wounds for what? Pocket change. I staggered through the maze of alleys. Each step was a battle against blood loss, forcing me to find a spot to tend to my injuries. No one came to my aid; I had no choice but to heal myself.

The nights that followed were a haze of agony. I stayed in an abandoned storeroom on the outskirts of town, behind stacks of forgotten barrels. The air reeked of stale wine and mold, but at least it was peaceful.

I tore strips from my shirt to bind the wounds. My hands shook, blood slicking my fingers as I worked. Philip had taught me not to rely on anyone else.

My time in Florence was a lesson, showing me that independence was a strength required to be a Phylax. I needed to be in control of my pain, my recovery, and my survival. I embraced the solitude as a necessary burden.

Now, in this desolate corner of China, I find myself injured again. My wound here is perhaps a little more serious than those in Florence. I don't know if I would have survived on my own. For good or ill, a stranger found me, dragging me into this shelter. Her motives are unclear. I loathe the taste of helplessness it brings.

I will have enough strength in the morning to slip out of town before sunrise. Florence taught me that I can overcome injury. Alone.

Xia is back in the room. She steps closer, kneeling beside me. She pulls back the blanket. Her fingers move with an efficiency that borders on surgical. Her touch is that of someone who has patched up worse injuries before. She knows how to keep steady under pressure.

"You're healing better than I expected," she says, her voice carrying a lyrical cadence. There's an undertone I can't quite place. It isn't the dialect itself; it's the measured way she speaks. Her words sound rehearsed. Or maybe it's my nature to be suspicious.

I study her, searching for answers in the subtle shifts of her expression. She keeps her head down, focusing on the wound. Whatever it is, she's more than she appears. Perhaps a healer with the experience of someone who's seen more than her share of danger.

When Xia finishes tending to my wound, she retrieves a small writing desk. She follows it with a roll of parchment, an inkstone, and a thin brush. She sets them up methodically beside me.

"How are you feeling?" she asks.

I dip the brush into the ink, watching the dark liquid pool at the tip. I've been learning to write Small Seal Script for two years, but the characters are complex. I do my best to form the correct words. *Better. Thank you for helping me.* I turn the parchment toward her.

She leans in to read, a smirk tugging at the corner of her lips. "Your Chinese is awful," she says with amusement. "Where are you from?"

I stick to the story I've crafted for times like this. *I'm from Eastern Scythia, exploring the world.*

She nods slowly, accepting the vague explanation for now. Her gaze remains thoughtful, perhaps weighing whether to probe further. Finally, she does.

"What happened to you?"

I quickly concoct a story. *Bandits ambushed the caravans I traveled with. We were outnumbered. I barely escaped with my life.*

I study her reaction.

Xia moves to the window, where any trace of a smile fades. Tension forms across her forehead. "Is that why the Imperial Army is coming? Because bandits attacked your caravan?"

A chill runs through me. I have no answer for her other than to shrug. *What army?* I write, my strokes less steady.

Instead of replying immediately, she stares at me. Her glare is piercing, making me feel exposed. I'm relieved when she finally looks away. As she leaves the room, she calls over her shoulder, "Maybe I'm imagining it. Just in case, we should be ready to leave."

I know she's not imagining it. A knot tightens in my stomach. The Imperial Army— they must be searching for Qin's assassin. I debate whether I can trust this woman. What if she's setting a trap, hoping I'll reveal my part in Qin's death? If the guards come and I'm too weak to defend myself, will she turn me in? Or is she simply trying to protect herself by keeping me hidden?

The reality is I need to regain my strength before making my getaway. One more evening of rest, that's all I need. In the meantime, I'll use my oath as a shield between us.

The hours pass slowly. Xia helps me sit up to sip at a bowl of thin broth she prepared. It's tasteless, barely more than warm water with a hint of some root or herb. I force it down, knowing I need the sustenance.

She keeps her words to a minimum, asking basic questions like whether I need more food or if the pain is manageable. I respond with the appropriate gestures. Throughout the day, she frequently peeks out the window. Periodically, she stashes bundles of herbs and other supplies into a sack.

Outside, the light shifts as the sun arcs through the sky. Morning gives way to the hazy brightness of midday, followed by the slow descent into late afternoon. Shadows stretch across the room, their edges softened by the dimming light filtering through the window. The sounds of the town beyond our walls change, too. The early clamor of voices fades into a subdued whisper. An underlying tension hangs in the air, as though the town is holding its breath.

Xia moves to the window again, her face partially obscured by a drape. She stays there for an extended interval, frozen, listening. I strain to pick up what she hears. I might have detected something carried on the wind, but it is too indistinct to understand. Whatever it is, my muscles tighten in response.

"Soon, you must trust me," she says softly. The seriousness etched across her visage seems to age her.

I reach for the parchment and write, *Why would I do that?*

Frustration crosses her features. "Really? After I saved you? You don't trust me?"

I write, *You seem to know too much. How do you know the Imperial Army is on its way?*

She searches the room for answers. Her voice drops to barely more than a whisper when she starts. "I've had to hide from these soldiers before," her voice wavers. "When Qin unified China, he went region by region, tearing down anyone who stood in his way. My parents were administrators in the Chu Kingdom. Our army was particularly tough. When Qin finally overcame our resistance, he was unjust to our people. The Emperor condemned my entire family to the Great Wall—forced to work until they died."

She pauses, growing distant while recalling memories. "Do you know how many dead slaves are in that wall?" she asks, her tone sharpening with a mix of sorrow and anger. "Probably a million. Maybe more. My parents are in there somewhere."

Her hands clench into tight balls as she looks

down. "I was only a child. My mother hid me before they came. She ensured they wouldn't find me, even if it cost her everything. I've been alone since I was seven. Still, they continued to come after me." Her voice cracks, a tear slipping down her cheek. She doesn't move to wipe it away.

"I can sense when that army is coming," she whispers. "I am certain they are near."

She glares at the door, her back stiffening. I almost expect soldiers to burst through now. "At one point, they finally caught me. They beat me, humiliated me, did worse. That's how I ended up with this scar," she points to the spot under her eye. "Somehow, I managed to escape. I told myself I would never let that happen again."

Perhaps I am safer here than I expected. Something tells me that this woman is always prepared for the worst.

I watch, struck by the rawness of her confession. Xia's story stirs something within me—a painful echo of my past with the Renegades. As the rulers who should have protected Xia harmed her, my community betrayed me. At least I had Philip to help me. Xia had no one. Her pain mirrors my own.

No, I must brush the feeling aside. Why am I making this connection? I don't need to relate to her story. In the morning, I'll leave her behind. That will be the end of it.

"I cannot stand those bastards and what they

do to people, which is why I will help you." she turns back. "Anyway, you need to rest."

She doesn't wait for me to agree; instead, she busies herself by cleaning up. Her movements seem more of a distraction, a way to keep occupied.

The room dims as dusk approaches. In the fading light, the walls take on a bluish hue. Chatter from outside hushes to an eerie stillness. As I relax on the mat, a rhythmic thudding carries through the air. At first, the sound blends into the hum of life beyond these walls. Slowly, it becomes more defined until it is a drumbeat through the earth.

Xia is on her feet, rushing to the window. She peeks through the narrow gap, tensing as she scans the horizon. "No," she whispers, almost to herself. "No, no, no."

I force myself to stand. Sharp pain shoots through my ribs. For the first time since we met, I see fear in her.

"We need to leave," she says, urgency tightening her voice. "There are many of them."

The room spins with my first steps, my body protesting every movement. It is a struggle, but I will manage. I must because the sound of boots grows louder, now accompanied by the clinking of weapons.

Xia rushes to my side, grabbing my arm to steady me. "We don't have much time," she mutters, her eyes darting around the room. She grabs the bag she's been packing throughout the day. "Can you walk?"

I have my doubts at first. The next few steps are marginally steadier. I glance toward the window. Whoever they are, I'm not ready to meet them.

Xia hands me a cloak. "Put this on. You need to cover up if you are going to blend in."

I wince while pulling the rough fabric around my shoulders. The marching is now accompanied by the bark of commands. We both freeze, listening.

"They're right outside," Xia whispers. "We need to hurry." She grabs my arm, pulling me toward the back of the room. I stumble forward, clutching at her shoulder for support.

As we reach the back exit, the air fills with shouts. My instinct is to fight, but that would be a losing battle today. Xia doesn't hesitate. She pulls me along with an iron-tight grip.

"Come on," she hisses, leading us toward the gloom.

The world outside is a cacophony of danger. A storm is rushing towards us. I peer back inside the house at the bed where I was lying, contemplating that I might not survive this.

Again, Xia yanks me forward. We plunge into the unknown, the approaching army echoing in our ears.

FIVE

Darkness presses in as Xia and I move cautiously through the narrow street. The night amplifies every sound—the rustling of fabric, the crunch of our footsteps on uneven ground, the distant murmur of voices. We hunch low, staying out of sight.

Torchlight casts distorted shapes along the alley's edges, making it harder to judge how close the soldiers are. The rhythmic thudding of their boots echoes in my ears.

Each step feels more laborious than the last. My body aches, and pain proves my vulnerability. My focus narrows to putting one foot in front of the other. Even walking is a slow drain of energy threatening to consume me.

Xia reaches out, steadying me. Her urgent grasp is gentle amid the chaos. I catch her outline in the light. She controls her breathing, a stark contrast to my ragged gasps. We exchange a brief look—no words necessary. We scan ahead, searching for the next safe spot to hide.

The alley twists, narrowing even further

until we have to squeeze past a gap in the stonework. I bite back a groan as pain flares in my ribs. A few more steps; I can make it a few more.

When we stop, Xia flattens herself against the wall. She pulls me close beside her. What I see in the open square makes my blood run cold. Torches burn in a hazardous sea of light, each carried by a soldier. Dozens are fanning throughout the streets. Their presence turns the square into a maze of danger.

Xia and I lock onto each other, the torchlight allowing brief glimpses of our profiles. She doesn't have to say it; I already know. This is a hunt. We are the prey.

We hurry away from the square. I search for any possible escape route, but the buildings loom high on either side. Xia moves ahead of me at a steady pace. I can't shake the gnawing belief that we're moving toward a trap.

My heart sinks when my prophecy comes true. We come to a halt, blocked by a wall of stone. My hands ball into fists as frustration surges inside me.

Xia doesn't flinch. Instead, she marches forward, approaching a section of the wall that appears no different from the rest. She turns back to me, her eyes gleaming in the faint light. "Trust me," Xia whispers before knocking on a thin piece of metal hanging from a rope. Three slow thuds, then two quick ones, and finally a single, forceful slap.

For a moment, nothing happens. My muscles tense with anticipation. Then, from the gloom, a figure materializes. I reach for the dagger at my side.

Xia moves quickly, stepping between us before I can act. "It's okay," she hisses, her arm stretched out to block my path. "He's on our side."

The stranger stays hunched, his form swallowed beneath layers of tattered fabric. A hood drapes over his face. His posture suggests a spine twisted by age or affliction. The stranger's attention shifts to Xia. Bony fingers peek from the folds of his shawl.

Xia pulls a small pouch out of her tunic. She tosses it to him, and it jingles as it lands in his palm. Without a word, he pushes against a façade of stones. A concealed door swings inward, revealing a staircase descending into the ground. A damp, musty smell wafts up from the depths, filling the air around us. The stranger steps back into obscurity.

Xia's voice is a drawn blade. "Let's go."

I pause, casting a wary glance at the stranger.

"Now," Xia urges.

The army behind us is closing in, so I follow her into the passageway. The stone steps are slick beneath my feet, forcing me to use the walls for support as we descend. Murk closes in around us, swallowing the sounds from above as the door creaks shut behind us. We're inside, enclosed in a network of tunnels that stretch out like veins beneath the town.

The stranger stays behind. I am unsure of why he is helping, causing tension to stretch between us before he seals off the entrance. The last trace of the surface world disappears, leaving only the sound of our hurried footsteps. Each stride echoes off the narrow walls as we descend deeper underground.

The narrow passageway stretches onward, dimly lit by sporadic torches anchored to the walls at irregular intervals. The flickering light casts distorted images, turning the stone into a writhing serpent. I move behind Xia, who leads the way. It is challenging to keep up. Her pace is quick and sure-footed despite the oppressive darkness.

Our footsteps are a rhythmic beat magnified by the corridor. My hand slides along the damp wall for support. The stones' chill numbs my fingertips.

From elsewhere, a noise breaks through— a muffled clash followed by restrained shouts. The sound is a menacing growl rolling down the passage, reverberating off the walls. Someone else has found a way into the tunnel. I freeze, the blood draining from my cheeks. I am not prepared to fight. My intuition beckons me to meet the danger head-on despite my weakened state. Thankfully, my mind knows this is folly.

Xia stops, tilting forward as she listens. Her lips purse. She waves for me to keep moving forward.

We pick up the pace. The passage shrinks at points where I have to duck to avoid the low-hanging ceiling. The walls close in, and rough stone scrapes against my shoulders. The urgency bears down on us, dread twisting in my gut.

A metallic clang echoes, this time from behind. Violence draws nearer. The tunnel is not a safe passage; it's a trap, a maze with danger around every corner.

It reminds me of a mission when I was twenty-two.

The Phylax sent me to the Palace of Knossos to kill King Rhadamanthys. The palace was a sprawling structure, rumored to be the home of the legendary half-man, half-bull, Minotaur. Its corridors twisted unpredictably, creating a labyrinth that confounded even the greatest warriors. These tunnels feel eerily similar. Every corner potentially leads to a dead end or ambush.

I remember how I crept around the tangled passages of Knossos, nervously listening for any movement. Back then, I felt the same cold sweat running down my spine, the same sense of a hunt. Here, beneath this ancient city, it's as though the maze has come alive again. This time, I am not the predator stalking my prey—I am the prey, scrambling for any chance of escape.

We round another bend when two soldiers emerge from a side tunnel, blocking our path. Torchlight glints off their drawn blades. The world seems to freeze. My muscles coil, but I'm slow to react.

Xia, however, doesn't falter. She first engages the larger man who is at least a foot taller than her. In a blur of motion, she lunges forward. Her movements are a deadly dance in the dull light. The soldier swings his sword. Xia twists her body effortlessly, slipping under the strike. She drives her knuckles into his throat with more power than someone of her stature should. At first, he wheezes, but Xia silences him with a kick across his head. He drops to his knees and then collapses to his side. I'm not sure if he will ever wake up.

Before the second soldier can react, Xia's arm snaps out like a whip. She strikes the nerve cluster just below his collarbone. He jerks back, off balance. With the same fluid motion, she drives a devastating side-kick into his knee. The joint buckles with a sickening pop, sending him crashing sideways into the stone wall. His head bounces off the rock with a dull crack before he crumples to the ground. His legs twist unnaturally beneath him. Neither soldier can follow us.

I stand frozen, unable to look away. Healers rarely know how to unleash such violence. I struggle to comprehend what I have witnessed. Xia, the woman who has been tending to my wounds, has easily dismantled two trained soldiers. This fierce, lethal figure replaces the healer. Her actions have an efficiency that speaks of formal training. Where has she learned to fight like that?

Doubt digs its claws deeper into me. I want to trust Xia—she has saved me. Yet, I know almost nothing about the person leading me into this maze of uncertainty.

The tunnel finally widens, and the air freshens as we near the exit. A glimmer of moonlight spills in from the opening ahead, casting a silvery glow on the walls. When we emerge into the open air, I stumble to a halt. My interest locks onto the sight before us.

Horses stand tied to a post, a perfect means of escape. This is no coincidence. Someone has planned our exact route. My gaze shifts to Xia, who moves to untie the horses. The image of her shifts again in my imagination, becoming more confusing. Who is she really? A healer, a warrior, or something else entirely?

Before I can think any further, a figure steps in from the dark. A lone soldier blocks our path, his weapon gleaming in the moonlight. Xia moves to intercept. She is ready for combat. The soldier wastes no time, launching into a series of strikes that force Xia back. She dodges, except I can already see that this fight is different. This soldier is more skilled and relentless.

The advantage is his. Xia loses ground, her fluidity buckling to his brute strength. I watch as she narrowly avoids a swing that would have cut her down. She needs help, but I'm barely standing. The remnants of my stamina ebb with each exhale, yet I cannot watch her die. I will be next on the soldier's kill list.

I gather my strength to creep forward, keeping out of the soldier's periphery. Every step sends pain through my battered body. The clashing of steel fills the air, each strike an echoing anvil. The soldier pushes harder, a true predator.

As I inch closer, Xia stumbles, her foot shifting on loose dirt. The soldier sees his chance. His blade rises high for the final strike. Time seems to slow, every second stretching thin.

I rush forward. Adrenaline surges, numbing everything except the need to act. The soldier's focus remains fixed on Xia; he doesn't notice me until my fingers are already on his belt. My fingers fumble before closing around the hilt of his dagger. Surprise flashes across his face as I rip the blade free.

With all the strength I can muster, I drive the dagger upward. The blade finds a gap beneath his dark armor, sinking into flesh. Warm blood gushes over my hand. The soldier chokes out a strangled mix of disbelief and agony. Before he falls, he lands an elbow into my side, where my wound struggles to heal.

For a flash, our eyes meet—his full of shock, mine filled with pain. Then he collapses into the dirt, lifeless. I stagger back, the dagger slipping from my trembling fingers. The world sways. Dizziness claws at my vision. It takes a minute before I can force myself to steady.

Pain flares through my side; blood soaks into my clothing. Xia approaches, cautiously scanning me.

"You saved me," she whispers.

Just as she saved me.

"I don't leave my debts unpaid," she says firmly before untying the remaining horse. "Quick, get on," she urges.

I wipe my bloodied hands on the hem of my cloak. Xia steadies me as I mount the horse. The danger closing in on us leaves no time for hesitation. We spur the horses forward, racing into the cover of night.

As we gallop away, the echoes of shouts and pursuit fade behind us. I hold my side as we ride. Pain flares with each stride of the horse. Being re-injured will delay my departure by another day. I know I must carry on by myself as soon as possible, especially considering Xia's discreet talents. The scene replays in my imagination— the stranger at the tunnel's mouth, the soldiers, Xia's deadly skills. The mysteries around her grow deeper with each passing heartbeat, leaving me to wonder how much more there is that I don't know. The desert's darkness stretches on, pulling us into whatever lies beyond.

SIX

The desert scrub gradually gives way to drier, barren plains. Hills flatten into endless stretches of cracked earth. Here, the wind sweeps across the desolate land, whispering of dangers yet to come. Dust clings to my sweat-dampened skin, forming a gritty layer that stings with every movement. We are heading west, further from the Imperial Army's reach, although I don't know how far this new legion's influence stretches or how determined they will be to find us. Does Qin's successor even care who I am?

We traveled the entire night—ten hours of pushing through pain and exhaustion. Thankfully, a swollen moon had cast enough light to guide us along a cautious path.

Dawn broke with us leading the horses. The rising sun casts long shadows before us. The journey is grueling, but the constant ache in my side fades enough that I can leave Xia tomorrow morning. One night's sleep will give me enough strength to travel alone.

Xia rides ahead, her posture impressively

upright. She scans the horizon with practiced vigilance. The wind catches her hair, whipping it behind her like an obsidian banner. I watch closely. She keeps her secrets, and I keep mine.

The hours pass in a steady rhythm of hoofbeats and shifting sands. The sun drifts overhead. Xia speaks nothing more than a few words. The only other sounds are the distant call of birds. Vultures hoping to find an afternoon meal. They ride the hot currents above us, circling lazily. Their presence is a worrisome omen looming in the wind.

After a full day of travel, the sun dips behind a distant ridge, painting the sky in golden hues. We make camp near a cluster of weathered boulders. The fire crackles weakly, its warmth holding back the chill that seeps in. Xia sits across from me, her eyes reflecting the flames dancing across her features. I stretch out, leaning back against a rock worn smooth by time. I drift to the horizon, where stars begin to pierce the twilight.

Xia finally speaks after a long pause. Her voice is restrained. "You're probably wondering how I managed to arrange our escape back there," she begins, fixed intently on the flames. Why she's waited this long to explain is anyone's guess.

"I arranged my safe passage well before you showed up. I even purchased two horses for a faster getaway. On the run, you learn to have an exit strategy ready before it's too late. I feel like I'm always dodging pursuit."

I find myself nodding slowly. The logic of her words resonates with my own experiences. Always plan in advance. Always have an exit strategy. It's a lesson I've lived by.

She pauses, the lull stretching between us. "Qin's army has been hunting me for so long," she whispers. "I always have to be ready for them. Ready to vanish at a moment's notice, leaving everything behind."

When I remain silent, frustration crosses her features. "Would you say something? Anything?" she snaps, the veneer of composure cracking.

She already knows I won't break my silence. She sighs, and her shoulders sag. The fire highlights her frustration.

"Because I've been running for so long, I also know those soldiers weren't Qin's army." She studies me. "I don't know who they were, but I'm certain they weren't after me."

I know she is right about both things. The soldiers weren't Qin's. Qin is dead. This new Imperial Army looks different—more deadly. She is also correct in assuming they are after me. Unless Xia has more enemies than she claims.

When she glances to gauge my reaction, I wear an impassive mask. My gut tells me there's more to Xia's story than a simple need for survival. I can't shake the feeling that she knows more about me than she's willing to reveal. Even though she wants me to talk, she seems to expect my vow.

Eventually, Xia falls quiet, turning her attention back to the fire. The night grows colder. Our shadows stretch out beyond the camp, creeping across the desolate landscape. I lie down, staring at the stars scattered across the sky. Sleep doesn't come easily. It never does.

I attempt to trace the constellations. The scholars of Qin believed the heavens were a celestial court mirroring the Chinese empire. They imagined heaven as an orderly bureaucracy. Gods and spirits governed the cosmos like provincial ministers answering to the Jade Emperor, their supreme deity. Even time had administrators recording the fates of mortals, keeping accounts in a vast imperial ledger.

I wonder where I fit in that system now.

Qin Shi Huang called himself the *Son of Heaven*. He was the link between the celestial order and the ordinary world. He carved his laws into stone, building his empire to last ten thousand years.

I ended him. I silenced the emperor who claimed divine authority, erasing his name from the cosmic ledger before heaven had the chance. So, what does that make me? A rogue scribe in the records of time? A thief who stole the emperor's fate before the gods could collect it?

I prefer to think of myself as someone carrying out orders of an unseen instituation.

Yet, the emperor's blood was real. His life was not an entry in a book nor a name in a ledger. It was warm, staining my hands, and ultimately, it didn't matter. The Celestial Administration endures whether or not Qin sits on his throne. The stars do not waver. Neither should I.

Xia quickly settles down, exhaustion overcoming her as she wraps herself in a blanket near the fire. Soon, her respiration softens into the rhythm of sleep. I watch her before turning back to my wound. The fire helps me inspect it.

I begin to unwrap the bandages from my torso. The wound is healing, but the bandages are stained. I cannot risk infection. I need clean cloth. My interest shifts to Xia's belongings lying out of her reach. I know she has packed extra. I will change the dressing, then leave her behind. She has saved my life, so I will spare hers.

I move toward her bag and open it. Inside, I find several expected supplies: herbs, dried food, and a small vial of liquid medicine. I dig deeper, my fingers brushing against something soft: a bundle of bandages, as I hoped.

I should stop here. I should close the bag and go back to the fire. Instead, my fingers drift further into it, searching for something I can't name. As I fumble through the contents, my fingers graze against something stiff—a smooth piece of paper that doesn't belong in this time.

Out of curiosity, I hold it up to the light of the fire.

The air leaves my lungs in an instant. It's a photograph. My heart thuds in my chest as I examine it, trying to understand what I see. Photography doesn't exist in this era. Xia shouldn't have anything like this in her possession. Yet, here it is, in her bag.

I force myself to focus on the image. It's a picture of me standing somewhere I have never been. Perhaps America around the year 2000. In the background stands a young woman, half-shrouded. A chill crawls down my spine. I squint, straining to make out her features. An uneasy realization strikes me. I have seen this woman before; however, I can't place her.

The image of the woman stares back. Even after a few minutes, I cannot recall how I know her. My grip tightens around the photograph. This isn't a coincidence. Xia ties into something far more significant than I realized. She isn't merely a fugitive or a healer; like me, she is out of place and time. A cold knot twists in my gut.

I watch Xia sleeping soundly by the fire. Every action of hers replays—how she helped me, arranged our escape, the contacts she claims to have, and her skill in combat far exceeding that of the average person. Now, this photograph. It is evidence that she has a more significant plan.

My hand impulsively drifts to the branding

scar on my forearm. I should be traveling alone. I feel anger welling up. How could I be so naïve? I've let my guard down by accepting her help. It goes against every teaching the Phylax has instilled in me, every rule of survival. I was right to be suspicious of her.

I turn the photograph over, hoping the back might reveal more answers. It is blank. My grip tightens around it, and an undeniable realization settles into my bones: I must confront this truth. I need answers, and then I need to kill Xia. After that, I will be as I should be: alone.

I slip the photograph into my tunic pocket and slowly draw my knife. The weight of it comforts me. The blade shines against the fire's flickering light. I rehearse the next step: I will bring the knife to her throat and force the answers from her. I will beat them out if I have to.

My jaw tightens as I imagine it. After I have my answers, a quick, precise slit across Xia's throat will end the ordeal. Warm crimson will flow. I will silence her forever. It will solve my problem, ridding me of this uncertainty.

The Phylax has taught me to remove any obstacles to the mission. Xia is now an obstacle. I step toward her, ready to unchain my wrath. I stare at her throat, where the pulse of life beats steadily beneath her skin.

Before I can begin my task, the air around her shimmers. It is a ripple in reality, distorting space. I freeze mid-step, staring in disbelief. The fabric of reality twists, an unnatural disturbance that tugs at my senses. The rift causes a faint hum. The fire wildly dances as if recoiling from the anomaly. Before I can react, she vanishes into the ripple. The hum dissipates, and the camp plunges into an eerie stillness.

I stand there, knife in hand, air caught in my throat. The desert feels colder. I struggle to grasp that a time distortion has happened. Here. Now. It took Xia away from me before I could get my desired answers.

The sharp whinny of spooked horses pierces the night. I turn in time to see one bolting into the void. The remaining horse rears, its eyes wide with fear. I press a firm hand against its neck, caressing its mane. Gradually, its trembling subsides as it leans into my touch.

Nothing has gone right on this mission. Every move, every decision, has led me deeper into chaos. I should never have trusted an outsider. Philip would chastise my lapse in judgment.

I have one option now: get to the Acropolis. The Phylax must know every detail of what happened, including that a rogue traveler has made contact. This traitor may have changed the parameters of my mission. The Phylax will demand a full report.

Get to the Acropolis. Tell them everything. For now, that is all that matters.

SEVEN

I used to think time flowed. One moment leads to the next in a river rushing forward. That's the simplest story we tell ourselves: the past is gone, the future's out of reach, and we are stuck in the present. But I've seen enough to know that time doesn't flow at all. I believe it's more of a solid block—a four-dimensional tapestry where past, present, and future all exist simultaneously.

We travelers can float over the neat illusion of the river, if only for an instant. It's not that we move through time. Time's already there, laid out in a cosmic novel. The way I see it, our consciousness simply riffles through to a new chapter in that book. That's what time-travelers are able to do: slip between slices of spacetime that were always there, skipping from one chapter to the next.

This begs the question: if everything is there already—past, present, and future—does that mean our lives are fated? Was Qin Shi Huang always destined to search for immortality, only to meet his end by my blade? Did I have any choice in my missions, or am I just playing out a role someone else wrote? If the entire universe was laid out in the moment of the Big Bang, then maybe every outcome is as inevitable as sunrise.

But the universe is an immense place—maybe infinitely big. If it is truly infinite, perhaps every outcome is our fate. I find comfort in that contradiction: that every possibility exists, even if we only experience one thread at a time. If each possibility exists, maybe I'm not doomed to be just one version of myself.

All I know is that when I jump through time, I can feel the edges of that block. It's similar to pressing my palm against a glass wall. It's there, but I'm still free to move my hand along its surface, choosing my slice of "now." Maybe that's enough. After all, no one—not even the Phylax—cheats death to live forever. We only see the bigger picture for the briefest of moments, stepping from one chapter to the next.

The Taklamakan Desert stretches out before me, an unforgiving expanse that swallows the horizon. They call it the *Sea of Death*. It is a place where the sand buries secrets and devours the unwary. Tales speak of travelers venturing in and vanishing without a trace. Now, it is my turn to cross this desolate wasteland, a journey that demands everything I have left.

The wind whips sharp dust against my

skin. On the horizon, ominous clouds churn, an oncoming threat. It's a tempest, a reflection of the one roaring within my soul.

I don't know how long I've been riding. My horse's pace has slowed to a plod. I lean forward, patting its neck, urging it on. The creature has held up admirably, bearing me across the rough terrain without complaint. Sadly, I can feel its strength waning until it finally stumbles.

I pull on the reins, trying to steady it. It is too late; the horse's knees buckle. With a pained whinny, the animal collapses onto the ground. I scramble to the animal's side as it lies still. Exhaustion glazes its eyes. Desperation grips me as I kneel beside it, dirt sifting into my boots. I pet its neck, feeling the shallow pulse slow, then stop.

My hand hovers over its neck, uncertain whether to offer comfort or simply acknowledge its passing. A harsh voice in my subconscious tells me to get up, to move, to survive. Except I can't. Not yet.

I reach for the saddlebag, then pause, staring at its lifeless body. It carried me this far. I owe the horse more than leaving its discarded carcass in the desert. For a moment, I think about burying the animal. Unfortunately, the dunes are endless. Time isn't mine to waste.

I don't feel this way for people. Not anymore. Sadness for animals, especially this horse, is different. They aren't pawns or enemies. They are pure.

I take a deep breath, forcing myself to my feet. I sling the satchel over my shoulder and grab the remaining food. My steps are heavy as I walk away. I don't look back—I can't. Their deaths stay with me in a way human ones never do.

I look toward the horizon. The storm clouds loom larger, their dark masses threatening to engulf this wasteland in their fury.

Steeling myself, I adjust the strap of the waterskin across my shoulder. Each step sinks into scorching sand, draining what little strength I have left. The oasis town of Sachu lies somewhere ahead, hidden beyond the endless dunes that test my resolve.

I trudge onward. It's not the heat that bothers me. My thoughts keep circling back to the photograph I found in Xia's bag—the image of myself captured in a place I have never visited.

I allowed her to get close, to help me when I was vulnerable. In doing so, I violated so many rules. I can see Philip's stern reprimand. *You let your guard down. Flashes of weakness will end you.* The fact that she vanished before I could confront her reeks of more failure. I should have known better.

At least I am surrounded by emptiness now. The vacant expanse gives me time to think. I appreciate this time alone. Here, there are no distractions, no deceptions—only the raw reality of survival.

The wind kicks up more, stinging dust against my legs. Like the Phylax, the arid plains are brutal, demanding everything. Despite its harshness, I find grim comfort in its simplicity.

If one isn't careful, the waves of sand can play tricks on the senses, confusing even the most seasoned traveler. Out here, landmarks are rare. The sun can be a deceitful guide, rising and setting in ways that make it easy to lose track of direction. The wind erases footprints almost as soon as they are made, similar to how memories fade with time. Except for our most formative experiences, like the first time Philip taught me to traverse time.

After saving me from the Renegades, Philip brought me to a farmhouse in Greece to recover. It was a place far from their reach. He was patient with me, never demanding more than I could give. That didn't mean I trusted him. After what happened in that church, trust wouldn't come easy.

I recovered over the next couple of weeks and then decided to slip away. It wasn't about Philip; I wanted to be on my own. When I set out to leave, I was surprised to find him sitting on the front porch, waiting. The late hour concealed his presence.

Philip clapped to get my attention, then signed, *Leaving so soon, lad?* He turned to face me.

Before you go, can I show you something? Just one thing. After that, if you still want to leave, I won't stop you.

I stared at him, naturally suspicious. What could he want to show me? I figured it was nothing more than some last-ditch effort to change my resolve.

Reluctantly, I agreed.

Philip rose from his seat. His movements were gentle. He feared breaking my fragile trust. When he placed his hand on my arm, I initially pulled back; however, his light touch reassured me.

Don't be afraid, lad, Philip signed. *This is something you need to see.*

He gestured for me to follow, leading me into the cool night. We moved through the sleeping city. I kept my distance from him, my skepticism lingering. Yet, curiosity tugged me forward.

We reached the base of the Acropolis, its towering cliffs rising against the twilight. Philip paused, tilting his head toward a narrow path that climbed upward. I followed him as we scaled the rough terrain, carefully avoiding loose stones that could slide away and betray our presence.

At the entrance to the Acropolis, Philip stopped. Guards patrolled the area, their flashlights were restless fireflies in the distance. Philip guided me along a less obvious route, slipping between ruins that served as makeshift cover. I followed his lead.

When we reached the top, the city spread out below us, shimmering in the sea of silver. The Parthenon loomed nearby, its grandeur softened by age. The ruins of older structures stood as remnants of what they once were. Philip motioned for me to stand beside him.

Again, he placed his fingers on my arm, this time gripping me tightly.

Then, the strangest, most disorienting, beautiful thing followed. Time spread in front of me like the pages of a book. To my left, the past shimmered. To my right, the future stretched until 2051, when everything abruptly ended.

Beyond that, there were no pages, merely an abrupt void where the story should continue. I was too amazed to ask questions then, so I didn't understand its meaning until later. I remained in awe as I stood above the flow of time.

My senses spun as the present blurred with the past. Philip's grip tightened. His stare never left me, perhaps gauging whether I was ready to understand the enormity of what he revealed. *This is your gift*, his expression seemed to say.

When he finished the theatrics, the current slowed. I tried to steady myself, to make sense of what happened. We were standing in the same place in Greece, except with an entirely different landscape. Beneath me, the ground felt firmer. When I looked out, the sight was breathtaking.

The Parthenon stood in its prime. Its marble columns gleamed in the sunlight, adorned with vivid carvings of gods and heroes. Nearby, the Erechtheion glowed as if blessed by Athena herself. These buildings were not ruins. They were alive with unparalleled grandeur.

My mouth fell open in awe. Nothing could have prepared me for the magnificence of these structures in their full glory. The city of Athens spread below us. The Agora bustled with the energy of ancient life.

Come, Philip signed, gesturing toward one side of the hill. *We have a challenging walk in front of us.*

The experience dazed me. I fought the urge to pull away from Philip's grip, wary of falling victim to another manipulation. Yet, I felt cracks forming in the walls I had built. Deep inside, a serene voice whispered that this was something good—something familiar, like a nearly forgotten song from childhood.

As we walked down a steep path, Philip fell into step beside me. *You can travel through time too,* he signed. *It's why the Renegade sect wanted you—to use you to manipulate time for their gain. They try to accumulate power, wealth, and control over everything. That's not the purpose of the Phylax.*

I said nothing. I was still trying to process that we had stepped back into ancient Greece. All of it was overwhelming.

Philip explained, *The Phylax exists to protect humankind. In 2051, at precisely 3 a.m. on July 1, the Sigma Event occurs. It's the end of humanity as we know it.*

I stiffened at his words. *What caused it?*

Philip continued, *We believe humanity destroyed itself. We triggered our own collapse through war, greed, or sheer negligence. The Sigma Event is the result of everything we failed to stop.* His signs became more forceful. *Our mission is to find the error, correct it, and prevent the Sigma Event from happening. No one can travel past 2051 because there's nothing left beyond it.*

He spoke with a heavy sense of responsibility that was muffled by my loitering skepticism. The Renegades told me too many lies by the time I was thirteen. I wasn't ready to believe Philip yet.

We walked for a while, the sounds of ancient Athens rising around us—the clatter of carts on cobblestone streets, the distant hum of voices, the melody of lyres playing somewhere in the city. The grandeur engulfed me.

Our steep path was overgrown. Eventually, it led us to a scattering of stone fragments. Philip pointed toward the base of the cliff, signing the word *descend*.

We climbed down to a spot where it appeared a giant boulder rested on a plateau. As we drew closer, I saw that it was actually a deeply worn groove in the stone. Nestled within the rut was a heavy door. Its design was simple and timeless.

Standing before it, an unusual feeling stirred within me. It was something I had never experienced with the Renegades. Belonging. I couldn't explain it, but deep down, I knew this place was for me.

Philip signed to me that this place was called the Sanctum. After gaining entry, he greeted a small group gathered near the entrance. When they moved, their robes gently flowed with them. One stepped forward, raising a hand to greet me.

Welcome, Adam, the figure signed. *We've been waiting for you.*

My heart raced, but not with fear. These people radiated warmth, enveloping me in a soft embrace. This wasn't the cold, manipulative organization that betrayed me; this was something pure, something real.

The ceremony that followed was powerful. The group formed a circle and pulled me into the center. They gently placed their hands on my shoulders as a gesture of acceptance, as if welcoming me home after a long journey. Their skin was warm, and their touch reassuring. The air filled with a subtle reverence, an acknowledgment of this pivotal occasion. It was nothing like the harsh, punishing rituals I had endured before. There was no pain, no fear, only peace.

The Archon approached, his gaze locking onto mine with an intensity that made me feel small. The others melted into the background when he neared. The Archon held my branding mark, his touch sending a subtle warmth through my skin. His stare pierced my spirit; his voice was a thunderous anthem:

"The past binds us.
The future calls us.
The present bends to our will."

Heat surged through my arm. A faint red glow spread across my skin, emanating from the branding mark. The warmth intensified, flowing from my arm into my chest, filling me with a radiant energy. Something shifted deep within me as the others stood around in a gentle communion. A long-buried part of me had awakened, an unfurling bud blossoming in spring. Warmth spread from my scar. With it came a seed of doubt. Could I trust this feeling, or was it another deception, a kinder mask for control?

When the ceremony ended, the members addressed me with serene smiles. Philip signed, *This is your beginning, lad. You are part of the true Phylax now.*

I nodded slowly. Was it gratitude, wonder, or optimism? I didn't know how to articulate what I felt. But I felt it in every fiber of my being.

When we left the Sanctum, light faded into the evening. In the distance, the ancient city's sounds disappeared. Philip signed, *We are unable to move through time near the Acropolis. There are devices inside that prevent it.* He paused before adding, *Each of us can travel once every three years. It takes a lot of power to travel; it drains us. That means you will have to bring us back to 2023.*

Before we descended the steep path, I asked, *What do you mean?*

Philip smiled softly. *When the Archon held your scar, he unleashed your ability. You can travel through time, like me. Now that we're here, it's up to you to get us back, lad.*

I blinked, stunned. *What? I don't know how to do that.*

You do, Philip signed with patience. *You need to unstick yourself from the present. Start here.* He placed his fingers on my arm over the branding mark. *This mark is a key to unlocking the power that flows through you. Use it to remove yourself from the here and now. You will feel like you are floating. When you let go, commit to that sense of drifting. The ripples of time will appear, spreading in front of you. That's when the gateway opens. You can take us back to our present."*

The possibility of using this power terrified me. I recalled the pull I felt when Philip brought us here—the sensation of time shifting around me. Anxiety knotted in my stomach. The responsibility felt immense, almost crushing. Yet, beneath the fear, there was a spark of curiosity. If I could tap into that sensation, perhaps I could bring us back.

I closed my eyes to focus on the brand on my arm, feeling the rough edges beneath my fingertips. I imagined stepping out of time. For a second, I assumed it was ridiculous. Then warmth spread through my body. I saw the gateway to the past and future open up. It was the same as when Philip brought us here. I grabbed onto his wrist. We shot through time, landing at the exact moment we had left.

I stumbled, disoriented. My senses struggled to catch up with the sudden shift. Philip caught me before I fell.

You did it, Philip signed with pride. *I knew you could.*

I couldn't believe it. I traveled through time. The power was mine.

Philip stepped back, giving me space. *This is just the beginning. You have so much to learn, but you've already taken the first step.*

I did not try to escape from Philip after that day.

The wind shifts, yanking me back to the present, to the endless void before me. Each step is a battle against exhaustion. I continue, relying on the survival skills drilled into me. It is second nature.

Then I see it: a raging tide of earth and wind closing in on me. The storm's shifting sands churn in a monstrous tide. My pulse quickens with anticipation. It isn't something to dread; it's a test, an opportunity to absolve myself. If I can withstand this, I can prove I have the strength to continue.

The wind picks up, stinging my face with the first bits of grit. I scan the surroundings and spot a dune, its steep slope offering some shelter. I move quickly, crouching down on the leeward side as the storm sweeps in.

The wind roars, slamming against me with a force that rattles my bones. Silt lashes out in every direction, creating a swirling, chaotic dance that blurs the world into a murky haze. I hunch down, wrapping my cloak tightly around me, using it as a shield against the onslaught. The noise is deafening.

The wind tears at my clothing. Sand stings my skin. My inhalations come in short, ragged gasps. Doubts swirl with the gusts. The storm forces them to the surface and then scatters them into nothing. The wind howls. I greet it head-on, feeling the force of nature grind against my resolve. This is my test. Endure it. I must prove my worth.

EIGHT

When sleep finally comes, it is unkind.

It's the same dream, but for the first time, there are differences.

I'm crouched in a wide clearing at dusk, leaning against a towering stone figure that looms above me. My fingers press into the rough surface, and I feel as though this carved giant is the only thing keeping me from drifting off into the purple sky. I only know I'm scared, and this stone shape offers a fragile sense of safety.

Beyond the statue, I glimpse someone else: the woman from the photograph. She clings to a tall figure who is veiled in shifting darkness. She grips its hand tightly, and I sense she's bracing for a calamity neither of us can name. They both seem to search the clearing, scanning every inch as though a threat will erupt at any moment.

It does. Two violent gusts spiral out of nowhere, crashing straight into the statue with a thunderous crack. I flinch as a jagged fault runs across the stone until chunks begin to fall away. A streak of crimson trickles over the statue's surface, staining it in a way that makes my stomach clench. The giant figure lurches forward, slamming to the ground with a sickening thud. Its protective weight is gone in an instant.

Before I can scramble backward, one of those swirling gusts seems to grow hands, seizing me around the waist. The grip is iron. My feet leave the ground; I try to fight, but it's like wrestling a storm. The sound of my own heartbeat drums in my ears, and the clearing dims around me. I manage a final glance at the woman in the distance—she's staring straight at me with urgency in her eyes. Then the wind yanks me away into the gloom, and everything vanishes.

I jolt awake. I don't know where I am. The wind, the woman, and the unease all feel more real than the cold earth beneath me. One thing stands out above it all: the woman. She's the one in the photograph.

Who is she?

I rub a hand against my branding mark, trying to steady my breathing. The vision has been the same for as long as I can remember, a loop playing in the background of my life. But now, it has shifted. The woman in the photograph was never there before.

I close my eyes and try to summon the earlier versions of the dream. Wasn't it a child's silhouette? Was there always the same sense of fear? I was always an observer, never in the action. It is smoke slipping between my fingers, holding onto something that was never solid to begin with.

Augustine of Hippo once wrote that the past does not exist. We cannot revisit it like a fixed point on a map. The past only exists in memory, and memory is unreliable. He argued that we hold time only in our minds: the past is a fading impression, the future an expectation, and the present a vanishing moment too brief to grasp.

I shudder.

This is only a dream, not my past.

I stare at the soft glow of dawn creeping over the horizon, trying to anchor myself to something real. I clench my fists. If the dream is changing, does that mean the past is shifting? It must. The Phylax changes the past so that humanity can survive in the future. Or maybe I am the one who is changing, and the truth has been waiting for me to finally see it.

I shake off the remaining anxiety. There's no time to dwell on dreams. Sachu awaits.

I reach for my supplies and pull out a strip of dried meat, slowly chewing a few mouthfuls. I have to reach Sachu before my supplies run out. It will be close. I take another small sip of water, feeling the urgency in every drop that slides down my parched throat.

The air is cool before the day's heat begins its relentless assault. I know this is the best time to make progress. I can't waste it.

The sun rises behind me, casting golden light across the sand. It illuminates the dunes. Each one is another obstacle to conquer. I move with measured steps, conserving my energy. I sweep the terrain for any signs of danger.

The golden sea is tranquil in the morning light—a deception. I know that beneath its surface lie countless threats. I focus on the path forward, carefully choosing my route through the dunes' slopes. The calmness stirs a memory of Philip's lessons in the art of survival.

I remember the shift in his posture when he surveyed the terrain. He could see things that were invisible to me. He raised his hands, signing, *Never trust what you first see, lad. Calm can hide danger.*

We were in a forest then, the opposite of this barren wasteland. The same principle held. The trees were dense, their shade masking everything beneath the undergrowth. I was young and overconfident despite my lack of skill. I believed I had spotted everything—the footprints trailing to a stream, the bent grass hinting at a recent crossing.

When I stepped into the clearing, proud of my keen intuition, Philip grabbed my shoulder. I froze as he crouched and pointed to the ground.

He signed, *Trap. Look closer.*

I squinted, scanning the patch of earth I

judged was clear. Then, I saw the glint of a wire nestled among the grass. A simple snare, perfectly veiled, waiting to snap.

Philip signed, *An undisturbed surface means nothing. You must read the signs beneath. Look twice, then again. If you miss the signs, you die.*

The lesson has stayed with me. It is even more relevant now than it was then. I scan the dunes again, the soft morning light unable to fool me. The desert camouflages its secrets, yet it won't catch me unprepared.

Neither will my memories.

Philip's lesson wasn't only about survival. It was also about perception, the ability to see what is hidden and trust the signs others miss.

Some philosophers argued that time is not something external, ticking away in measured intervals. We feel time, which is shaped by experience and memory. We do not exist in a sequence of disconnected moments. We carry the past with us, and it defines who we are.

I recall the most significant details of Philip's lesson. If memory is unreliable, then what do I have left? If time is just a collection of moments, memory is the thread that stitches them together. What I recall is real because it shapes me.

I glance at the horizon, where the dunes rise and fall like ocean waves, slowly changing with the continuity of time. The past is similar

—always there. Even as the wind reshapes the surface, the foundation remains.

No, the past is not gone. It is alive in me. And that is something I can trust.

As the morning wears on, the light reveals details I hadn't seen in the dawn's earlier softness. That's when I notice something unusual in the sand—a pattern cutting through the otherwise smooth desert floor.

I pause, crouching to get a better angle.

Tracks.

They stretch across the dune, a mix of footprints and hoof marks. I brush my fingers over the indentations. They're fresh, the edges still sharp where the wind hasn't touched them yet. Whoever made them passed through a few hours ago, at most.

I trace the tracks as they weave across the ground, disappearing over the next ridge. Traders? A caravan, maybe? It's the most direct route from here to Sachu, after all. I search the horizon for movement. The expanse remains motionless.

The hoofprints are heavy, pressed deep into the sand—a sign of loaded animals. Likely, three horses, judging by the width. The footprints are uniform and evenly spaced. My stomach tightens. These aren't the tracks of wandering merchants or harmless travelers.

They're soldiers.

The realization sharpens my focus. Soldiers

out here, on this route? There's solely one reason for that. They're hunting me.

The footprints are numerous. Five or six men are present. Their steps are also heavy. They will not be fast enough to outpace me.

I smirk to myself. These soldiers have made a mistake by passing me, leaving tracks so easy to follow. They might as well have lit a beacon in the open, inviting me to find them.

If I'm their intended prey, then the hunt is on. Except they have miscalculated. I'm no longer a cornered animal. I am the predator.

Excitement sparks. The fatigue in my legs vanishes. I roll my shoulders, feeling the tension shift. These soldiers don't know who I am.

A new kind of clarity settles over me. The soldiers set the terms of this hunt, but the favorable outcome will be mine. My steps quicken as I follow the trail.

NINE

The desolation gives its travelers too much time to reflect. Every gust of wind whispers of the future. Every grain of sand carries memories. It pulls me back to General Tiberius Cassianus' dimly lit chambers.

He had maps spread across his desk, their edges curled from use, each bearing the marks of military strategy. The man himself was not present yet, so I took the time to let my eyes wander. A general's quarters always told a story. This one whispered of precision, control, and a man who valued the chessboard above the battlefield.

Then I saw it.

A small, ornate object hung above the narrow desk. Its bezel was etched with strange, intertwining patterns. In many ways, the symbols resembled the Mark of the Phylax: two spirals entwined in an eternal dance, their textured curves flowing endlessly into one another. They suggest harmony, transition, and the timeless rhythm of existence.

The talisman was unlike any I'd seen. It pulsed with a turquoise luminescence, a glowing heartbeat that felt alive. As I stepped closer, the light intensified. It was as though the object recognized me, responding to my presence with an unspoken acknowledgment.

Intrigue flared, a dangerous ember I had learned to extinguish. My fingers hovered over the talisman, but I stopped myself. The Phylax taught me that the mission was all that mattered. While on a mission, questions were luxuries we could not afford. However, the pull of the object was undeniable.

The sound of footsteps broke the spell. Tiberius Cassianus entered, his presence filling the room. He was a man built for command—stone-faced, broad-shouldered, and carved from stone. It wasn't his stature that struck me. It was his demeanor: peaceful and resigned, as though he had seen the end of this encounter before it began.

He didn't reach for a weapon. Instead, he walked to the desk, his attention shifting to the talisman before settling on me. "I know why you're here," he said, "I won't fight you."

I didn't move. Cassianus' composure was disarming, yet I held firm.

"You're not the first," he continued, leaning on the desk as though addressing an old acquaintance. "You won't be the last. The Phylax never stop, do they?" He let out a small, bitter laugh. "They'll send soldiers until the mission is complete. That's their way."

His words tightened something within me. I didn't let it show.

"You don't see it yet," Tiberius said, his tone carrying pity. "You are on the wrong side of history."

Of course, he would see it that way. He was somehow tied to the Sigma Event, though the Phylax never provided me with specifics. I only knew his actions would contribute to the death of billions. True evil always obscures itself in righteousness.

Tiberius straightened. "One day, you'll see the truth. When you do, I hope it doesn't destroy you."

I could not endure his foolishness any longer. My blade cut through the air with all the force I could muster. He fell without a sound, his body a puppet with its strings severed.

I carefully lifted the talisman. The rhythmic pulse of its light drew my attention once again. Its hypnotic glow was infectious. Curiosity breeds hesitation, and hesitation is fatal for someone like me. I let its glow fade as I left the room. The talisman's powers remained a mystery.

Why are these memories surfacing now? I've walked the desert countless times, always focused on the present. Yet, these unbidden fragments of the past are clawing their way back.

Many physicists argue that the past isn't fixed. The act of observation can change what has already happened. They call it the *Participatory Universe*—the idea that the universe does not fully exist until something interacts with it, shaping its nature.

It sounds absurd, but a footprint in the sand does not exist until I step forward. The stars overhead do not shine in my vision until I look up. The universe is unfinished, uncertain, waiting for someone to give it form. What if time is the same way? What if my past is not a road I have already walked but something still taking shape beneath my feet?

I think of my recurring dream and its shifting details. Or the picture of the woman pulled from another time. Now, this—the memory of the talisman and the strange way it pulsated. I took nothing with me from that room. Yet, here in the silence of the desert, the memory refuses to let go of me. The more I think about it, the more it is an ember rekindled into a flame.

Maybe the past isn't resurfacing. Perhaps it's responding. If these physicists are correct, every moment I recall is an interaction with history. It is a thread being pulled from something unfinished. Maybe the talisman is more than something from my past.

I return to the tracks, which become more distinct as I push on. They cut a path through the dunes. I still count three horses, and I am confident there are five men. My instincts thrum with the thrill of pursuit. I am closing in on my target. I climb the next dune. Sweat beads on my brow despite the early hour.

Cresting the ridge, I pause, squinting into the distance. Far ahead, a small cluster of figures moves steadily across the landscape. Even at this distance, I can see how controlled their formation is. Unlike the scattered patrols of Qin's army. The sunlight catches flashes of dark metal that doesn't match the worn brown leather that Qin's soldiers wore. It's impossible to make out the details, but my gut twists with recognition.

The way they sweep the terrain feels eerily similar to the soldiers who came for me in the village with Xia. I can't see the golden trim or the Imperial Mark from here, but I don't need to. I've seen enough to believe these are the ones who replaced Qin's forces. The new power. Why they care about hunting down a ghost from a fallen regime is still unclear. One thing, however, is certain: they'll be dangerous. I need to know more before I act. If they belong to the new Emperor, then I must be careful.

I stay low, fixed on the soldiers as they march across the desert. The contours of the land provide some cover. Each dune is a chance to slip out of sight. They remain disciplined but lack the urgency of someone being pursued. That means they don't know I'm behind them. At least not yet.

Far in the distance, the outline of Sachu wavers in the heat and teases the edge of my vision. It has to be the town, though I know the sun-baked terrain is a master of illusions. The sight sends a spark of hope for resupplying. It also carries a warning. If those soldiers reach Sachu, they'll have an advantage over me. I need to catch up with them before they cross into the town. Tonight is my window to strike.

The sun dips lower, cooling the air. Shadows stretch across the ground. I watch as they make camp, settling in for the evening. Soon after, their fire flickers in the twilight, allowing me to hone in on their position.

My muscles coil with anticipation. Nighttime is my ally, the cover I need to close in without detection. I watch their camp, the silhouettes of soldiers moving around the flames. My time will come soon enough.

I stay behind a dune, locked on the sentries, standing watch at the camp's edge. They move lazily, not expecting an intruder in this void. It's a mistake I intend to exploit.

The sand cushions my footfalls, absorbing any noise. The first sentry comes into view. I close the distance quickly, my knife slipping from its sheath without a sound. In one fluid swing, I bring the blade up, covering his mouth with my free hand as I draw the knife across his neck. His body goes limp. I ease him to the ground, listening for any sign that his fall has alerted the others. Nothing.

I creep toward the second sentry, who stands several paces away, oblivious to the fate of his comrade. The darkness veils me while his outline looms against the light of the fire. He shifts, glancing in my direction. I freeze, noticing how young he is—too young to be out here. He squints, shrugs, then turns his back to me. I can't believe he didn't see me. I almost feel bad taking the life of someone not yet ready to shave. Unfortunately, this small detachment has chosen to hunt me. I close in, repeating the kill, my knife swiftly finding its mark. After he drops to the ground, I grab his sword.

With the sentries down, I slip deeper into the camp. The fire crackles softly, casting light across the sleeping forms of the remaining soldiers. I am a phantom, circling the fire's edge to where two men lay on their bedrolls. Their chests rise and fall with the rhythm of sleep.

My dagger hovers over the first one. I see a worn piece of parchment sticking out from his cloak. A letter, most likely. The ink-stained edges and careful folds tell me he cares about the note. Perhaps someone waits for him back home— someone who will never see him again.

I plunge my knife deep into his neck. Warm blood seeps over my fingers. I instantly swing the sword in a wide arc. The blade meets flesh and bone, decapitating the second soldier before he can stir. Both kills are quick.

I retreat toward the edge of the camp when suddenly, a force yanks me back. A hand clamps around my throat, squeezing with incredible strength that chokes the air from my lungs. My vision narrows to a tunnel of blurred images as the world constricts around me. I twist sharply, slamming my elbow into the attacker's ribs with all the force I can muster. The grip around my throat loosens enough. I drop low and drive my sword upward, deep into the soldier's side. My blade glides through his flesh.

He falls to the ground, gurgling on his own blood. His strength slips away. I stumble back, gulping for air. The taste of dirt and blood is thick in my mouth, burning my throat.

It's done. The camp is quiet once more, except for the crackling fire.

I stand among the fallen, my grip loosening around the hilt of my sword. Then, I see a lone figure stationed across the glow. He is different from the others. His jet-black armor is far more ornate, with intricate gold accents that catch the firelight. The Imperial emblem gleams on his breastplate. His helmet, crafted to resemble a crown, marks him as someone of great power. A golden mask cover his face, which is tilted at an awkward angle. An unsettling aura of authority surrounds him. A chill runs down my spine because I believe this may be the new Emperor.

It's strange to see a man of such importance wearing sleeveless armor, his muscled arms exposed. My sight drops to his shoulder. There it is—the Mark of the Phylax seared into his flesh. Or is it? I cannot tell with certainty, but his brand appears mutilated. The firelight dances in his eyes as he watches me, his lips curling into a smug, arrogant smile.

"Ah-ha, traveler," he begins, his breath stinking of contempt. "Even though you failed your mission, the legendary silence of the Phylax remains." He takes a deliberate step forward. The fire casts twisted images behind him. "You think you're worthy of it?"

I say nothing, my oath binding my tongue. This man isn't following the creed. The sole Phylax permitted to speak is the Archon. This man does not hold that title.

His laugh is chilling. "Not even a twitch, of course." His focus bores into me, searching for any reaction. "Do you even understand what you've done? What you've failed to do? The Chinese were supposed to believe Qin died by the sword of his Imperial Guards. Now the world knows an outsider killed him. The Phylax do not take kindly to that level of failure."

I keep my muscles taut, attention never leaving his. Is he a Phylax? How else would he know of my mission? Of my failure?

"Look at you," he sneers. "Stumbling through the desert like a lost child, all because you couldn't complete a simple task." He gestures around the camp with a flourish, mocking the carnage I've wrought. His laughter is cold. "You don't even know, do you?" he continues, taking another step closer. "The Phylax chose me to clean up your mess. Your failure makes you part of that mess, of course." His hand moves to the hilt of his sword, the firelight gleaming off the blackened metal.

He lunges without warning. I duck, bringing my sword up in a swift arc. He matches my speed. His blade slices through the air, forcing me to twist away. The clash of metal reverberates across the dunes, thunderously ringing out.

He moves with precision. Each strike is relentless. His sword arcs toward my legs. I leap backward, the sand shifting beneath my feet. The firelight casts our chaotic dance across the dunes. I aim a strike at his exposed side. He parries effortlessly. His counterstrike knocks my knife away, the force exploding through my wrist.

Pain blossoms up my arm as I stagger away. He presses the advantage, his attacks growing more vicious. A sharp blow to my ribs sends me sprawling onto the ground. I am thankful he hit the side opposite my wound. Regardless, the world blurs as the soldier hovers over me.

My muscles scream in protest as I fight to keep consciousness.

The soldier pauses, savoring his triumph. His sword gleams in the firelight as he raises it, poised for the killing blow. A twisted smile spreads over his lips. "The silence of the Phylax," he sneers. "What a fitting end for you."

I wait, the moment stretching endlessly as the sword begins its descent. My hand shoots along the ground in a desperate thrust, snatching a fistful of sand. I fling it upward with as much speed as I can muster. The grains erupt in his face, catching him mid-swing. He reels back, clawing at his eyes with a howl of rage. As he twists, the armor on his arm shifts, revealing the heavily scarred mess in the spot where the Mark of the Phylax would typically be.

I roll hard, the world tilting as adrenaline takes over. I need to rise. Before I can, the air around me wavers. A low hum vibrates through the ground. The fire's glow dims to an ember. The soldier stumbles toward me, his outline blurring.

The air collapses inward, pulling at my senses. A searing, twisting force wraps around me, dragging me into the rippling void. The soldier's outstretched arm wavers out of focus, his enraged shout swallowed by the distortion. The dunes melt; the stars above twist into a vortex.

I'm falling—or maybe I'm rising. The sensations blur together; the desert, the soldier, and the fight all peel away. A dream dissolving into wakefulness. Then, nothing.

TEN

No matter how much I wish otherwise, time travel has two unbreakable rules. The first rule is that my ability to move through time takes precisely three years to recharge, down to the second. We all have the same limitation, except for the Archon. I've tried countless times to break that limit. Every attempt has failed.

I came here two years, two months, and three days ago. If I could have left earlier, I would have. Especially when that soldier's sword was poised to end me. I couldn't pull myself through time.

When I move through time by my own will, it feels controlled, like flipping through the pages of a book. Being pulled through by someone else is disorienting. The world yanks me off my feet, leaving me with no sense of control.

I've experienced it twice before, both times with Philip. The first was when he took me to the Acropolis, introducing me to time travel. The second was three years later when we went to ancient Egypt. Each time, I was nauseous.

This was different. No one was with me

when the pull stopped. Whoever did this had enough skill to eject me from the flow of time while continuing on their path, leaving me stranded. I didn't know such a thing was possible. If they were here, I might thank them for saving me. They're not, so I'm left alone to understand where and when I've landed.

I need to take stock.

The man who tried to kill me claimed the Phylax contracted him. The mark on his arm suggests he might have been one of us, yet his speech hinted otherwise. Could the Phylax really have hired him? If so, the implications are troubling. I am a dead man. However, I'd expect the Phylax to demand every detail of what has happened, not end me in the middle of nowhere.

There are other explanations. His dark armor suggests he is associated with the Chinese army. The new emperor probably wants me dead. It would help prove his loyalty to the former regime and deflect any suspicion that he played a role in its downfall. Or he might work for someone else, reducing his costume to confusing theater. If that's the truth, then who could it be?

Assuming the soldier isn't with the Phylax, I have an even more significant problem: reporting these events. The Phylax expected me to return within a year of completing my mission. By all indications, I am now centuries late. The hard-packed road beneath my feet and the larger city of Sachu on the horizon suggest

I've traveled at least four hundred years forward from my starting point. It could be even longer.

Despite everything, Athens remains my destination. While reporting this to the Phylax is risky, it's still the safest course of action for now. I must admit, it's not a plan I'm particularly fond of.

It is difficult to adjust to the scorching sun after being ripped out of the cold night. I pause for a rest before making the final push to Sachu. As I set my satchel down, the picture I took from Xia slips into view. I pick it up, thinking briefly about Xia and the woman in the image. There isn't anything new to consider, so I put the picture back. I have more urgent concerns; Xia's mystery can wait.

I take a long drink of water, savoring the relief as it slides down my throat. It's enough to steady me, to keep me moving toward the city on the horizon.

My footsteps are slow while my senses adapt to Sachu's atmosphere. This place has changed significantly from when I first passed through. Before, the buildings were simple homes with some merchant activity. Now, imposing structures with curved roofs loom against the skyline. Their silhouettes provide a welcome contrast to the flat desert I have traversed. Wooden beams lined with ornate carvings and doorways flanked by stone guardians point to the Northern Dynasties period. Yet, I am unsure how far into the future I've traveled.

I advance onward into Sachu. The streets bustle with activity. Merchants peddle their goods, their voices rising in a cacophony of haggling. Shoppers move between the market stalls. They speak Middle Chinese.

I scan the crowd, cataloging people and noting exits. *Stay focused*, I tell myself. Every step through this maze of people makes me feel vulnerable. In the wilderness, I can move unseen.

I pass a stall draped in silks that boasts a vibrant rainbow of colors. Another vendor displays metal that gleams on a weapons stand. As I weave through the throng, I feel the undercurrent of unease grow stronger.

A particular stall draws my interest. Unlike the others, it is cluttered with various relics, including tools, trinkets, and scrolls. Each seems plucked from history's grasp. A rusted blade lies atop a pile of leather-bound scrolls, while strange gemstones with faded carvings glint under the light. It is a collection gathered from the corridors of time.

There is something about these items that I find provocative. The merchant watches me intently from under the privacy of his stall's tent. He juts his head forward, tilting it at an awkward angle, tracking my every move.

"You seek what is lost," his gravelly whisper

chills me. "To find it, you must embrace what you fear." The words hang in the air, cutting through the market's noise. I stop. His tone has a malevolent edge.

I move closer, gesturing for something to write with. I need to ask a few questions.

The merchant looks down at my hand, a hint of a smile curling at the edge of his lips. It is not warm or friendly.

He reaches into the folds of his coat, producing a small brush and a scrap of parchment. "Ah-ha, a silent guardian," he says, "that always makes for an interesting conversation."

I ignore his comment, taking the writing instruments from him. I scribble my question: *What is the date?*

He takes the parchment back, reading it with amusement. "Why do such things matter to one like you?" He waits for a reaction. Is he goading me into revealing something about myself? If so, I do not give him the satisfaction.

He answers, "The third year of Xiaochang, the year of Dingwei. We are in the second month, on the fifteenth day. A time when much is in motion, and the past is eager to change."

My guess was not incredibly accurate. This is the late Northern Wei period, somewhere around 527 CE, over seven hundred years after my mission.

As I glance over the relics again, a

turquoise luminescence catches my awareness. The talisman hangs from the edge of the stall. Two opposing spirals locked in an eternal loop etch its surface. This is the exact item that once belonged to General Tiberius Cassianus. The glow intensifies when I near it. I forgot how alluring its call was.

The merchant's smile widens into something more of a grimace. "It calls to you, traveler," he says as though he is speaking of a curse rather than an object. "It has a way of finding people and things that walk between times."

He reaches out, plucking the talisman from its place. He holds it out toward me. "Go on, take it. It wants you."

I hesitate. The talisman is no ordinary trinket. I reach out, my fingers closing around it. It's warm to the touch, almost alive, pulsating against my palm. I feel compelled to keep the item.

I take the parchment back from him. *Who are you? Where did you get this?*

The merchant chuckles softly. "My name is unimportant. The talisman's origins are older than you or I can imagine. Some say it comes from the space between seconds, where time itself was born. Others say an ancient order of some kind."

I doubt that I will get a straight answer from this guy. I know Tiberius once held this relic.

"A compass," the merchant continues, his tone trickling with malice. "For those lost in the currents of time. A guide, or perhaps a trap, if not careful. It depends on the choices you make."

My grip tightens around the talisman. I fight to keep my expression stoic while trying to figure out what this trinket is.

"You stand at a crossroads, traveler," he whispers, leaning forward. "The guardian, the wanderer, the fool who seeks to bind what should be free." His voice grows colder. "Tell me, what will you do when you find the family you've forgotten?"

His words freeze me in place. What does this merchant mean? I know my family—my mother didn't care about me. My father broke my bones. That's all there is. To whom does he refer? Philip?

I force a nod, slipping the talisman into a pocket under my tunic. His words have unsettled me, but showing it is a weakness. I must not show anything other than indifference.

He leans back, folding his arms into the sleeves of his coat. "Very well," he murmurs. He drifts away as though dismissing me. "Use the talisman as you see fit. It may guide you. Or it might bring you right back here." Something sinister shrouds him once again. "When you are ready, of course."

With that, he retreats into the depths of his stall, leaving me standing amid the bustling market. I take one last look at him, wondering about his cryptic words. *The family you've forgotten.*

When I step away from the stall, the talisman's pulse mirrors the rhythm of my heartbeat. The object is alive and attuned to me. It resonates with my body, seemingly aware of how I feel. How did the merchant explain it? *It has a way of finding people and things that walk between times.*

Could it be that time travel knocks people out of sync with the natural rhythm of the universe? Like plucking a guitar string in the wrong key, a displaced traveler would vibrate at a slightly different frequency, creating tiny ripples in spacetime. The talisman could be calibrated to sense those ripples—a temporal resonance. A quiet hum that only something designed to listen for it would pick up.

The talisman may act akin to a spectrum analyzer, measuring frequencies that are out of sync. If a traveler is slightly out of phase with the present, the device resonates with your mismatch, zeroing in on whatever shouldn't be here and now. That would explain why it feels alive in my hand. It is listening for those echoes from another time.

The market swallows me with activity: vendors continue to shout, coins clink, and children weave their laughter through clusters of shoppers. The air is thick with the scent of spices, incense, and humanity—an oppressive mix that sifts in from all sides.

I keep my pace steady. Each step carries me deeper into the mob. My unease doesn't fade. Not while in Sachu. I peer around the crowd, searching for the source of my apprehension. The faces blur together, indistinct in the shifting light of the market.

Then I see him. A figure draped in dirty robes stands near a fruit stall, obscured by the bustling crowd. His posture is as rigid as a drawn bow. His dark complexion contrasts sharply with his vivid green eyes—an unusual combination in Sachu. The talisman's pulse quickens. Its heat intensifies until it threatens to scorch through my cloak.

The figure turns, a hood lowered to his brow. Two words escape his lips: "Dahr-khoday."

The words strike my interest. I have never heard anyone use the term before, but I latch onto its Pahlavi etymology: Master of Eternal Time.

Pahlavi? Here in Sachu? It's not a common language in these markets. My hand brushes against the talisman. Its heat is almost unbearable.

Dahr-khoday. The word refuses to fade. Is it an accusation? Introduction? Perhaps it is a warning or prophecy. The world is never short on dollar store prophets.

I force myself to keep walking. I don't dare look back. I don't want any more problems on this trip. Cold crawls up my neck, icy fingers tracing my spine.

The talisman's quickened pulse continues. I weave through the crowd, staring at the exit at the far end of the market. The noise fades into a dull roar. I move swiftly, resisting the urge to glance back.

The edge of the market comes into view. The talisman's heat fades as I leave the crowd behind, hoping for a moment to collect myself. I turn and see him. The figure stands at the far end of the street, staring at me.

It's not until the sounds of the market have dimmed behind me that I finally allow myself to relax. I keep walking, each step putting distance between me and whatever danger lurks back there. This talisman might be helpful.

ELEVEN

For nearly two months, the desert stretches on. Each day blurs into the next: sand, heat, thirst. At night, the temperatures plummet, transforming my exhale into ghostly mist. The monotonous expanse of dunes and rocky outcrops push me to the brink. At least nothing disrupts my journey: no ambushes, no pursuers —just the peace of the journey.

As dusk settles, I stumble upon an abandoned campsite tucked between two jagged rocks. I pause to survey the area. In the center lie the remnants of a fire pit, its scattered ashes long cooled by the wind. Worn footprints crisscross the ground, almost swallowed by the shifting dust.

For the first time since leaving Sachu, the talisman pulsates. Its rhythmic energy sends my senses to high alert. I scan the campsite, gripping the talisman tightly as I move. Is it reacting to something nearby? I tread carefully, the pulse growing stronger. It sends a signal up my arm. I see a sliver of metal, barely visible beneath the sand.

I crouch, brushing the grains away to reveal a small, tarnished brooch. The talisman's vibrations raise the hairs on the back of my neck. I freeze temporarily before reaching for the brooch. As I pick it up, I see an unmistakable mark on its surface: a jagged dent cut across a stag's body. I remember how my blade caught the brooch at the end of my scuffle, denting it before it fell to the forest floor. I had practically signed my name on it.

I turn the item, ensuring it is not merely a similar trinket. As suspected, the phrase Rex Invictus is etched on the back in faded Latin.

Unconquered King.

This was William Rufus's stag brooch.

The memory unfolds.

William Rufus called for help, his voice unanswered by the mute forest. Cornered, he fought back with all the ferocity he could muster, but it was futile. Each of my strikes drove him closer to the inevitable. Finally, with one decisive blow, he collapsed. The brooch—this brooch—tumbled from his tunic, landing with a thud among the leaves.

The item is laughably crude, as if crafted by an apprentice fumbling with their tools. The stag etched into the metal has misshapen antlers. I later learned it was likely a gift from Malcolm III of Scotland, part of a diplomatic exchange to solidify ties between the two kings. That knowledge didn't make it any less hideous to me then, and it certainly doesn't now.

The talisman hums louder, more insistent, urging me to uncover something I've overlooked. There was something peculiar about that mission, a detail buried beneath the haze of time. Then, clarity strikes.

I drop the brooch as though it pierces my finger. My hands fumble as I search my pockets, desperate to retrieve the photograph I've carried since Xia and I departed under the most enigmatic circumstances.

The woman in the photograph.

It can't be.

Deep down, I already know it is.

Before I found William Rufus in the forest, I noticed a shimmer in the air, like ripples on a disturbed pond. It was the first time I had witnessed a temporal distortion from the outside rather than being enveloped within it.

A woman appeared—barely visible in the shaded woods. Her presence defied logic; she moved as if the flow of time bent to accommodate her.

"You're making a mistake," she whispered. "William Rufus doesn't deserve to die. The Phylax isn't telling you the truth."

Before I could respond—before I could even begin to process her words—she vanished. She had simply ceased to exist, dissolving into another ripple of distorted air.

I stood frozen, struggling to piece together an explanation. The woman was a stranger, yet she knew me. She wasn't a Phylax—that much was certain. Still, she moved through time with ease, appearing and vanishing effortlessly. The three-year rule was immutable, but somehow, she had broken it.

Regardless, I did what my training demanded. I buried my questions, forcing the encounter beyond my conscious mind. When William Rufus died, I returned to the Acropolis as ordered.

Protocol demands full disclosure of a mission's events. I recounted the incident to the High Council, describing the woman and how time shifted around her. I expected them to react urgently, demand an investigation, and perhaps even commend my vigilance. Admittedly, I left out the cryptic warning the woman gave me.

That's impossible, one Council member signed as her focus darted away from me. *Only a few outside the Phylax can travel through time; we know each of them. You must be mistaken.*

While the Council's words were decisive, the discomfort etched on her visage told a different story. It was the first time I had ever seen a Council member falter in their certainty.

I wanted to demand answers to my questions, but I knew better. The Phylax does not tolerate insubordination. So, I feigned understanding. The unease lingered temporarily; however, the memory didn't take long to fade into nothingness.

That confusion feels fresh again while standing here with the photograph in my fingers. The woman's words echo: *They aren't telling you the truth.*

I pick up the brooch again. How did it end up here?

Some physicists speculate that matter doesn't exist in a fixed state. Instead, it flickers in and out of reality at an imperceptible scale. On the quantum level, particles emerge from nothing and vanish just as quickly, like fireflies blinking in the dark. Typically, this happens at such a small scope we never notice. Given the right conditions, what if objects—or even people—could slip out of one place or moment and reappear in another?

If that were true, then maybe the brooch isn't always buried beneath the leaves of that distant forest. Maybe it phased out of existence and surfaced here. It could be carried by the unseen current of time itself.

I turn it over again, staring at the familiar dent. If objects can flicker through time, who's to say the same thing couldn't happen to a person?

But that's just a theory.

More likely, the merchant had possession of

this relic, too. He could have sold it to some careless traveler. There is no way to know. Aside from jogging my memory about the woman, the brooch means nothing now.

I've delayed my travel for too long. There's no immediate threat here. The talisman's vibrations subside, aligning itself with my steady rhythm. I slowly exhale worries away. Dwelling on this serves no purpose. The priority is clear: keep moving to the next resupply point. Samarkand is a week ahead.

Again, the following days blur into a steady rhythm: dawn rises, footsteps fall, and the endless dunes yield nothing except their cruel monotony. While I love the solitude that the desert brings, I am exhausted. Each night, I collapse beneath a sky filled with the stars' cold indifference.

By the time the sand shifts to firmer ground, my pace quickens. Minor signs of life emerge— a distant caravan winding along the horizon, the outline of walls rising against the blue haze of midday. Samarkand.

When I finally crest the last hill, the city unfurls before me, bustling with life. Tall, domed structures dot the skyline, their intricate mosaics glittering in the early afternoon sun. In many respects, this city is the same as Sachu. The smells, noisy merchants, and crowds all set me on edge. While I understand the traders speaking Chinese, the locals here speak Sogdian.

Its clipped consonants are unmistakable, though the meaning of these words escapes me.

Samarkand is a melting pot of cultures. Persians, Turks, Mongols, and travelers from distant lands cross these narrow streets. The place is alive with the constant hum of movement, which should be comforting after so many weeks alone. Instead, it heightens my caution. There is always danger in a crowd.

I stop at a stall selling dried food, pretending to inspect the goods. The bustling marketplace stretches out, a chaotic dance of movement. People weave through the crowd. Nothing seems out of the ordinary.

Then, beyond the mass of people, I spot him again. I'm sure it's the same man from Sachu—half-hidden beneath a worn tunic, standing at the corner of a narrow alley. He is too rigid. His gaze is fixed on me. I catch a flash of his dark complexion and piercing green eyes.

Dahr-khoday. That's what he said.

I am confident this man is following me. Is he a Phylax?

I pretend to haggle with the vendor as I gather my composure. If this man is on a mission, he's working alone. Something in my gut tells me I'm his target. I sense he's trained to hunt, track, and strike in the same way I am. For all I know, he has already set the trap.

I slip down an alley; my footsteps muffled against the uneven stone. The noise of the marketplace fades behind me, swallowed by the soundless passage. The walls press in. My hand moves to my belt, fingers brushing the hilt of my knife. It's a comforting weight, though I leave it sheathed for now. A fight here would be messy, but I'll be ready if it comes to that.

I glance back, catching stillness in the alley behind me. Yet the tension coursing through me refuses to ease. If I'm being followed, they will know this route better than me.

The path soon narrows into a dead end. The walls are unbroken—no doors, no windows, nothing to slip through or climb over. I rush to the most concealed corner, crouching low behind a stack of broken crates. It's not much of a refuge; however, it will give me an extra minute to assess the situation. I position myself with my back to the wall, fixed on the entrance.

My breathing slows as I force my body to remain motionless. The entire city seems frozen with anticipation. Then, I hear a shuffle—not one but two sets of footsteps.

As the sound gets louder, my grip tightens on the hilt of my knife. I can almost feel them pressing into the alley. The talisman pulses in my pocket with an insistent vibration. They are time travelers.

I strain my ears, catching the soft rustle of fabric and a boot scraping against stone. A bead of sweat slides down my temple. They must be with the Phylax. Or, is the Dahr-khoday something new to worry about?

A shadow appears at the alley's mouth, stretching across the wall. Another follows. The shapes of the two figures merge briefly before separating again.

The first figure steps into view, a hood pulled low over the face. Their posture isn't openly hostile. The second follows close behind, movements sharper, more aggressive. Both pause to scan the alley. I keep my eyes on their hands—empty for now, but I know better than to assume they're unarmed.

The talisman's vibrations act as a warning. I adjust my grip on the knife, readying myself for what's to come. I wait. The longer I stay, the more I might learn.

The woman raises her hands higher. I notice the subtle gestures of the Phylax sign language. *We've come to talk.* Her fingers quiver as she forms the words. Her companion shifts his weight, glaring at the alley's entrance as though expecting someone else. *We don't want to fight.*

Phylax? If they are, why are there two of them? Am I that dangerous? Something in the way she moves suggests she is telling the truth. They aren't here for a fight. Not yet, anyway.

I step out from my hiding spot, still keeping my distance. The tension in the alley crackles between us. I keep my focus on the woman. She is the leader. Her fingers quickly weave through the air in a series of signs. *You need to come with us.*

The Council will explain everything. She hesitates, then adds: *It's safer if we travel together.*

Safer for whom? I wonder.

I watch her closely, waiting for a catch or an attack. I fight to maintain my cold detachment. What could be so wrong? It must be significant if the Phylax is sending scouts to find me. Or this is a lie.

Your safety is at risk, she signs. *Ours depends on you as well.* The implication is clear: if they fail to bring me back, it will mean trouble for them.

The man starts to sign something but stops halfway. His fingers hang in the air. He looks at the woman, who shakes her head almost imperceptibly. The rest of the message remains unsigned.

I check them over for weapons. They both stand with open stances. Still, I don't let my guard down. They could strike at any moment. This could all be part of a trap.

The woman signs, *We don't have time. You have to come with us. It's not safe here.*

If something has gone wrong within the Phylax, it could mean chaos or betrayal in the ranks. Why would they need me to fix it?

Before she can start signing again, I lift my arm. I've heard enough. *I won't go with you,* I sign back. *I'm traveling to the Acropolis anyway. I'll get there on my own.*

The idea of traveling with them, under their unnerving vigilance, makes my skin crawl. I will follow the Phylax creed: always travel alone.

We have to go together. The Archon is worried. He thinks something will happen to you on the way. She hesitates before continuing. *He needs your account of what happened with Qin.*

The mention of Qin stops me cold. I study the woman. How many people know about my clandestine mission? Everything we do is supposed to remain in the dark—even from other members of the Phylax. Yet, here they are, following me, asking for details they shouldn't even know to inquire about.

No. I sign the word with more force than intended. *I don't need your help. I'll make it there alone.*

The man shifts slightly. With folded arms, one finger nervously taps against the opposite bicep. The woman, however, doesn't back down. She is more insistent this time. *This isn't about your pride. The Archon needs you there alive.* She adds, *We both do.*

I sign to the man, *You spoke to me in Sachu. You said, 'Dahr-khoday.' What is that supposed to mean?*

The woman signs to her partner sharply, *Did you see him in Sachu? Why didn't you tell me? Why did you speak out loud? We could have handled this back there.*

He rolls his eyes, then signs to his partner, *I thought he would talk to me instead of running away.* His focus shifts back to me. *The Dahr-*

khoday is a dangerous group of radicals the Archon has discovered. He fears they have interfered with your mission. He thinks they might be trying to kill you.

My attention darts between the pair standing in front of me. I've never heard of the Phylax sending two agents to bring in one. It's not our protocol, and I have difficulty believing them.

The woman signs one last time, each word punctuated with worry. *We have our orders. We will bring you in.*

I tell them once more, *I will go on my own. You two can go ahead. Inform the Archon I'll be there soon.*

An unspoken plea hangs between us. Shortly after, it seems the woman decides she needs to follow orders. She draws her knife. I won't be taken in.

The man's knife and mine slide into our palms in a synchronized motion. My hands remain steady. He surges first, his blade sweeping toward my midsection. I twist my hips, feeling the rush of air as his steel whistles past. Our knives meet in a brief clash, the impact reverberating through my wrist. I feint high, forcing him to bring his arm up; then I slash low. He jumps back just in time.

He tries for another rush, but I can already sense his intention. I sidestep, letting his momentum carry him too far forward. Seizing that split-second, I slam my elbow into him, knocking his knife off course. My blade comes up beneath his guard. The point slips between his ribs, and his breath catches in a sharp gasp. His eyes go wide, searching for something—mercy, maybe—but I've already finished what I started.

The woman charges me. I twist aside, barely dodging her strike. An upward slash touches her arm. She hisses, more in frustration than pain. I am surprised by a swift pivot, followed by a blow to my wrist that knocks the blade away. The knife clatters to the ground between us. We both move for it. She's faster, kicking it out of reach.

Before she can press her advantage, I drive into her. She tries to grapple with me, her hands clawing for control. I manage to trap one of her wrists, twisting it hard enough that her grip falters. The weapon slips from her grasp. She snarls and counters with an elbow to my ribs, knocking the wind from my lungs.

Staggering back, my hand brushes against something on the ground. It's a discarded leather rein, half-buried in the dust. I snatch it up. She charges again, and I shift with the rein clutched tight. Momentum carries her forward, and in that brief opening, I slip behind her and whip the leather around her throat. I yank it back hard. She thrashes, fists swinging, nails clawing at the strap, but I hold fast. Her fight ebbs, legs buckling, until I'm left holding the full weight of her limp body.

I tell myself she chose this fight, but the justification feels hollow. I wonder if they believed this mission was worth their lives. While unsure of their true identities, I believe they were Phylax.

I crouch beside them, searching for clues. My hands move quickly, checking their pockets until I find an ornate scroll sealed with the Mark of the Phylax. I hesitate, my thumb running over the broken wax before unfurling the scroll.

The instructions inside are cryptic. My name is scrawled across the parchment, accompanied by detailed notes tracking my movements. They've been watching me since I left Qin's encampment. One location catches my interest the most—Merv. They set a meeting for two weeks from now. The exact purpose isn't mentioned, except I don't need it spelled out. I'm on their agenda.

I wind up the scroll. Merv. It has always been a waypoint on the trek to the Acropolis. It is more important to me now. Making it there in two weeks will require my total effort. If I want to find real answers, I have to make that push.

I walk back into the bustling streets of Samarkand, slipping into the crowd. I select my supplies: dried meat, water skins, and a fresh cloak thick enough to shield me from the winds waiting outside the city. My fingers brush over the coarse fabric as I hand over the coins. My talisman is still; however, I still scan the streets for any sign of the Phylax. The people in this city are unaware of the real storm brewing. What will happen to everyone else if those who protect humankind are under siege?

With my provisions secured, I rush to the outskirts of the city. The noise begins to fade as I approach a stable nestled between the last few buildings in the town. The stableman agrees to sell me a sturdy chestnut mare. Her legs are strong, built for endurance. She'll carry me across the sands faster than I could manage on foot.

I tighten the saddle straps, securing the bags. I lead the horse toward the edge of the city. The walls of Samarkand loom behind me as the horizon stretches out.

I check the talisman beneath my cloak. It is calm. I rub my arm where the Mark of the Phylax is embedded, thinking of the two I killed. I wish I could feel regret for what happened. I don't. They should have taken my advice and moved ahead of me. I will make it to Athens on my own.

TWELVE

Merv defies the desert. Its massive walls, built from sunbaked mud brick, stretch out in both directions. It is a fortress against the sand's relentless encroachment. The towers are vigilant silhouettes watching over the countless lives within.

The city's tangled streets wind through clusters of buildings. Architectural styles from every corner of the world come together. Spires and domes lend an exceptional beauty to the town. Their polished surfaces are jewels that glint in the sunlight. The houses are built low, with thick mud-bricked walls to repel the heat. Only a few grander homes rise above the rest. Their lush inner courtyards are visible beyond ornate wooden gates, hinting at the opulence within. Wealthy merchants have carved out sanctuaries in this city of trade. They bury their riches behind walls adorned with intricate carvings that speak of distant lands.

The diversity of Merv's people is striking. People from every imaginable culture fill the streets: Sasanians, Arabs, Göktürks, Northern Wei Chinese, and even the odd Slav. The cacophony of languages surges, then fades, overlapping in a constant hum that never seems to cease.

Beneath the façade of all this life, there is something else. A city this significant—standing as a gateway between East and West—is a place where secrets trade as freely as spices. Merv is a city of influence, where whispered conversations forge alliances behind closed doors. Fortunes can rise or fall with the flip of a coin or the slip of a tongue. To most, this place represents opportunity—the chance to acquire wealth and power. To me, it feels dangerous.

Except, I need answers. The scroll's cryptic instructions pulled me here toward a Phylax meeting that's soon to happen. Somewhere in this maze of people, I will uncover mysteries.

I slip into the quieter part of the city, away from the chaotic din of the marketplace. The energy of Merv fades behind me, replaced by wind rushing through the narrow alleyways. The sounds of haggling give way to the muffled footsteps of a few passersby. I move with purpose, pulling out the scroll once more. Scanning the words, I note the location carefully: *two buildings south of the Zoroastrian fire temple on the west side of the city, near the outer wall. Look for the mark.*

I tuck the scroll back beneath my cloak. The

west side of Merv is more secluded, its streets are veins winding through the ancient city. Centuries of wind have worn the walls, and the faded exteriors tell stories of generations long gone.

The fire temple's tower comes into view, its golden spire gleaming in the afternoon sun. The temple's bell has tolled. A few latecomers hurry toward the entrance, encouraged by the gathering chant inside.

Each weathered building blends into the next. In moments like this, I can't help but appreciate the efficiency of modern city planning. Finding this place would be far easier if the ancients had numbered their buildings. Instead, I'm left chasing brief descriptions and relying on intuition through a puzzle of near-identical structures.

Eventually, I find the building not far from the temple, nestled against the city's outer wall. It resembles any other structure in this district. As I approach, one detail stands out: a crude Mark of the Phylax etched into the doorframe. I touch the scar on my arm, feeling the raised edges beneath my fingers.

This is the place.

I keep a grip on the dagger. Stepping closer to the door, I notice a latch embedded in the weathered stone disguised as part of the old structure. I move to open it until I realize this may be a trap.

I search the perimeter for another way: a window, a side entrance, or anything else to avoid walking into an ambush. The structure is sealed tight, offering no alternatives. Our safehouses are often built this way. There is security in providing only one passage. Time is slipping away. I have no choice except to take a chance.

My hand hovers over the latch. Prepared to fight, I push on the mechanism. With a low groan, the door shifts inward, revealing a narrow staircase that slopes downward.

I pause at the threshold. There's no telling what awaits inside, but turning back isn't an option. I've come this far. The answers I need are within reach. With a final glance over my shoulder, I step inside, closing the door softly behind me as I descend into the depths below.

I navigate the narrow stone platforms, each step as hushed as possible. The air is cooler here, heavy with dampness and the scent of mold. The flickering light of a few scattered torches guides my way. My senses heighten as I move deeper into the chamber. The enclosed space amplifies every sound. The distant water drip whispers while the rustle of unseen creatures skitters along the edges of my awareness.

The steps lead to a small landing. Beyond it, the room opens into a vaulted chamber with arched ceilings that disappear into the gloom. The building seems insignificant from the outside—a modest shell of weathered stone easily overlooked. Beneath its plain exterior lays this space of unexpected grandeur, a new world carved into the earth, hidden away from prying eyes.

From somewhere deeper within, I hear feet shuffling. The talisman pulses under my robe. I already know these people are from another time.

I crouch to stay within the alcove's protection. In the center of the room, three Phylax agents gather around a worn table. I can see their hands moving. Swift, deliberate gestures suggest this is an intense conversation. They use the Phylax sign language, holding to their vow, even in this enigmatic place. In a way, it is comforting.

I watch as a woman signs to two men. Her missing index finger gives her sign language an unusual slur. *The agents from Samarkand haven't arrived.* The signs hang heavy with implication. *We must move forward without them.*

The group shifts uncomfortably.

They were supposed to bring Adam in, the woman continues. *Their failure means no more negotiation. Adam must be captured and brought to the Sanctum. Alive.*

One of the men gestures with urgency. *If the Archon shares details like this, the problem must be severe.* I can see the tension in the other agents' jaws, clenched so tight that their muscles twitch.

He then signs something that makes me freeze. *During Qin's assassination, there was a mistake in the operational synopsis. The Dahr-khoday altered the scenario after we finalized our plan. They installed a signal string inside the yurt. It should not have been there.*

Yes, that's why we need Adam, the woman signs. *He's the only one who can tell us what happened. This failure has worsened the Sigma Event.*

If this Dahr-khoday can manipulate missions, it means they hold significant power. They are a force that could challenge the Phylax, which helps to explain why so many know about Qin's mission. It concerns us all.

The extent of their reach remains unknown, but it must be vast. The thought gnaws at me—how many of my missions have they manipulated? The idea is a splinter lodged in my brain. If we've been fighting to save humankind from the Sigma Event, then the Dahr-khoday must have set something nefarious into motion.

The instant Qin pulled the alarm string, I knew there was a problem. I expected punishment for my failure, but I never imagined it could escalate into something that threatens the survival of all life on Earth.

I'd give anything to go back and fix it, except it breaks the second immutable law of time travel: we cannot return to an event we've already altered.

Time does not allow contradiction. If I were to step into a moment where I had once stood, I would be nothing more than a shadow. The past has already accounted for my presence. It has no room for another.

They called it Novikov's Principle, a law of physics that no one can break. If I were to try to grab a weapon, my fingers would slip through the hilt like smoke. If I were to call out, the air would swallow my voice whole. The universe would fold around me, ensuring that events happen correctly. It would be as if I was never there, at least not the second time.

Regardless, if my actions have jeopardized the future of humanity, then...

I wouldn't want to be him, the woman signs.

And I agree.

The leader continues, signing something I find equally concerning. *What about this family member?*

The room shrinks with tension strangling me. Is this the same family member to whom the merchant referred? It's hard to imagine that they matter in my life now.

To my parents, family meant pain. They delivered discipline with the back of a hand or worse. I remember one night vividly, though I wish I didn't. I had left streaks on the plates after washing them. My father saw it as an excuse to teach me a lesson. He yanked off his belt, the metal buckle clanging against the chair as he whipped my back. Each lash cut deeper, the sting burning into my skin. My mother sat coolly at the table, not lifting a finger to intervene. She didn't flinch, didn't speak—until she saw the blood soaking through my shirt.

That's when my mother pulled my father away from me. She wasn't concerned for my well-being, just upset that she'd have to soak the bloodstains to clean my shirt.

That's family. At least, that's what the word means to me: pain, control, submission.

There's something else—something buried so deep it feels more of a dream than a memory. It nags at me, pulling at the frayed threads of my past. A whisper of something softer, more hopeful. It's a hand on my shoulder—not to punish but to comfort. A voice promising to keep me safe. There's something there, out of reach.

I shift my boot on the floor, causing sand to scrape on the stone. It's audible enough for one of the agents, mid-sign, to freeze. He listens to something the others don't hear. Air catches in my throat; my pulse hammers in my ears.

The room falls deathly calm.

An agent scans the alcove with suspicion. Slowly, his fingers move, signing to the others: *Did you hear that?*

They examine the alcove. Every muscle in my body tenses as I prepare to move. I've already lost the element of surprise.

The room explodes into action.

All three agents rush toward me, their hands grasping their weapons. I don't wait to see what comes next. My feet are already moving, propelling me out of the alcove as I bolt toward the passageway.

The chase is on.

I sprint through the chamber, their footsteps thundering behind me. The echoes of their pursuit bounce off the stone walls, filling the narrow space with the sound of chaos.

The taller one is a brute with bouldered shoulders and heavy footsteps. She's built to smash through walls if needed. The smaller one moves with unsettling grace, his knife glinting like a predator's fang.

I throw myself through the front door. My fingers graze the stone walls as I twist around the corner. I need to keep moving. The other Phylax won't tire quickly.

They're herding me. One cuts to the left, forcing me down a narrower path, while the other veers to the right, boxing me in. They are wolves, coordinated, silent, and closing in—leaving me with diminished options.

The city is a twisting web of alleys. There's no time to think. I can hear them getting closer. No matter how fast I run, they don't falter. Their steps drum in perfect unison, closing in with every second. They're wearing me down, waiting for me to make a mistake.

THIRTEEN

The uneven cobblestones beneath my boots force me to be careful. A miscalculation comes with the risk of falling into their hands.

Their boots pounding against stones are louder now. The Phylax agents are too close. All three of them refuse to let up. I ignore the burn in my legs and the ache in my side. I catch a glimpse of their shapes elongated on the walls beside me. I can't outrun them much longer.

I duck into another alley, even narrower than the last. A wooden stall sits overturned in the middle of the path, its contents spilling across the ground. Leaping over the broken pottery expends more effort than I wish to use.

A figure breaks through the crowd, moving toward me with surprising speed. Their dark clothing sends a surge through my nerves—at first, I think it might be the soldier from the desert, back to finish what he started. Or worse, a fourth Phylax I hadn't accounted for. Realizing who it is does nothing to assuage my fear.

Xia.

"Adam!" she shouts, urgency ripping through the air. "Follow me!"

I don't slow down. I can't. My gaze darts to Xia, then to the shadows creeping beside me, calculating my options. The Phylax agents are too close.

If I stop and fight, I'm outnumbered three to one. Xia might be here to kill me as well. If I keep fleeing, my chances of escaping all three are slim. That leaves one option: move forward with Xia. I can't trust her, but I have no other choice. I make my decision, change course, and run straight for Xia. If she plans to betray me, I'll encounter that fight soon enough.

When I'm within reach, she extends her arm and grabs my wrist. Before I know what is happening, a sharp, tingling sensation spreads over my limbs. My head spins; a wave of nausea grips me, causing me to stagger. The world around me wavers, the colors bleeding into one another as if the fabric of reality unravels. My ears ring with an almost unbearable pitch, drowning out the pounding footsteps behind me.

Xia had shifted us through time. My heart races as I slow to a walk, breaths escaping in bursts. The sun hangs in the sky as before, and the stones underfoot feel the same.

"It's a week after the chase," Xia says. "We're pretty sure the Phylax agents are gone. For now."

I straighten myself, anger burning inside. My

arms fly up, furiously signing the questions that have haunted me. *Who are you? Why are you here? Why should I trust you?*

Xia stops me before I can finish. "Don't bother," she says, her voice unnervingly calm considering the chaos we escaped. "I don't understand your sign language. If you're patient, we'll explain everything."

Frustration simmers beneath my skin. She knows something crucial; I can feel it. And why does she keep saying *we*?

"Come on," Xia adds, nodding toward the now-empty street. "We're close to the safe house. Let's hurry. The Phylax might be gone for now, but they will figure out we're here soon enough. If they haven't already."

I consider walking away from her. Why should I follow?

When I glance at the empty street, a grim certainty settles over me. I already know what comes next—more running, fighting, and unanswered questions piling up, an open grave of bodies in the dust. The Phylax and the people who claim to be my allies won't stop. Every step forward tangles me further into a web.

More than that, she knows something. The way she speaks, the certainty in her voice. I take a breath, suppressing my frustration. For now, I'll follow. But Xia will have to start talking soon.

The safe house feels frozen in time, its walls

steeped in an eerie past. Shelves hold old scrolls with frayed edges and rusted coins from distant eras. Tools are carefully displayed, each bearing the marks of ages past. If this were a time for leisure, I would be fascinated. Everything here tells a story, each object a fragment of time. My talisman pulsates.

People who move through time must use this place. The artifacts tell the story of travelers like me. Yet, there's something different here that doesn't align with the Phylax. This space doesn't carry our rigid order or cold discipline. It feels even more secretive.

The Phylax led me to believe that aside from a few enemies, only we held the power to move through time. They taught me that we were chosen to protect the past and, more importantly, save the future. Ever since this mission began, cracks have started to show. My thinking has been too narrow. I have been blind to the possibility–the probability–that others could do the same. The truth might be much different than I imagined.

There are more people with this ability, although I don't know how many. Some must be walking through time without the Phylax's knowledge, slipping between epochs unnoticed. And then there's Xia—her ability allows her to break the first *immutable* law of time travel: it should only be possible once every three years.

Xia stands by the door. "She won't be long."

I place my palm on the hilt of my knife, preparing to unsheath it if necessary.

The door opens, and a woman rushes in. She sees me, offering a brief smile before her eyes land on Xia. They share a caring gaze.

The woman strides further into the room. She is friendly and distinctly different from Xia. While Xia carefully plans her every move, this newcomer carries herself with brash confidence. It's clear she thrives on interaction; her presence fills the room instantly.

"Well," she says with a grin. "Seems like we've all made it. That's something."

Her casual, almost playful tone sharply contrasts with the tension in the air. I observe her. Something strangely familiar about her tugs at the back of my mind: I should know who she is.

I study her closely. Her hair is cropped in an easy, textured bob, framing cheeks that hold a hint of color. Her smile lifts, etching deep laugh lines around her mouth and eyes. Her eyes—there's something in their shape or deep blue color. No, it's the way she looks at me.

It hits me: she's the woman from the photograph I found among Xia's belongings. She is the same woman I saw during my mission to assassinate William Rufus. The memory stirs: she appeared in the forest not long before I killed Rufus. She tried to stop me—said I was making a mistake, that Rufus didn't deserve to die, and that the people I served weren't telling me the truth.

I sign questions at her in a flurry. I demand to know her name, why she has been following me, and what I am doing here. Before I can even get halfway through, she raises a hand, stopping me with that warm, easy smile.

"Hold on," she says, rummaging through a small bag at her side. She pulls out a modern notebook, flipping it open before giving it to me with a grin. "I thought you'd appreciate a real pen and paper. It's much easier to write with this than the stuff they have around here."

I blink, taking the notebook from her, unsure what to make of her casual demeanor. This isn't something I'm used to. She seems almost excited. It's unsettling.

She turns toward Xia, her face softens, then snaps back at me. "I'm Clara. I believe you've already met Xia," she says, gesturing toward her with a smile. "My wife." She coily blows a kiss to Xia.

Wife? I shift to Xia, who stands a few steps back, arms crossed, watching.

Clara continues, "I asked Xia to help you because we knew you'd need it. We've been monitoring the Qin mission for years. The Phylax's mistake was inevitable; however, we don't know what caused it. I have to admit, we were both a little disappointed when you tried to kill Xia. Even though we knew you were going to." She giggles as if this moment isn't serious.

She softens even further as she recounts the details. "Xia's done more for you than you realize," she says, glancing back at her wife. "Remember when that soldier in the dark armor was about to kill you in the desert? Xia pulled you through time. She saved you."

I clutch the notebook tightly. I have a thousand questions to ask. I scribble quickly, keeping to the topic at hand. *Where did that army come from? Is that the new Imperial Army?*

"They aren't, but they have replaced the Imperials. We stopped tracking them and have no idea who is in control now. They emerged out of nowhere after Qin died."

Who are you? Why should I trust you? I scribble across the paper and then point to Xia. *She has been hiding things from me.*

Clara sighs. "Because we're trying to protect you, Adam. The Phylax has lied to you your entire life. I tried to warn you in that forest long ago, but the Phylax were chasing me. It's time you knew the truth about who you are." She pauses, meeting my gaze. "I'm your sister."

Time stretches as her revelation sinks in. *Sister?* I stare at her. The notion is almost laughable. I respond, *That's impossible. I was raised in a Renegade commune.*

I'm taken aback when I see Clara's tears well up. "I know that's what they told you. It's not the full story," she says, her voice wavering. "The

Phylax kidnapped you when you were five years old, Adam. I was there. I saw it happen."

I don't believe her. My pen touches the paper, ready to challenge her claims. She continues before I can write more.

"I'll tell you what I remember," Clara says, growing distant as she begins describing an unsettlingly familiar version of events.

"You were in the backseat of our car. You were so small—only a kid."

She seems to search me for any sign of recognition. As Clara recounts the memory, I feel the edges of something familiar pressing into my memory. It's a faint reflection. Could she be telling the truth? Or is this another layer of manipulation I can't see through yet?

"Dad was in the front seat waiting for me and mom. We were getting ready to go somewhere. I don't know where. Mom never told me. I remember we were in a hurry."

She pauses, sadness passing through her before continuing. "I was on the sidewalk, holding onto mom's hand. We were about to get in the car. She was terrified about something. I could feel it in her tight grip."

Clara's voice sounds weighed down by the memory. "Then everything went to hell."

A sense of foreboding settles over me; I know what comes next.

"There were two strangers who came rushing toward the car. One of them jumped

into the front seat. Suddenly, dad was dead."
She swallows hard, forcing the following words
out. "He was slumped forward on the wheel,
blood sprayed across the dashboard. I remember
thinking how unnatural it looked on him." Her
voice trembles for a second before she steadies
herself.

"Mom started screaming. It was this
awful, guttural sound like someone had ripped
something out of her. Then I saw this man in
the backseat. He reached for you and yanked you
so hard it made me want to scream. Then, you
disappeared.

"I wanted to run or do something. Instead,
mom held me tight. She whispered, 'Not right
now.' She carried us through time. She had the
ability, too. Because of that, we lived in secrecy
for the rest of my youth."

Clara wipes her tears away. "In a way, they
took you, dad, and even mom from me. I've spent
so many years trying to find you, Adam. When
I did, I knew it would be hard to bring you
back from those bastards. The Phylax has really
messed you up."

She describes a version of the nightmare that
has haunted me for as long as I can remember:
the towering stone figure that shatters and
bleeds, the figures off to the side, and the wind
whisking the boy away. I never understood what
it meant, only that it filled me with a fear I
couldn't explain. Now, hearing the details from

her lips, something shifts. How could I have lived my life without knowing I once had a family? Without knowing there was a life before the Renegades—before the abduction? The images in my dreams were buried memories. Because of this, I decide to give her one chance. I scribble in the notebook: *Prove it.*

Clara says, "I can. But before we do anything, we need to remove your anchor."

I shrug, confusion knitting my brow. I have no idea what an anchor is.

Clara's hand slips into her pocket before she folds her arms again. It's subtle. Her eyes meet Xia's for a fleeting moment, an exchange passing between them before Clara steps forward. "The anchor is a device that the Phylax implanted under your branding scar."

Xia explains further, "The anchor regulates exotic energy buildup in your body. It is designed to limit how often you can time travel. It works by using Casimir Energy Regulation, constantly leaking away the exotic energy that time travel requires. It ensures that you never have enough stored up to travel freely. I bet the Phylax says it's a biological limitation, but it's artificial. The anchor acts as a pressure valve, releasing just enough energy that it takes three years for your body to build up enough to make another jump. Without the anchor, the energy buildup only takes a minute."

The Phylax told us three years was a natural

limitation. This anchor Clara and Xia speak of sounds torn from a work of fiction.

"We learned this from a man who helped us find you," Xia says. "He knows more about time travel than anyone else we've met. He knows about the Phylax and this device. Without it, you'll be able to jump like we do, whenever we want. You'll have full control."

The more she talks, the colder I become. It's all too much—too fast, too convenient. Distrust is a shield that keeps me alive. I write, *I don't believe you.*

I tear the page out of the notebook, shoving it toward her. Her features twist as she reads it.

Clara steps closer. "Adam, this is why they could track you in the desert, Sachu, and Samarkand. The anchor leaves an imprint every time you travel," she explains. "A signature the Phylax can detect by the energy released when you jump. The anchor sends out a signal pinpointing your location in time and space. They always know where you are."

My fingers instinctively brush against the scar. It could be true. There were moments when I felt watched. Sometimes, it was a shadow in my periphery. I told myself it was paranoia, just the natural tension of the job. Now, I'm not so sure.

"You'll never be able to outrun the Phylax until it is removed." Clara pauses. "By taking the anchor out, we can show you what actually happened."

I do have questions about my past. Still, I shake my head firmly. I will not let this woman defile the Mark of the Phylax. For all I know, this is a setup. I scribble down a final message: *I don't believe you. I won't let you carve into me.* With that, I rise to leave them.

Xia has been watching me carefully. She steps between me and the door. "We're not manipulating you, Adam," she says. "We're trying to free you."

My hand slides toward my knife. Trust is a hard-won thing, and this is not how to earn it.

Xia sighs, turning to Clara. "I told you he wouldn't accept the truth."

Clara shrugs, a hint of resignation in her posture. "We prepared for that."

Before I fully grasp the meaning of Clara's words, they signal to each other. Clara reaches back into her pocket. She pulls out a small metallic disc and flings it at me, striking me square in the chest. It sticks there, adhering to my clothing. Clara pushes a button in her hand. Suddenly, my body seizes up. I remain conscious as I drop to the floor, unable to control any muscles. While I feel no pain, panic shoots through me. What the hell did she throw at me? I can't even grit my teeth. I'm trapped in my own body.

Clara kneels beside me. "I'm so sorry, little brother. The stasis disc is temporary. You need the anchor out, and you need to watch."

Damn it. There's nothing I can do.

Xia kneels on my other side. She slides my tunic off enough to reveal the short-sleeved shirt underneath. She then rolls my sleeve up to my shoulder, exposing the Mark of the Phylax branded into my skin. Lastly, Xia tilts me so that I have to watch Clara. "This should help you understand," she says softly.

Clara leans over me, fixed on the scar burned into my arm. From the same bag she entered with, she pulls out a scalpel. Without hesitation, she makes a precise incision over the scar. I feel the pressure but not the pain—a small consolation amid this utter violation.

It's not as simple as she made it sound. She mutters something I cannot make out while her fingers probe inside my arm. She struggles to grasp whatever might be lodged within.

Every second that ticks by feels forever. I am powerless, and it terrifies me. A blurry memory surfaces: I am a child, strapped to a chair, unable to move. It produces an overwhelming sense of confusion.

Finally, Clara pulls something free. It jars me back to the present: a sliver of metal no larger than a fingernail clipping. It drips with blood. She holds it up, letting me see the cursed object that was buried in my flesh.

"See?" Clara says in a tone that I imagine is often used between siblings. "I told you so." She chuckles.

I don't feel as humorous about it. I stare at the tiny piece of metal. Rage and disbelief churn inside me. Is Clara right about the Phylax? Has my life been a lie?

FOURTEEN

This place is a prison, not a safe house. I continue to lie on the floor, powerless and unable to move. Clara bandages my arm where she carved out the anchor. The wrappings squeeze me tight as if trying to contain my anger. They do not. I don't know who I want to hurt more: my so-called sister and her wife for violating me or the Phylax for what is becoming the worst betrayal I could imagine.

I want to let the fury rip out of me, but I don't have a complete picture of what's happening yet. What I do know is that Clara and Xia appeared right in the middle of all this. I don't believe in coincidences.

Clara shifts her weight from one foot to the other. She moves into my view, opening her mouth to speak. When she looks at me, she seems to know I'm not taking this well.

I would love to yell at her, but I refuse to abandon my oath—the cursed oath that keeps my voice locked away. Right now, no one deserves my words—not Clara, Xia, or the

Phylax.

Clara kneels beside me, brushing hair from my damp forehead with a foreign tenderness. A strange sentiment fills her voice. Is it warmth? Kindness? "They've been tracking you with this, Adam," she says, holding the device for me to see. "As long as it was inside you, they would always know your exact location in time and space. Now that it's gone, you can freely move through time whenever you want."

The words land like stones in my gut. I've always sensed that the Phylax tracked me—they always seemed to know what I was doing, but limiting my ability? They told me it took time to recharge my power. Am I a fool?

I want to lash out, call her a liar, and tell her she's making all of this up. Sadly, her words resonate with too many things I've seen, especially over the last few months.

Clara walks to the far side of the room. "I need to get rid of it properly," she says over her shoulder as she exits the building.

I watch the empty doorway.

What is Clara doing with the anchor?

Soon, she steps back into the room, her hands empty, her shoulders loosened. A smile tugs at the corner of her lips. "It's done," she says. If she seemed comfortable before, she's utterly serene now. "They won't be able to track you."

She returns to my line of sight, speaking

directly to me. "I hid the anchor," Clara says, her voice softer. "I buried it outside this house about two hundred million years ago. I thought seeing Merv during the Triassic Period would be fun."

Two hundred million years? That's as good a time as any, I suppose.

Clara adds, "If you want it back when this is over, you'll find it waiting. Although, I suspect your Phylax friends will be searching for it."

I'm surprised by the open invitation. Having options is not a luxury I'm familiar with. A strange combination of relief and apprehension settles within me like oil and water. Right now, I feel no freer than I did with the anchor in my arm. I remain on the ground, my body useless, while the stasis dart keeps me in chains.

Clara kneels beside me again. She is earnest. "You can travel whenever you want," she says. Her eyes drop to the floor. "I know I shouldn't have done it without your consent. I didn't want to hurt you, but you wouldn't have let me otherwise," she says softly. "In a few minutes, I will stop the stasis dart from paralyzing you. When it stops, you can go wherever you want. We won't try to stop you."

She pauses, moving even closer. "I hope you come with us." There's a vulnerability in her words. She knows there's a good chance I will walk away forever. "Because if you do," her voice trembles, "I can prove who you are. I know where and when you were kidnapped. I've spent so long

trying to piece it together, waiting to show you."
She holds hope for what I will decide.

Despite my anger with her, I have to admit I
am intrigued.

If I go with them, it may lead me to many of
the answers I seek. Or I could leave. Run. Test this
freedom for the first time. Put as much distance
between myself and everything—everyone—else
as possible. It is tempting. I don't trust the Phylax
right now. I also don't trust Clara. I need to keep
my guard up.

My need for answers pulls at me with a force
I can't ignore. If she is telling the truth—if this
is my chance to understand who I am—I can't let
it slip away. I let out a sharp exhale; something
loosens a little.

Clara reiterates softly, "It's your choice." Her
words are barely audible. Without another word,
she pulls out the small device she used to activate
the stasis dart. She deactivates it.

The control in my limbs quickly returns.
I flex my fingers slowly, testing my regained
freedom. I roll my shoulders to shake off the
lingering numbness. My arm, however, throbs
with a dull ache. Impulsively, I rub the
fresh bandages, fingers brushing over the scar
beneath. It feels different.

I glance at Clara, then at Xia. They've taken
liberties of which I disapprove. If I'm going to
stay, it'll be on my terms.

I grab the notebook from the table and

quickly scrawl a message. Tearing the sheet out, I hand it to Clara. *Okay, let's see this proof.*

A swell of defiance rises. It is unfamiliar, but I must admit it's exhilarating. I'm consciously making decisions that contradict the Phylax's codes. I'm not following orders. I'm not on a mission. It is liberating.

I meet Clara's gaze, nodding once to let her know I'm ready. A slight, almost imperceptible shift passes between us—an acknowledgment of what's to come. The path forward may be dangerous, tangled with memories and lies, but it's a path I've chosen. In a life stitched together by others' lies, the only true freedom comes from the first decision you make for yourself.

Clara's fingers hover over the bag as though uncertain about its contents. Finally, she holds up a worn, plastic figure. I feel a strange connection to it. It's a toy that she handles for a while before giving it to me. She is almost apologetic. "Before we go, I thought you might want this. Mom left it with a note saying that you need to have it if I ever found you. Do you remember this Dalek?"

The talisman vibrates when Clara hands me the toy. Its silver paint is chipped, and one of its arms is missing. A hint of recognition stirs in my memory. I can almost see myself sitting on the floor, making the toy exterminate imaginary foes.

Is that my memory or something else? The

line between what I remember and want to remember feels impossibly thin. Perhaps Clara's suggestion conjures a world of make-believe.

"You loved this thing," Clara says. "You carried it everywhere, even slept with it under your pillow. Mom used to joke you'd grow up to be Dr. Who."

The Doctor never saw time as a straight line and never believed in the kind of rigid order people try to impose on it. He said time was a tangled mess of paradoxes and possibilities, a great wibbly-wobbly, timey-wimey ball of chaos in which events don't always happen chronologically. The future could slip into the past.

I glance at the toy again. Maybe time really is unruly and unpredictable, less of a strict sequence, and more of a bad joke with missing punchlines. If that's true, then what does it matter if I remember this Dalek.

I stare at the toy. Dangling a piece of a life I cannot fully recall feels cruel. That life seems more of a story someone told me than something I lived. I know this isn't Clara's intent. I suppose this gives me a taste of the life the Phylax stole from me. A knot of sadness tightens.

"We should get going," Clara says. "We came here on October 14th, 2024. If you return to that day, we'll have a car waiting."

The prospect of wandering through another endless stretch of desert makes my muscles ache.

While I have always loved the solitude of the expanse, modern transportation sounds more appealing than another sandstorm. Besides, I would appreciate a break from this scorching heat.

Clara steps in close, waiting expectantly. I reach out, placing one hand on Clara's shoulder and the other on Xia's arm. I feel a strange, fragile connection forming between us.

I close my eyes. A sensation unfolds around me: the pages of an ancient book opening. To my left, the past stretches back to the earliest moments of life on Earth. To my right, the future stretches forward until its vivid chapters suddenly end in 2051, torn away by an unseen hand. It is an unfinished story. The Sigma Event stole the ending.

A sense of relief blooms—it's working. The three-year rule is a lie. This realization fills me with a kind of joy, a reassurance that, for now, I remain untethered.

The feeling is magical. It is always magical, as though I'm floating above the great manuscript of time itself, every thread of possibility laid bare before me, waiting for my hand to guide us to the next chapter.

Then it happens—something I don't expect. As the pull of time takes hold and I guide us forward, I feel an unfamiliar tug at the corners of my mouth. It's subtle, barely noticeable, but it's there. A hint of warmth spreads across me. *Am I smiling?* It's as if my body remembers an emotion I've long forgotten.

I try not to dwell on it as the world bends, pulling us into a new time. Whatever lies ahead, whatever we find, will be on my terms.

FIFTEEN

When we step into 2024, the dry warmth engulfs me. My feet crunch on the cracked earth as the ruins of Merv surround us. Time has stripped the ancient structures down to skeletal remains of their former grandeur. The outer walls rise in jagged, defiant angles. Beyond these ghostly ruins lies the hum of cars rolling along a highway. Modern buildings gleam under the same sun that once bore witness to empires long gone.

Xia points past the ruins of this tourist attraction. "The visitor's parking lot is that way."

Clara pulls a key from her pocket and tosses it into my hand. "Hope you remember how to drive." She grins, always a hint of sarcasm dancing on her lips.

The insinuation irks me. Of course, I know how to drive. I'm a time traveler, not someone plucked from the distant past.

The engine rumbles to life. Soon, we're driving toward the city of Mary. My attention drifts as the landscape transforms. Old gives way to the new. Ancient ruins become gas stations, blinking traffic lights, and rows of boxy buildings. Cars zip by, their drivers lost in whatever worlds occupy their minds. A motorcycle growls past us, the rider's music blasting loud enough for us to hear, even with the windows closed.

Clara is nearly bouncing in the passenger seat. Xia leans against the door in the back seat, one arm draped lazily over the seat.

People romanticize the past because they haven't been there. The truth is, the past is hard. It's simpler, I'll admit that. Today's modern conveniences make life far more comfortable.

I'm not talking about televisions or entertainment of any kind. I mean things like transportation. Take my journey from China to Merv, for example. It took me nearly three months to get this far, a journey fraught with danger, bandits, and never-ending thirst. If I made that journey in the modern era, driving would take three or four days. Even in a compact car, it would be a relatively plush trip.

The world outside this car is the mirage: plastic signs, smooth pavement, bustling markets. Returning to my present always feels unnatural, as though these things don't belong. Except, I'm the one who doesn't belong. I seep through the cracks between time.

As we cross a narrow bridge, Clara nudges

me with her elbow. "Hey, Earth to Adam. Don't miss the upcoming ramp."

Snapping back to the present, I catch the sign that points to Mary and head that way.

Clara looks back to Xia with a playful grin before saying, "Since you're not going to ask, I suppose I'll tell you how Xia and I met."

She jumps into the backseat and wraps herself around Xia. I can see in the review mirror that her features soften while reliving the memory. "It was 1786 in Vienna. We were both sneaking into the premiere of *The Marriage of Figaro*—one of Mozart's early operas. I was posing as a noblewoman's daughter, which was easier than you'd think with the right wig. And Xia? Well, we ended up sitting next to each other. Let's just say she stood out. There weren't many Chinese women wandering around 18th-century Austria," Clara giggles.

"Neither of us spoke German, making it difficult to be in Vienna. What are the odds that two time travelers would land in the same place and sit next to each other? Funny how fate works, huh?" She smiles at Xia. "I knew a little Chinese—enough to embarrass myself—so I tried introducing myself. When that failed, I switched to English. I said, 'My name is Clara.' To my surprise, she replied, in perfect English, 'Your Chinese is awful.'"

Clara leans back with a playful smirk. "After the opera, we decided to explore Vienna. A few guys threw racist slurs at Xia—we didn't know what they were saying, but we understood the tone. Xia told me she wasn't comfortable with these guys around. She asked if I was up for an adventure. Of course, I said yes. She took my hand, and we jumped to 2003. Not knowing she could time travel, I found it funny. I didn't give her the satisfaction of my shock, though. Instead, I asked, 'Why here?' Then I touched her arm and pulled her to 2036. She couldn't believe that I could travel, too. The rest, of course, is history."

Clara pauses. It seems like her story is over until a renewed smile takes over. "We had so much fun together. I knew I had to marry her. Across all the years, one moment felt right—a moment where our relationship mattered. So we chose June 26, 2015, in New York. The day after the Supreme Court legalized same-sex marriage. There, we were a part of an important historical milestone."

She glances out the window as the city of Mary draws closer. "We could have done it in some exotic place in a fairytale time, dressed like ancient queens from a forgotten empire. It felt right to make it ours—in a time where it meant something, where we could finally exist together without pretending."

"She's exaggerating," Xia says with a smirk, leaning forward. "Clara has a way of turning us into heroes in some grand story. Half the time, we're running from one disaster to the next." Xia meets my line of sight in the mirror, her smile widening. "You know how she said we planned our wedding on June 26th, 2015? She forgot to mention that we almost missed it because she wanted to *borrow* a dressmaker from the 19th century."

Clara groans, throwing her arms in the air. "I think I made the right choice."

Finally, the talking stops. The engine's hum fills the car, which is more than enough noise for me. All this chatter is static that I cannot tune out. Even if I did enjoy her story, I still prefer the quiet.

It doesn't last long. Clara starts up again. She dives into stories about her adventures:

"There was the time we saw Mount Vesuvius erupt. The ground shook so hard I thought it would split beneath us. Ash drifted down from the sky, coating everything in a choking gray haze..."

"...Jimi Hendrix at Woodstock? That was a different kind of chaos. The smell of damp earth mixed with the sweet tang of marijuana. Mud clung to everyone's feet. The crowd was alive, a single entity swaying under the pulsing lights..."

She discussed the construction of the Great Pyramid of Giza, the destruction of the Berlin Wall, and walking among dinosaurs during the Jurassic period.

Xia interjects, "That was scary! Although,

the higher oxygen in the air was interesting. Do you remember how lightheaded we were?"

Clara turns around with a playful glint. "I do! The humidity—my God, the air was a wet blanket. Do you remember the pterodactyls? The way their wings cast shadows over the ground? Their screeches were bone-chilling. We were also terrified that something bigger than a pterodactyl was stalking us. But tell me it wasn't worth it."

I catch Xia's smile in the rearview mirror. "It was worth it."

When the muted lulls sneak back in, I'm grateful for the respite. It never seems to last long with Clara in the car.

Finally, we make it to Mary Airport. Clara jumps back into the passager seat so she can look in the glove box. "Aha!" she exclaims, pulling out three passports. With a triumphant grin, she waves them in front of me. "I knew we would need these. Let's hope they work."

I assume these passports are less than legitimate.

Mary International Airport is small but alive with movement. Travelers drag luggage, agents make announcements, and carts squeak as they roll by. It's a different universe—one that doesn't care who we are or where we've been.

While the agent flips through our passports at the check-in counter, Clara says, "We'll fly to Ashgabat. From there, we can go directly to Baltimore. It's the quickest way back."

When we finally board the plane, I sink into my seat, letting the cabin's hum settle into the background. Air travel is strange: hurtling through the sky in a pressurized metal tube at impossible speeds. People cross the planet in hours with nothing more than a ticket.

The plane takes off. Clara nudges me before I lose myself in contemplation. "You know, as soon as they took you, mom didn't stop to think. She grabbed me and jumped to 2027. We ran and hid in the hills of Montana. She figured it was the best way to stay safe. Mom said they might come for me next—or maybe even for her—because of our abilities. So she kept me close, way too close. I felt like I was a prisoner in my own life."

"There was nowhere to go, nothing to do," she continues. "I was terrified to travel through time by myself. I was scared they'd find me, or worse, that I'd never find my way back. Mom —she stopped living, except for one obsession. Finding you. That's all she did. Every day, she'd sit with books and maps, gathering everything she could about what might have happened to you."

I try to picture her face, her voice, the way she might have smiled at me. The memories are more feeling than fact. Admittedly, I am curious to know more about her. I want to remember the way she held me. I want to hear her laughter, but it's gone—all of it. Clara holds onto fragments I'll never have. That hurts more than I assumed it would.

"Mom came across a name mentioned in conspiracy books: the Phylax. She kept digging, uncovering more than I believed possible. She found that they kidnap children whom they believe can further their agenda. They usually kill time travelers who aren't part of the Phylax.

"Mom knew you were in a commune but couldn't locate one. She knew a little about your missions and the Phylax's obsession with the Sigma Event." Clara shifts in her seat. "She even learned that those who crossed over the Sigma Event at 3:00 AM on July 1st, 2051, never returned. By then, she wasn't herself anymore. She was so wrapped up in it that nothing else mattered."

She lets out a sigh as if releasing the pain she has carried for too long. "When I turned seventeen, I couldn't take the isolation anymore. I knew I had to get out of that bunker. I sought adventure, trying to forget about everything. A few years later, when I met Xia, things clicked. For the first time, I had more than fear driving me." A small, genuine smile touches her lips. "Xia knew me better than I knew myself. When I told her about you, she was the one who said it was time to help. I knew she was right, even though it scared me."

Clara's voice falters for the first time. "When

we went back to Montana, the house was empty. All that remained was a neatly stacked pile of notes on the kitchen table, with a letter resting on top. It said, 'Going to save Adam. I don't know when I'll see you again. Love, Mom.'"

She wipes her eyes with her palm, her usual bravado slipping. "We kept returning to the day the Phylax took you, hoping to find her watching. She never showed."

Clara has lived an exciting life, seeing things I can merely imagine; however, her pain stands out. She's carried this story with her across the years. For her, it's a burden. I envy her strength.

She is glassy with unshed tears. I might be tempted to do the same if I knew how to cry. Instead, I sit there, absorbing the magnitude of her story. My mother cared for me and might have given everything to find me. What kind of woman does that? Was she strong, or was she broken? I try to imagine her hunched over maps, chasing a son who might as well have been a ghost. Did she truly believe she could save me, or was she clinging to a desperate hope because the alternative was unbearable? Regardless, she's likely gone forever.

Xia reaches over and holds Clara's hand. I am tempted to hold the other one. I stop myself.

Clara wipes her eyes one last time, then digs into her backpack. She pulls out a fresh notebook and pen, shoving them into my hands with a grin. "Okay, I've told you enough stories. Now you go."

I take the notebook from her and fixate on the blank page. What can I possibly say? That I was beaten as a child? That I have committed several assassinations in an attempt to prevent humanity's end? I cannot think of a moment I want to share with others. After a minute, I write, *It has been a difficult life*. It's the most truthful thing I can come up with.

Clara squints at the page. "That's it? That's all you've got?"

I think about it. What more is there to say? My life has been missions, silence, and obedience. I scribble down, *Yes.*

She throws her chin back to laugh. "Alright then. If that's all I get from you, I guess it's my turn again." She leans closer. "Let me tell you about when Xia and I attended the first Heraean Games. These were the Olympics for women. Xia, do you remember when that was?"

Xia answers, "Around 694 BCE."

Clara continues, "Did you know that there were such games? Only unmarried women could compete."

I have to admit, I did not know about the Heraean Games.

Clara's story continues. She is animated as she recounts the races, the vibrant parties, and the elaborate religious ceremonies. She paints a vivid picture of the festivities, from the crowd's cheers to the torchlight illuminating the temple of Hera. In fact, she just keeps talking.

I stare out the window, watching the clouds roll past beneath us. My mind drifts elsewhere. If I were to time travel right now, what would actually happen? Would the plane come with me? Would I land safely at my destination, skipping the hours in between as if I had just fast-forwarded the flight? Like dragging others through time, I am touching the plane, so perhaps that would work. Or would I move independently of it, leaving the plane behind while I travel?

If that's the case, then I'd be in trouble. The plane might keep flying without me, and I'd find myself right here, thousands of feet in the air, with no plane to hold me up. Just a sudden, stomach-dropping plunge into the ocean or the expanse of some unsuspecting city below.

I exhale, staring at the endless sky beside me. At least, as I plummeted to my inevitable death, there would be a brief moment of silence. *That's a joke*, I tell myself.

"Time travel isn't always as exciting as Clara makes it sound," Xia says. "It's disorienting, sometimes. You lose track of what is real. Sometimes I get to one place, thinking maybe I shouldn't be there." A soft smile spreads over Xia as she looks at Clara. "Other times, I want to stay in one spot. Just to enjoy it for a while."

Clara holds Xia's hand.

I know what Xia means. Time travel can be a series of disconnected fragments. I have seen so much but never feel a part of it. I watch people move through their days, knowing I'll never truly belong. Clara may have given Xia something to hold onto. For me, there hasn't been anything. I cannot imagine what it would feel like to stop wandering, to find a place where I fit in.

Before I settle too deeply into the thought, Clara is talking again. I close the notebook, letting the hum of her voice blend with the engine noise. Stories about foreign lands, wild escapes, and Xia's clever schemes spill from the unstoppable river that is Clara. I settle into my seat, realizing the chatter won't end until the plane lands. I enjoy the silence; that much is true. But I might be able to get used to this.

SIXTEEN

Goddammit, there's no way she can be my sister. She's loud, funny, not nearly serious enough. She fills the gaps with stories, sarcasm, and an endless stream of questions—the complete opposite of me. Where I am quiet, she speaks an infinite stream of words. Yet, there's something familiar about her too. In the way she refuses to let things drop, her stubbornness mirrors mine. As much as I try to resist, I feel a tug that makes me think maybe I could care about her.

After an endless flight, we finally arrive in Baltimore. The rush of airport crowds presses in from every direction. Typically, all this noise would wear on me, but right now, it barely registers. All I can think about is Jean Street. I need to get there.

We leave the airport in a cab. Clara tells the driver where to drop us off. When we get there, Xia grabs our arms. The familiar sensation washes over me. Letting someone else pull me through time is still disorienting.

The alley warps; the air shifts around us. Nearly everything is the same, except it's a warm summer morning. July 7, 2015, 10:20 AM. We walk out of the alleyway. Baltimore is humming with life. Jean Street feels so recognizable, except I have no recollection of ever being here.

The street is the same as the picture I found in Xia's backpack—the houses, the cracked sidewalk, even the faded street sign. I scan the area, expecting to see someone taking the picture. I do not find anyone holding a camera.

Clara, Xia, and I stand in the shade of a nearby tree as the scene unfolds. A younger version of me, a small, wide-eyed boy, walks down the street, holding a woman's hand. My breath catches in my throat. That's my mother. The girl, young Clara, clings to her other hand. They're walking toward a car parked at the curb. The man in the driver's seat must be my father.

I watch as the younger me climbs into the back seat, oblivious to the danger closing in around us. My mother tenses, something catching her interest. She pulls Clara back as two figures emerge from the shadows, rushing toward the car with terrifying speed.

An overwhelming urge grips me—to run toward them, to shout, to do something. My feet shift. Clara clamps onto me, wrapping her arms around my waist in a tight hug. "No," she whispers, her voice barely audible. "Xia and I have already tried. We can't do anything for them. We've already been here, and we can't change it." I guess the second law of time travel is immutable.

My entire body tenses. Every muscle is ready to snap. One of the figures comes into focus. I can't believe who it is. My savior. My mentor. Philip. The punch of realization hits deep in my gut. He's known. He's always known.

Philip is at the center of my abduction. This man shaped me into who I am today. His lies run too deep. He knew about my parents and Clara.

The scene grows even darker as chaos erupts. The second figure—a woman—slips into the front passenger seat. Without hesitation, she raises a weapon and executes my father, a cold shot that echoes through the street. His head slumps forward onto the steering wheel, the horn blaring incessantly. For a moment, I am paralyzed.

Philip grabs me from the back seat, pulling me away before I know what's happening. My mother screams, her expression twisted in panic. She shields Clara. The little girl peeks from behind her, frozen with fear, clinging to her mother's leg. Then, in an instant, Philip disappears, and I along with him.

The silence that follows is deafening.

I stare at my mother's happiness draining away like a punctured vessel. She will never be the same. Seeing her floods me with memories—fragments of a life I didn't even know I'd lost.

I remember her scent—lavender and warmth, with the soft, lingering sweetness of vanilla clinging to the air between us. It's the smell of safety, of home. I remember the warmth of her hand on mine, the way her fingers would gently trace circles on my palm to soothe me.

She used to hum as she worked, a tune I can't quite place but feel I've always known. When she spoke my name, the world slowed down, her words wrapping around me.

I can see her sitting by the window, the sunlight catching the golden strands of her hair. She used to tilt her head when she laughed. The way the corners of her face wrinkled placed me at the center of her world. The image is so clear it is overwhelming. It all surges through me, bringing with it a crushing sadness and rage.

Anger burns in my chest with an intensity I can barely contain. My skin is hot; tears stream down my cheeks. I try to scream. The sound gets stuck inside me. My jaw clenches so tight it hurts. My hands shake at my sides, fingers curling into fists.

I try to scream again. Still, no sound comes out. The words knot in my throat, suffocating me. I'm locked in place, watching the pieces of my past shatter before me. In that silent, agonizing moment, Clara's steady presence pulls me back from the edge.

Some time later, Clara leads the way, guiding us down the street to a small, unassuming house. Its worn exterior is similar to all the other houses on the block. "This is it," she says, approaching the front door. "This is where we lived before they took you."

Clara unlocks the door, and I follow her inside. It is an elusive dream. I walk through each room slowly, running my fingers along the furniture. The chipped edges of a picture frame, the worn fabric of a couch: each touch stirs something within me. Memories ripple beneath my façade, too faint to fully grasp but enough to leave me off-balance.

The pieces of my past don't fit together anymore. The child in the car doesn't translate to the man I've become. I am a series of fragments from different lives, none genuinely mine. I wonder who I am without the Phylax. I'm not sure I want to know the answer. My hands tremble, trying to steady myself against the rising tide of anger, confusion, and loss.

I try to speak, to force words out, but my throat locks up. Have I forgotten how to talk? Why can't I make a sound? No matter how hard I try, the words refuse to come.

With a frustrated exhale, I reach into my pocket and pull out a small notebook. The broken Dalek tumbles out with it, landing in my palm. Its chipped silver paint and missing arm are no different than the pieces missing from my memory. I run my thumb over its scuffed surface, feeling the ridges of its battered shell, hoping to unlock something buried deep in my mind. When nothing comes, I slip it back into my pocket.

I open the notebook and scribble a quick message for Clara to read. *I need to know more. I need to find out what else happened to me.*

Her eyes reflect understanding. "It took me years to make sense of your abduction. I want you to find your answers." She places her hand on my shoulder. "Let's meet back here in two days. At sunset."

I consider asking them to join me, but navigating the commune will be easier if I'm alone.

"Xia and I need to gather some information while you're gone," Clara says. "We met someone who helps us with time-traveling matters. He's odd. We don't trust him much; however, he helped us find you. He might have information on what the Phylax are planning next. If we're going to take them down, we need as much information as possible." When she finishes talking, she disappears toward the entrance.

Take them down. I hadn't considered that before. While the prospect of destroying them is intriguing, it may be crossing a threshold from which I will never return. I sense that this is the beginning of something terrifying. I am not yet convinced this is the correct path.

Clara's strength, her ability to hold onto hope after everything she's been through, amazes me. She fights for answers, as does Xia. Watching them makes me wonder if I could find something to hold onto.

Clara reappears with a set of car keys. "I think it's in the garage," she says.

Before parting ways, Xia adds one word: "Godspeed."

I inhale deeply, grounding myself for what lies ahead. The truth awaits, buried in the years stolen from me. I know I can't stop until I recover it.

The garage door groans as it lifts, revealing an old Mazda. I slide into the driver's seat. The engine starts with a low hum—a steady rhythm that seems too relaxed compared to what's inside me. I grip the steering wheel, feeling the worn pleather beneath my palms ground me in the present.

The Renegades live in the Black Hills of South Dakota. It has always been a distant place I never wanted to see again. Now, it's the place that might hold the answers I need. My hands tighten on the wheel.

I pull out of the neighborhood, leaving behind the house that vaguely reminds me of a different life. The city fades in my rearview mirror as the highway stretches westward. Mile after mile, the urban sprawl gives way to rolling fields, then patches of forest, and eventually, open country where the sky seems endless. The hum of the car engine becomes a backdrop to my pondering.

The rage that burns is all-consuming. An unwelcome thought worries me as the miles stretch on: when the anger runs its course, what then? What if emptiness is all I feel?

I grip the wheel tighter, shaking the thought away. The answers won't come from sitting here, spiraling. They'll come from facing the people who stole everything from me.

The solitude should feel comforting. It doesn't—not now. I've walked alone through deserts and mountains, where there were no sounds but my own footsteps. I never felt lonely. Yet here, on this long stretch of road winding into the unknown, loneliness is a spear slipping into my soul.

In the rearview mirror, a black SUV appears for the third time. It trails me at a steady distance. It's probably nothing—a coincidence, I tell myself. It creates a tension that coils into the two-headed serpent seared into my flesh. Every so often, the vehicle vanishes, reappearing hours later.

A memory emerges.

The man I once called father at the Renegade compound was caught in a state of fury. I can't even remember the reason; not that he ever needed one. His wrath left me with the gift of a spiral fracture winding through my forearm. The community nurse set it in a cast. Life went on. To her, it was another routine injury. To me, it wasn't. It has always been an unanswered question that gnaws away. Why? Why did he do it? Why any of the other beatings? There was no reason, merely his rage crashing down on me repeatedly.

If Philip had never taken me from my real family, none of that would have happened. Now I know Philip was part of it. He was the one who ripped me out of my family's grasp, putting me into the hands of those who abused me.

The hours stretch endlessly. The ache in my shoulders grows sharper with every mile. My hands cramp from gripping the wheel too tightly, yet I can't seem to let go.

The road becomes a thin black ribbon stretching across fields of gold and green, broken by the occasional farmhouse or weathered barn. Dark forests rise in the distance, a watchful army standing at attention. The world peels away layer by layer. Memories drift in and out, some clear, others distorted. They slip between the cracks of certainty and doubt.

When we recall a memory, we aren't remembering the original event. We're remembering the last time we thought about it. Each recollection is a copy of a copy, warped by time, emotion, and repetition. Maybe that's why my past has always felt like a collection of half-truths. Whenever I pull an old moment from the depths, I might reshape it, unintentionally altering the details. How much of what I remember is real? And if memory is this fragile, how much of anyone's past is the truth?

I tighten my grip on the wheel, my knuckles aching. The past I remember is fractured, rewritten, pieces scattered across years of silence. Philip, the Phylax, the compound, the man I once called father—were they precisely as I recall, or have I filled in the gaps with whatever version of events made sense?

At least now, I don't have to rely on memory alone. I can step into the past and see it for myself. The thought should be a relief—finally, the truth. But what if the truth is worse than the memories?

The tires crunch over gravel as I turn onto the dirt road. I finally see it: a narrow turnoff nestled among the trees. An old wooden post indicates I am close. I slow the car as I approach. The symbol, carved deep into the wood, catches my attention. It's the same one that marks my arm—two serpents curling toward infinity. They look ready to strike each other. The Mark of the Phylax. A mar of betrayal.

I guide the car onto the dirt road. The closer I get, the more the landscape looks familiar. A stretch of forest here, a crumbling stone wall there. Fragments of childhood flash: running barefoot through fields and the sting of splinters from wooden fences.

The vehicle shudders. Towering trees crowd in from both sides, their branches forming a shaded canopy overhead. The path twists and curves as it pulls me further away from the present world, deeper into the past. After several miles, the forest finally thins. A sprawling compound nestled among the woods opens up.

A large metal gate looms, rust streaking its iron bars. Beyond the gate, I see several scattered buildings. A barn with weathered wooden slats. A row of small cabins clustered together. The schoolhouse where I learned history and language. Several other structures dot the landscape. What draws my attention most is the church, rising at the heart of the compound. It is larger than necessary for a community this size. Its steeple juts into the sky, reminding everyone here of something oppressively sacred.

Farther back, fields stretch out. Rows of crops sway in the fading light. Small patches of forest are woven between the farmland, creating pockets of shade.

This place is self-sufficient, a community built on survival and secrecy. Even though I lived here for nearly nine years as a child, I know nothing about it.

SEVENTEEN

The compound begins to stir as dawn breaks. I drift through the gloom, a ghost among the living, watching the Renegades come to life with the first light. Morning routines unfold: farmers venture to the fields, and workers gather tools from the workshop. I drift along the periphery as an observer, watching a world I once knew intimately. Time feels more fluid here, bending as I let myself slip between the present and the echoes of my past. I let the hours roll back, tracking the rhythm of the compound.

When ready, I slip toward the schoolhouse, crouching beneath one of its windows. I peek inside. The interior is simple: nine wooden desks arranged in three rows, a chalkboard scrawled with symbols, and shelves lined with battered books. The scene inside sends a jolt through me. As the children enter the room, they sit, hands folded on their desks. I spot the nine-year-old version of myself among them: young and obedient, absorbing every word the teacher communicates through sign language.

I'm surprised when the talisman starts vibrating once the children are inside, not when adults are near. When Philip explained how the commune was a Renegade sect of the Phylax, I assumed they were all time travelers. This, it seems, may not be the case. Or something is different here, causing the talisman to malfunction.

But when I spot her, none of that matters. Everything in me locks up.

Rasha.

Not a memory. Not a trick of the light. Her, exactly as I remember: eleven years old, seated near the back of the classroom. Her loose braid hangs over one shoulder and wisps of hair curl around her face. The delicate freckling across her cheekbones softens her expression. Even the confident way her fingers move as she signs with the others brings back memories. She carries herself with that same quiet defiance, like she's always bracing against something the rest of us have already surrendered to.

She meant everything to me. For that brief period, I was in love. We couldn't wait to get out of school, to slip away unnoticed and hide in the forest near the gardens, where no one watched. We'd sit for as long as we could, our fingers tangled in each's hand. She was my first kiss—soft, sudden, and unforgettable. We kept it hidden from everyone because affectionate relationships were forbidden. Love—whatever form it took—was weakness to the Phylax.

And then, one night, she was gone.

No warning. No goodbye. Her bed empty, her family's quarters cleared out like they had never existed.

I always wondered. Maybe someone found out. Maybe we were too careless.

I never did get an answer. Only silence, and the hollow space she left behind. I wish the outcome had been different—for both of us. But wishes don't bend time. They only haunt it.

Inside, the children shift in their seats as the lesson moves on. They start to talk about history, focusing on the Pax Romana—a time of peace that helped the Roman Empire reach new heights. When they explore the turmoil that follows this era and discuss Caracalla, will they tell the version found in all the history books? Or will they reveal that a Phylax named Adam Foster slit the emperor's throat? Either way, their history lesson will be tinged with hints of Phylax doctrine. Sacrifice and order are the path to survival.

The Renegades mold history into a narrative that justifies their existence. They use the past to shape our worldview, showing us how their mission is necessary. It made every lie they told easier to swallow because they were rooted in half-truths. When Philip freed me from the Renegades, he revealed that much of our education was untrue. Yet, I cannot see how this and the *true* Phylax differ.

I continue to watch as the children absorb these lessons. They were once blank slates forced to swallow the dogma fed to them. Glory. Sacrifice. Duty. Words hammered into us from the time we could understand them, shaping us into tools. We learned English, Chinese, Pahlavi, Greek, Latin, and the basics of other languages. One day, we will have to blend in seamlessly, no matter where or when we find ourselves.

A bitter taste rises in my throat as I realize how deeply these lessons have embedded themselves in me. How difficult they are to let go. Before I move on, I take a long look at Rasha and wonder what has become of her. Will I ever know?

I let time blur around me, pushing forward to the next scene that demands attention. The morning passes in fragments. Faces, movements, and sounds blend in harmonious cacophony. From a blind spot in the balcony of the communal dining hall, I observe the room below. It's an ample space lit by unsteady bulbs that cast long silhouettes over rough tables. The children, including my younger self, line up. They move in unison. There's no talking, no laughter, just the soft shuffle of feet and the clink of dishes. The children take their seats at the long tables, waiting obediently.

Maya Foster, the woman I once called

Mother, moves down the line of tables with the same robotic movements I remember. She places bowls of soup in front of the children without looking at any of them. She goes through the motions, her every action steeped in quiet resentment. The Maya I see here is even more miserable than I recall. I focus on her, searching for something beyond her wretchedness.

I remember overhearing one night when she warned Azar, "The Archon sees everything." Did she speak these words aloud? Whether spoken or signed, she was scared. "Do to the boy what they ask. Otherwise, we'll both pay the price."

The contrast stings. I recall the softness in my birth mother's touch and the pain when they took me. This woman, Maya, laughed as Azar nearly beat me to death. When they took me from my family, they gave me to this woman who was bound by duty, not love. They replaced my family with empty vessels, people with no real connection to me.

The creaking door pulls my attention back to the room. Azar, the man I was forced to call father, steps inside. All the children are tense. He has a reputation within the commune; even the other adults shrink in his presence. I see my younger self curling inward, trying to disappear.

Azar perpetually scowls. He strides over to the table, grabs a chair, and slams it aside before sitting. The wooden legs scrape against the floor, creating a harsh screech. He leans forward, elbows on the table, glaring at everyone. They have disappointed him already.

I watch, fury rising in me like a slow-burning fire. I've lived this scene before.

The children barely dare to lift spoons to their mouths. My younger self eats with caution. Even a minor misstep will bring punishment.

As the meal winds down, Azar explodes from his seat, grabbing the young version of me by the arm. I can see from here that the boy wants to cry out in pain. Azar drags him across the room toward the exit, the child's feet stumbling as he tries to match Azar's pace. Everyone else keeps their heads down.

The rage inside me boils. My hands ball so tightly that my knuckles whiten. I want nothing more than to step outside and tear Azar apart. I want to make him pay for every bruise, every scar. But I can't. I know that this young boy will survive. I have more to see here. Even with the second immutable rule of time travel protecting me, I cannot risk the Renegades being alerted to my presence.

I peer through a window in time to see Azar throwing the child to the ground. He strikes the boy across the temple. The boy crumbles without a whimper escaping his lips. He's already learned that it's safer not to make a sound. Azar doesn't stop. He kicks the boy, hammering in some lesson. I doubt Azar even knows what that lesson is.

The boy stumbles to his feet, glazed with hurt. Azar looms over him, breathing heavily. The act of violence seems to have satisfied some need inside him. He points to the church. The boy nods weakly, not even daring to wipe the blood from his lip. He shuffles toward the church without protest.

Azar stays behind, his composure fracturing as the child disappears from view. I follow his gaze, which drifts down the dirt path near his home. In the dim light, I glimpse a figure, half-hidden in a window, watching Azar. I am unsure if the voyeur lives in the compound; however, I sense that they do not. Before I can get a better look, they dart out of sight.

Staggering to the side of the building, Azar doubles over and retches. His shoulders heave with the torment of something worse than sickness. Eventually, he looks to the sky, tightening in a way that suggests he's cursing the unseen forces that bind him to his wretched role. Wiping his face with trembling hands, he regains his footing and then sets off in the opposite direction.

I've always known Azar as a man of ruthless certainty, unshaken by anything. I wonder if that certainty was a mask. Perhaps he was forced into this life of violence, bound by something I don't understand. Still, none of it matters. Whatever his reasons, he beat on a child. That is unforgivable.

I descend the stairs and slip through the back door of the community kitchen to follow my younger self. I trail the boy to the dimly lit church that crowns the commune. The windows glow, casting dull streaks of amber light onto the dirt path. I slip into this heart of darkness behind my younger self.

Inside, the nine children sit in neat, perfect rows, backs straight, hands folded in their laps. They are hollow vessels of obedience. An older man stands at the front of the room behind a wooden pulpit. The swaying light of a few lanterns illuminates his gaunt cheeks. He is the Renegade Priest who tricked me into speaking and then ordered the severe beating immediately afterward.

Above him, a large wooden plaque bearing the seared Mark of the Phylax looms on the wall. It towers over the congregation, a constant warning of the authority that governs their existence. That plaque could crush anyone who stood beneath it for too long.

The priest raises his hands for attention. Even when he signs, the words feel severe. *Society stands on the precipice of ruin. We stay in this community to save ourselves. Without the Phylax, you will be lost. Without the Phylax, humanity will be lost.* He pauses, his focus sweeping over the children. *The Phylax will stand between humanity and annihilation. We have been chosen.*

The priest's words are vague, supposedly

because he is a Renegade. That is what Philip said. The Renegades maintain a bastardized version of the Phylax doctrine. I can no longer believe anything Philip said.

The room remains frozen as the Priest continues, evoking fear and loyalty with every syllable. *Only the Phylax can avert the coming doom. Only through unwavering obedience and silence can we ensure survival. You are the future. You are the sword. When the time comes, you will stand, or all will end.*

My stomach churns as I listen. These words are familiar. I recall hearing many of these sermons before. I accepted every twisted word as truth. I didn't question it. None of us did.

I press my back against the wall, watching my younger self among the children. He rigidly sits, hanging onto every word as gospel. Indoctrination—that's all this ever was. Conquer the minds of the young, and loyalty becomes inevitable. They rewrote our thoughts before we even had a chance to think for ourselves.

The priest signs, *We are the architects of humanity's survival. Through sacrifice, we endure. Through silence, we are strong.*

I force myself to keep watching as the children respond in quick, mechanical gestures:

With fidelity, we protect humanity.

With fidelity, we protect humanity.

My skin crawls as I watch myself sign the words. He's too young to comprehend them entirely, but he believes every syllable. These words will become his reality.

I want to scream at him—at myself—to stop, to wake up. The boy sits there as the lie sinks deeper into him with every repetition. Somewhere deep in the pit of my stomach, I know the boy doesn't stand a chance.

The children rise from their seats in choreographed unity. One by one, they file toward the back of the church, guided by adults bearing lifeless expressions. I slip from my hiding spot, following at a distance. I don't remember this.

A narrow corridor stretches into nothingness at the rear of the church. The adults escort the children into small rooms along the hallway. After a few minutes, the adults slip down the hall. The sounds of their footsteps fade to nothing, leaving the church eerily quiet.

I stop at the room where my younger self is contained. I crack the door open enough to peer inside. The overhead light reveals bare walls, a thin mattress on the floor, and a single metal chair facing a wall.

A knot tightens in my stomach. I cannot recall this. Apparently, lessons from the pulpit were only a first step. The actual conditioning happened here, in these tiny rooms, out of sight from anyone who might question it. This room is where they broke me.

I stare at the horrifying sight. My younger

self sits slumped in the metal chair. His forehead is strapped into a crude contraption that forces him to fixate on the wall, his nose inches away from it. His tiny body is limp. Eyes half-lidded as if caught between sleep and waking. Tubes trail from his arms, feeding something into his system that keeps him docile.

On the wall, a video plays in an endless loop. Images flash in rapid succession, burning themselves into his subconscious. The Phylax symbol appears first. Then, the Acropolis gleams under a bright sky. It is an emblem of power. Phylax armies march with emotionless determination. Victory. Strength. Sacrifice. The rhythm of the video is a hammer striking.

Why is the Sanctum in this video? If these are Renegades, why highlight the centerpiece of the Phylax's power?

A voice drones over the images, weaving promises into commands. "The Phylax will never lie to you. Never trust anyone outside the Phylax. Emotions are distractions; they must be controlled. The Phylax is infallible. Never break the silence. Obedience without hesitation ensures survival."

My nails dig into my palms. These were the rules that bound me. They were my commandments, my creed, shaping everything I did. Here it is: the blueprint of my existence, reduced to flickering images on a screen.

Brainwashing is a slow erosion. The Phylax

made us repeat a lie until it became the truth. They stripped away what we were and replaced it with what benefits them. The mind can only hold so much before it overflows, and that's what they count on. Fill a person's head with enough of the same message, and eventually, new thoughts replace the old.

Psychologists say the brain is a system that constantly absorbs, adapts, and rewrites. The Phylax weaponized this idea. They didn't need to erase who I was. They buried it. They flooded my mind with their version of the world, their truths, and their commandments until there was no room for anything else. No space left for doubt. They filled my head with an unquestionable righteousness of our mission. When I finally accepted it, I became their creation.

Rage. They made me believe these lies through twisted repetition. Through punishment, the vow became inseparable from my identity. When I sat in that chair, I was no longer my own person.

I watch as the boy twitches with confusion. His eyelids flutter as each new image is forced into his brain. Meanwhile, I stand here, fully awake, my anger burning brighter than ever.

There are two more things I need to see here in this retched place—two final pieces that might help me stitch together the shattered fragments of my past. I must witness the beginning of it all, starting with my arrival at the compound. After that, I'll confront the Temptation. Maybe then, the pieces will finally fit.

I return to the nave, where the children file in after their conditioning. It is darker now, and the echoes of their footsteps sound emptier. I let the present dissolve, peeling back the layers of time to find the beginning.

Time swirls around me. I must focus. I need to see when I first arrived. I peer deeper, trying to ignore other events that happened here. I'm sure there are many other secrets. And then—

There it is.

Time snaps into place, pulling me to the memory I've been searching for. The echoes of the present dissolve, leaving the raw, unfiltered past. I'm five years old—small, scared, and shaken from being torn away from everything I knew.

This is where it all started. This was my first moment with the Phylax. I'm unsure what frightens me more—what I'll find here or the person I might become when I confront it.

EIGHTEEN

The priest stands tall at the pulpit, veiled by shadow. He exudes an air of unyielding authority while stepping toward a portable forge. Its orange glow casts an angry light throughout the room. From it, he withdraws a branding iron, glowing with a red-hot intensity that radiates violent power. He holds it aloft, judging its readiness. Satisfied with the searing metal, he slides it back into the furnace. The hiss of heat fills the room—a prelude to the upcoming anguish.

The congregation sits below him. Among them are Maya and Azar, who purse their lips in anticipation of what is about to happen. Maya gawks at the pulpit, her hands resting rigidly on her lap. Azar sits beside her, the muscles in his face twitching from the storm that continuously churns beneath his surface.

Maya and Azar sign to each other with hurried movements as if they are trying to keep the conversation to themselves. Azar's brows knit together. *This feels wrong*, he signs urgently.

His fingers tremble, betraying the fear he's trying to conceal. He glances at the furnace.

Maya's response is swift, almost mechanical. *It must be done. He is chosen. You will do your duty.* There is no hesitation in her gestures. She doesn't look at Azar. She directs her attention toward the priest and the ritual about to unfold.

The church doors creak open. There is no ceremony or music, just heavy steps echoing in the open space. The procession walks in single file. The congregation doesn't move. Each of them has witnessed this annual ceremony.

The woman who killed my father enters first. She looks as cruel now as she did in the car. Seeing her reignites the ire inside me. The gunshot that killed him continues to ring in my ears. I want to strike her down for what she did.

Then Philip enters with my five-year-old self. He grasps my wrists without any hint of compassion. Seeing him drag me down the aisle twists my guts. The boy is terrified.

Seeing Philip here reinforces something I believe: the Renegades aren't renegades. They are the foundation for this organization of lies.

The boy pleads, his voice trembling, "No. Please, no. I don't want to be here."

Philip tugs at the boy, a command to stop talking and hurry up.

I want to grab my younger self, to pull him away from all of this. Sadly, I cannot. The second rule of time travel prevents it. I will pass through the scene, unable to change anything because it is myself that I want to whisk away. Worse, the Phylax might sense my presence somehow. They will hunt me while the five-year-old version of myself will still be stuck here. Instead, I make a solemn promise: I will correct this wrong. Not for me, for the world. I swear it to my younger self.

Two more figures follow Philip: the assistants to the Archon. They move in perfect synchronization. Obedient tools, as I was meant to be. They take their places on the altar platform.

The Archon enters.

If there is any lingering suspicion about who the Renegades are, it vanishes at that moment. The Archon would never visit a dissenting faction of the Phylax.

His formal regalia gleams in the low light. The intricate patterns woven into the fabric reflect his deep understanding of time. The robes flow around him—the trailing edge of a storm in motion. He always publicly adorns this attire, inspiring awe, submission, and fear. As he walks, even gravity appears to bend to his will.

Each member of the procession moves into position around the chancel. The priest stands near the furnace. He looks smaller now. His unyielding authority falters in the presence of the Archon. Meanwhile, the Archon ascends to the pulpit. Every eye is on him now, including mine.

"Is the Mark of the Phylax ready?" the Archon asks. He is the sole member of the Phylax who wields the privilege to speak. His voice thunders through the nave.

The priest grips the branding iron's handle. Its head glows molten orange, palpitating with heat. The priest turns and raises the iron toward the Archon. The glow bathes their features in a grotesque hue. The iron hums, alive with purpose.

"For the Phylax," the Archon says with finality.

His gaze shifts to Philip. "Do you have the anchor?" The Archon's tone isn't a question; it's a command.

Philip steps forward. He retrieves a small box from a small leather pouch at his waist. He opens it to reveal a gleaming sliver of metal. It's the anchor, the same device Clara cut out of me. I brush the scar on my arm. The mark is a chilling confirmation of what was once inside me.

"For the Phylax," the Archon repeats as if the phrase alone could justify the horrors unfolding.

The Archon then addresses one of his attendants. "Bring me the knife," he orders.

An attendant steps forward, cradling a tray of crushed velvet, upon which rests a scalpel. The Archon takes it without ceremony, gripping it with the precision of a surgeon who has performed this ritual countless times. There is no reverence in his hold, only cold efficiency.

I feel a phantom pain creep up my arm. Skin prickles with dread and pity for the boy who will endure this.

Philip drags my five-year-old self toward the Archon. The boy is trembling, his small frame wracked with fear. He senses that something terrible is about to happen. He pleads through his tears, his voice desperate. "Please, I want to go home."

The congregation ignores the boy's cries. The Archon stands still as they force my younger self into a chair. The boy's arms and legs are pulled taut with leather restraints, immobilizing him. His panic fills the room. I stand helpless, watching fear consume him.

The Archon lifts the scalpel, holding it over the boy's trembling arm. The blade slices through his skin and into the muscle with ease.

Young Adam shrieks. The sound tears through the church. A pure, unfiltered cry of agony. It is the scream of a child who doesn't understand why this is happening, why these strangers are hurting him. The sound cuts through me in a way the scalpel itself could not.

I have blocked this part of my life out. Watching it now, I see a tragedy unfold— not mine, but one stitched into my memory. Yet, despite the detachment of memory, I feel connected to that boy in a way I hadn't imagined possible. My body aches with his pain. My heart reaches out to him across the years. His suffering is my suffering. It cracks something open in me. It is a raw understanding of human pain that I hadn't grasped before. Hot tears I hadn't realized I'd shed dampen my skin. Still, the worst is yet to come.

The Archon takes the anchor from Philip, holding the metallic device as if sacred. It shimmers in the light, its edges gleaming with the promise of something sinister. The Archon thumbs it deep into the boy's wound, embedding it into the sliced flesh.

Little Adam lets out another agonizing cry, his body jerking against the restraints. The straps hold firm. The congregation watches, their faces devoid of emotion. Unlike the boy, they know this isn't the end.

The Archon signals to the priest, who steps forward. The branding iron in his hands glows. The priest bows as he offers it to the Archon, who takes it with both hands. "For the Phylax," he says.

As the branding head nears the boy's skin, its glow makes his flesh appear translucent. The Archon forces the iron firmly against the raw, open wound, sealing the anchor inside. The sound of searing flesh fills the air, a sickening hiss that echoes off the stone walls. The acrid stench of burnt skin hangs in the room.

The Archon's voice cuts through the hiss. He utters the sacred words in Greek: "Με την πίστη, προστατεύουμε την ανθρωπότητα." *With fidelity, we protect humankind.*

The congregation signs back in unison, *For the Phylax.*

This moment marks the beginning of my training as a Phylax. The anchor and branding are the first layers crafted to bind, control, and forge our identities.

Young Adam screams. His tiny body convulses against the restraints while the nightmare-inducing screams reverberate through the nave. The cries go on and on until he finally passes out from the misery.

Phantom pain rises again, burning into me. I instinctively clutch my arm, feeling the scar that never really healed. The room around me blurs. My tears sting.

I think the ceremony is over. I prepare to move forward through time, but I'm wrong. When the boy stirs, waking from his brief reprieve, he sobs uncontrollably.

The Archon's assistants approach with something metallic—a crude collar lined with electrodes. They wrap it around his neck, snapping it into place. I do not understand what it might be.

The Archon steps closer. He leans toward young Adam. His voice is cold. "From this moment forward, you may no longer speak. If you do, you will regret it. That includes crying, Adam, so I suggest you stop now." Straightening, he stares down at the boy with contempt. "Never break the silence."

The congregation signs again, *For the Phylax.*

The Archon awakens the collar around his neck with a slow button press.

Shocks punish young Adam's sobs. Every time he makes a sound, the collar delivers another jolt, forcing him into obedience. The shocks come in rapid succession. The boy's cries dissolve into broken gasps. His body jerks uncontrollably, writhing in the chair. The agony continues until, mercifully, he loses consciousness once more.

I clutch my own throat as the spectral pressure tightens. I cannot breathe. So this is how they enforced the oath in my earliest days?

I'm not even sure if I'm capable of speaking anymore. Was the ability to speak taken from me completely? Maybe I've been fooling myself into believing my vow was a choice.

Trauma can bury itself so deep that the mind refuses to acknowledge it. It's locked away, walled off to protect oneself from breaking. The brain decides what must be hidden to survive; however, forgetting isn't healing. It's simply a delayed reckoning. Today, the walls have collapsed.

I've spent my life thinking my silence was a choice, a discipline I embraced. But here it is—the truth, stripped bare. They shocked the voice out of me. Every surge rewired and carved obedience into my nervous system until silence was my world.

My hand claws at the scar on my arm, hoping to tear it away—tear away the years of submission. Tear away these new memories. Unlike when I was a child, I won't forget this. There's no escaping the haunted screams of my younger self. His agony is my agony, burned into me twice: first, when it became part of my unconscious programming, and now, hearing his screams, realizing the truth.

I can't stay here, trapped in this scene. I wipe the tears away. My blood boils even as the edge of panic recedes. I can't change what they did to me.

As the trembling inside me slows, I shift time forward. There's one more thing I need to see in this place. One more event I must confront.

I must watch my Temptation.

NINETEEN

I sift through the pages of time, narrowing my search to the moment of my Temptation. As I approach it, something in the preceding moments catches my attention—a detail I hadn't anticipated. My curiosity grows as I notice the nave isn't as empty as I had assumed it would be. Instead of the priest preparing to greet me alone, I uncover an unforeseen exchange.

The priest stands draped in a black gown. A white Mark of the Phylax emblazoned across his chest contrasts sharply against the midnight fabric. Philip faces him, sloppily dressed in jeans and a worn leather jacket. His hair is damp with sweat that clings to his temples. His shallow breaths come unevenly. Each exhale accompanies a subtle tremor in his hands.

It's winter now, and the cold seeps into every crevice of the commune, including the church. I remember nights so frigid that I would shiver endlessly, wishing for the warmth of a summer that never seemed to arrive. Today, however, anger keeps me warm.

The priest signs, *The boy will break tonight. I've built enough trust with him. I'll ask him about his father. I promise it will get done.*

It had better, friend, Philip replies, his body betraying him. Tension vibrates in his movements; for a second, I think he might lash out to strike the priest. The crisp snap of his gestures makes his leather jacket creak. *The Archon believes the boy is destined for the Council of the Phylax. If that happens, everything we've worked for unravels. I have seen the world beyond 2051 with him on the Council. It's a future you and I do not want.*

Worry etches itself across the priest's forehead. Philip continues, *I'm supposed to be in the New Order right now. Everything is locked down; there aren't any gateways open. I was lucky to find an anomaly with my talisman. Do you know how dangerous they are, friend? How hard it is to travel through them? They aren't nearly as lethal as the Archon, though. If he finds out I'm here, we'll both be executed!*

Philip confirms it; the world doesn't end in 2051. If Philip returned, something still exists beyond the Sigma Event. The future is there—it's just locked away, and it seems the Phylax holds the keys. It isn't destruction that keeps travelers from reaching it; it's a deliberate barrier, something designed to keep us out. But why?

Until Philip mentioned it, I hadn't noticed the talisman dangling from his neck. The metallic bezel catches the light, revealing a design identical to mine. As I focus on it, I feel the rhythmic pulse of my own talisman intensify, almost as if it's reaching out, resonating with his. The vibration feels alive, insistent. Philip's focus remains elsewhere. For now, I feel confident that he's unaware of the connection.

Philip continues, *It's terrible news for both of us if the boy rises. He needs to break to prove the Archon wrong. Then, the Archon will have no choice but to make him an assassin. He will be assigned to me. Only then can I steer Adam onto the path that aligns with our goals, and we have to make sure it happens before the Convergence.*

Could it be true? Is there another version of me out there? Perhaps even countless versions, splintering off with every choice I make. Infinite Adams, each shaped by various decisions, some stronger, some weaker—some who never took the vow of silence. Infinite possibilities, infinite lives.

If this is true, I wonder which one became the better man. Can I still become the best of them all, rising above this tangled, fractured history? Or am I too far gone, just another shadow of what I could have been?

The priest's fingers hesitantly move as he signs to Philip, *Wait outside. Adam will be here soon.*

Philip shoots a threatening look. His eyes never leave the priest. *This better work, friend,* he signs before exiting the nave. The heavy doors thud shut behind him.

Left alone, the priest paces beneath the vaulted ceilings. His robes whisper against the stone floor. Nervous energy radiates from him. He turns to the entrance every few seconds—a solitary candle atop the pulpit flickers.

At last, the doors swing open again, and my younger self steps inside. Although he is thirteen, he still clings to Maya's hand. By this point, he had already learned not to trust the priest. Something felt wrong—the man insisted on speaking instead of signing. Maya's hand, however, remains limp in his grasp, her fingers slack and lifeless. She holds her arm still, waiting for him to let go.

She signs to the boy, *The priest wants to speak to you*, then moves toward the corridor where the children were given their special lessons. Instead of disappearing entirely, she pauses at the hallway's entrance, lingering in sight.

The scene unfolds in a half-remembered dream. A knot forms in my stomach. I don't want to relive this. I let time blur—like watching a movie in fast-forward.

The muffled sounds of a struggle snap me back. Philip bursts into the nave, engaging with the guards in a flurry of choreographed movements. To my younger self, this was a daring rescue; now, I see it for what it was— a staged charade. He dispatches the guards with ease. The guards' fake grunts echo in the vast space. It is a scripted symphony of deception.

Philip kneels beside the trembling child— beside me. Gently, he gathers the boy into his arms, murmuring reassurances. The boy clings to him, desperate for protection. I remember how safe I felt in that moment, convinced he was my savior.

I understand now. The Renegades aren't a failed offshoot, they are a training ground for the youth. They exist to harden a child, to mold them through discipline and loss. This place isn't meant to nurture. It is created to make sure that by the time a child turns thirteen, they already hate the world around them. Hate the rules. Hate themselves.

I know, because I did. The only good thing I can remember from this place was Rasha. And they took her from me, too.

That's the design. We're made to suffer until the Temptation, when we are beaten to the edge of death. When we're hanging there, a savior appears. A false one. A carefully timed rescue from the torment they created. We're told the Renegades betrayed us, lied to us, and abused us. Then comes the kindness—the first real kindness we've ever known.

A father figure steps in. The hand that lifts us up. The Council welcomes us with quiet smiles and makes us feel chosen. Special. Safe.

It's a ruse. A slow, methodical lie. One that

takes more than a dozen years to root so deeply we can no longer tell where they end and we begin.

That's why Maya's posture is unnervingly casual in contrast to the charged atmosphere of the nave. Her lips curl into a smile as she exchanges signs with the priest. *Azar did everything he was supposed to. I made sure of it.* The slight tilt of her head is almost playful. *Did the Archon say I could go back now?*

The priest waves her away. Maya doesn't leave immediately. First, her grin widens as if she is savoring a small triumph. Then, with a graceful turn, she steps back into the shadows, her figure disappearing into the corridor with a quiet finality.

Her grin haunts me—not because it shows malice, necessarily. It suggests she was in control in a way I didn't—still don't—understand. Of all the things I expected to find at the commune, the strange relationship between Maya and Azar wasn't one of them. How she spoke to Azar makes me wonder what choices he had to make. He always obeyed, and it caused him pain. Why?

At last, she slips out of the church, her figure swallowed by the encroaching darkness.

The priest withdraws, ready to vanish into the corridor. Before he is out of sight, he turns back. He proves how meaningless his oath is by speaking. "Back so soon?" he asks, probing for a response.

I hadn't realized it until that moment, but with my five-year-old self gone, I am no longer a ghost in this place. My throat burns with the effort of words I cannot speak. My silence will have to suffice. I stand there, stone-faced.

As I reach the door, the priest's voice follows me. "The Phylax will see you soon."

I do not acknowledge him. I know the fight will come to me. I'll meet it unflinchingly. Enemies riddle my path. I don't know if I'll succeed in destroying the Phylax. I don't know if I'm strong enough. At least I won't have to do it alone.

TWENTY

I pull up to my family's old house in Baltimore. The neighborhood is still, with only the occasional chirp of crickets breaking the calm. When I arrive at the front step, I travel back in time to the evening of July 9th, 2015, when we agreed to meet.

I made several attempts to speak out loud during my journey. Nothing came out. At the doorstep, I try once again to say anything. Still, no words form.

My hand hovers over the worn wood railing. I should continue my journey alone. I don't want Clara or Xia dragged into the danger I fear awaits me. The thought of either of them injured, or worse, is hard to take. I wrestle with conflicting emotions: the desire to protect them by leaving and the relief of knowing I won't face the future alone. Before I can resolve the inner conflict, the door creaks open.

"Adam," Clara says softly. Her eyes are warm, the way I think a home should feel. She wraps her arms around me.

I return her embrace, then attempt a smile, though I can't be certain if my lips obey.

In the kitchen, Xia is already seated at the table, her fingers curled around a steaming mug of tea. She understands the room's unspoken currents—she always does.

I reach into my jacket pocket to take out a notepad and pen. The one voice I have left. *I'm not sure how much time we have. The priest saw me leave the church; I'm sure he sent someone after me.* I hold up the note for both of them.

Before reading the words, a smirk tugs at Clara's lips as if trying to lighten the mood. "Still not talking, huh?" she says with strained laughter. She's trying to ease the tension for my sake. We both know how dire this is.

I shake my head while writing, *I've tried, but no luck.* I describe what I witnessed. As I put the memory into words, I relive it: the shock collar they fitted me with, the way it helped steal my voice. When I finish the story, I add, *I'm not sure I'll ever be able to speak again.*

Clara's hand rises to her lips. "Oh, Adam..." She steps closer, wrapping her arms around me. She holds me tightly. It feels strange to have someone attempt to shield me from my past, a past I've carried alone for so long. I am unsure of how to accept this gift.

"It doesn't matter if words come or not," she whispers. "You're here. That's what matters. We'll do this together."

She pulls away. Her fingers rest firmly on my shoulders. "What else did you see?" she asks. "Please, tell us everything."

Taking a seat at the kitchen table, I write quickly. I describe seeing my younger self at the commune—recalling the familiar school, the communal suppers, my father's simmering anger, and my mother's icy detachment. I explain how their relationship was nothing like I remembered. I outline how the Phylax shaped us into obedient followers, using manipulation and brainwashing to break our spirits. My fingers tremble as I detail the anchor they implanted beneath my skin and the branding iron that seared my shoulder. I reiterate the cruel shock collar. Finally, I expose Philip's deception.

Clara leans in, reading over my shoulder. I make it clear: *The commune is part of the Phylax. It is a training ground where children learn obedience and loyalty to the order. Everything I believed about my past was a lie.*

I relay what I've uncovered—how the Renegades aren't rebels, just another mechanism of control. A necessary cruelty designed to shape us. I watch her face as the details sink in.

"Those bastards," Clara hisses, her fists clench tightly. "They're monsters that must be stopped."

Xia sets her mug down with a clink. "We suspected this." She pauses briefly. "While you were gone, we met with the person who helped us find you. They know a little about the Phylax's history. After what you've seen, I'm sure you already suspect this: the Phylax aren't here to save humankind as they claim. They're the ones manipulating it. We believe they caused the Sigma Event."

She reaches out, placing a steady hand on my arm. "You're not alone in this fight, Adam. Clara and I are with you every step of the way."

I look back at her, grateful. I don't want them hurt, but I don't think I can destroy the entire Phylax alone.

When Xia mentions the Sigma Event, Philip's conversation with the priest comes to mind. I write, *Philip said the Archon hoped I would join the Phylax Council. Philip wanted the priest to push me hard enough to make me speak, ensuring I'd fail the Temptation. He claims to have crossed the time barrier beyond 2051. He said my presence on the Council would destroy their plans for the future.*

Xia's voice is unsteady, "That's impossible. No one who has crossed the Sigma Event has ever returned."

I consider her statement. *I doubt Philip was lying. He spoke to the priest. They have some plan in place.* After a moment, I add, *They have agents everywhere. If we're going to beat them, we'll need to come up with something impressive.*

Xia's expression hardens. "Then we outsmart them," she says. "Use their arrogance against them."

Clara grasps my hand, grounding me with her warmth. "We'll make them pay for what they've done—to you and everyone else they've hurt. We'll end those assholes."

Xia leans forward, fingertips tracing invisible patterns on the table. "Most who know about the Sigma Event believe some cataclysmic event ends humanity in 2051," she murmurs. "There's no proof. If an apocalypse were coming, wouldn't there be evidence of it before July 1st? I've traveled to June 30th, 2051. Everything is normal. People are living their lives completely unaware. The only thing I found unusual was the shutdown around the Acropolis."

I grip my pen. *That's where the Sanctum is. Something must happen there. Supposedly, no one knows; however, I think Philip does.*

Xia reads my note. She replies, "Our contact told us that the Phylax have created a device to stop passage beyond that date. They created something that blocks time travel past July 1st, 2051. Once that point is crossed, time travel in any direction becomes impossible. It's not the end of the world or humanity. It's something else."

Some physicists posit that spacetime isn't genuinely infinite. Instead, it has temporal horizons. A temporal horizon is a point beyond which no path can continue. It is a cosmic dead-end, where every route forward collapses into a wall of pure impossibility. If the Phylax has created or harnessed such a horizon around July 1, 2051, then crossing it would be walking off the edge of a cliff—there's no time to stand on. In practice, time travel to that date hits a hard limit, a lock that bars any further steps.

We experience time as though it's open-ended, but if some kind of technology enforces an artificial wall, it might manipulate the fabric of spacetime in a localized region. In doing so, this technology forms a horizon that no traveler can bypass. The result is that the timeline cannot be accessed beyond that point. It isn't that existence ends—just that the pages beyond 2051 are sealed shut, leaving the universe intact but hidden from any time traveler's reach.

A chill prickles at the back of my neck when I remember the meeting I interrupted in Merv. A piece connects, though the picture remains frustratingly incomplete. I write, *I eavesdropped on a Phylax meeting. They said the Dahr-khoday interfered with my mission in China, making the Sigma Event worse. Maybe Philip wanted my mission to fail, to twist the Sigma Event somehow. Have either of you heard of the Dahr-khoday?*

Clara glances at Xia, obviously puzzled. "I've never heard of them before. Have you?"

Xia shrugs, her fingers grasping the edge of her mug. "No," she says, her voice tightening. "No, I haven't," she says simply.

I add another line: *The Sigma Event, and I might be connected.*

Xia intentionally stares at me when she replies this time. "Maybe you are, maybe you aren't. The future is always in flux. Even the Phylax don't know how things will unfold."

I remain undecided about the Sigma Event. When I travel through time and see the blank pages of the future, I worry that this is all false hope. I write, *Maybe.*

Clara, who has been pacing, suddenly stops. She blazes with resolve. "This could be our chance," she says. "What if we visit the Sanctum in June 2051? We can observe what happens. If the Phylax are behind this temporal horizon, or whatever it is, then the Sanctum is where we'll find answers. We can watch from the outside, look for any unusual activity that explains what's really going on." Her excitement builds. "It could be how we break their grip on the timeline."

The enormity of her idea envelopes me. The Sanctum. It is the malignant heart of the Phylax's power. It is zealously guarded. Going there during such a pivotal occasion is suicidal.

"It's dangerous," Xia concedes, "although it might be our best shot. If we can discover what they're doing, maybe we can stop it—or at least find a way to undermine their control."

I tap my pen against the notepad, the sound anchoring me. I write, *Agreed. We must be extremely cautious. The Sanctum will be heavily guarded, especially at that time.*

Clara's lips curl into a determined smile. She winks at Xia when she says, "When have we ever let a little danger stop us?"

The porch creaks outside, followed by the shuffle of boots. I raise an arm to signal quiet. Clara and Xia become tense. Another creak.

"What was that?" Clara whispers.

Adrenaline races through my veins. I write rapidly, *Someone's at the front door. Probably Phylax.*

Xia slips toward the window. She peers through a narrow gap in the curtains. The streetlamp's glow stretches across her body. "There's a black car parked across the street," she whispers. "I didn't see it before."

Clara's jaw tightens. "We need to move. Now."

I scribble, *Get your bags. We'll get out of here quickly.*

We launch into action. The house's serenity shatters when we grab our go-bags. I shove the notepad into my backpack, grabbing whatever else might be helpful. Clara scoops up her phone and gear bag while Xia does the same with her stuff.

The floorboards creak softly beneath our feet as we gather in the kitchen. Somewhere behind us, I hear two or three sets of footsteps moving down the hallway. They round the corner with raised guns. I reach out, grabbing Clara's and Xia's shoulders. I focus, willing time to bend around us.

Suddenly, everything slows. The world stretches out like taffy. The Phylax assassin pulls the trigger. A flame blossoms out of the gun's muzzle. The bullet emerges as if moving through thick syrup. Its tip glints under the dim light. The shimmer of its wake hovers. The crack of gunfire unravels into a low hum, vibrating my body. An unnatural stillness settles around me. Time seems to create an invisible resistance. This is a new experience. Unfortunately, we don't have time for experiments or curiosity. We need to leave now before a mistake costs us our lives.

I concentrate harder, jumping forward, shifting into a quieter future. It is only a day later, but the sudden tranquility of the empty house greets us.

Clara's voice breaks through the hush. "How did you do that?"

I shrug.

"They'll be back soon. We need to get out of here," Xia says. "Let's get to the airport."

Xia is right. We leave immediately. Hurrying outside, everyone piles into the car.

"They'll realize we're gone any second," Xia warns.

Clara turns the key. The engine hums to life. "Then let's ensure we're far away when they do."

As we pull onto the street, I glimpse two shadowy figures rounding toward the back of the house. Xia watches them from the side mirror. She murmurs, "That was too close."

Clara's knuckles whiten around the steering wheel. "They're escalating. We must assume they'll stop at nothing to get to us."

I scribble in my notepad, then tap Clara's shoulder to grab her attention. *All the more reason to get to the Sanctum quickly. If we can uncover their plans, we might find a way to stop them for good.*

Streetlights blur as we speed along. The tension slips into a fragile calm. Clara and Xia's faces are illuminated by passing lights. They are warriors in this battle, bound not by obligation but by a shared resolve to see it through.

Xia says, "Our best move is to get to the airport immediately. If we hurry, we may stay ahead of the Phylax."

Clara asks, "You think we can catch a flight this late?"

Xia's fingers hover over her phone's screen. "I know how we can get a private flight. It won't be cheap, but it'll be off their radar."

I jot down another note for Clara. *Xia's right. The sooner we reach Athens, the better our chances. Hesitation helps them close in.*

Clara's eyes dart between the paper and the road. "Alright. Athens it is." She steps on the accelerator, merging onto the highway. We leave the city lights behind us.

Xia's already punching in a number on her phone. "I'm making arrangements now. Go straight to the airfield. With luck, we'll be airborne before they realize we've left the city."

I lean back, exhaling a breath I didn't know I was holding.

"Once we're in Athens, we need to move carefully," Clara says. "The Phylax will be everywhere, especially near the Sanctum." She fixes her attention on the road. "We'll figure out the details as we go. Right now, we need to get there in one piece."

The Sanctum is the Phylax's core. Walking into it is madness. I also understand there's no other way to bring them down. If we're going to stop their reign, it will be there.

I write, *Thank you both—for standing by me.*

Clara softens. "We're family, Adam. We look out for each other."

Xia reaches over, giving my shoulder a gentle squeeze. "We'll get through this together."

The city's skyline fades as we approach the private airstrip. The future is fraught with danger; however, I feel a renewed sense of purpose. We're on our way to Athens. I know I won't have to navigate whatever we find there alone.

Clara pulls up to the hangar. "This is it," she says, cutting the engine.

We exit the car, the cool night air brushing against our skin. The hum of jet engines rumble softly in the background. Xia leads the way into the hangar, where a sleek jet awaits.

"Ready?" Clara asks, coming to stand beside me.

A resolute determination settles within me. *Let's go*, I write, holding up the notepad with, I think, a smile.

"You need to work on that," she gestures to my face and laughs. "Athens awaits."

As we board the plane, I sense that we've made progress. My demons have surfaced, and I have lived to tell the tale. Yet, I'm not ready to put the past behind me. That will involve dismantling the web of control the Phylax have spun across time. Only then will I be at peace with my past.

As the plane lifts, I watch the world shrink away. Ahead lies Athens and the Sanctum.

TWENTY-ONE

A few blocks from the Acropolis in Athens, the air shimmers briefly as Clara shifts us forward in time. We arrive on the afternoon of June 30th, 2051, not long before the Sigma Event. At 3:00 a.m., the world will drastically change.

The sun hangs overhead in a cloudless sky, bathing the city in a golden light. Around us, the streets teem with life. Vendors call out their wares, their voices mingling in a chaotic blend of Greek and a cacophony of other languages. The laughter of tourists harmonizes with the hum of traffic. The Acropolis rises proudly, its ancient marble pillars contrasting sharply with the modern skyline.

I pull my notepad from my pocket. *The Sanctum's entrance is on the northern cliff, under the Erechtheion.* Clara and Xia lean in, reading over my shoulder.

"Understood," Clara says, tightening the strap on her backpack. "We should go that way before these streets get any busier."

We weave through cobblestone alleys, guided by the scent of fresh bread and roasting meats. Street musicians play cheerful tunes that drift through the crowd, adding a melodic current to the afternoon bustle. As we approach the northern side of the Acropolis, the lively atmosphere fades. Fewer tourists wander here; a strange hush settles over the area.

Metal barriers block the roads leading to the ancient site. Warning signs in multiple languages proclaim restricted access. Men dressed as police officers stand guard. Something definitely feels off.

Xia says, "This is how it was my last time here. It's the only time I have seen the Acropolis closed off."

I share her concern. Unease knots my stomach.

We approach the barrier slowly. One guard steps forward, his mirrored sunglasses reflecting our worry back at us. "The Acropolis is closed today," he says in accented English. "No entry permitted."

Clara smiles politely. "Closed? That's strange. We checked the schedule this morning. It said open."

The guard's tone is curt. "There was an accident. Come back another day."

I study his uniform. He dresses correctly, but his posture is too rigid, more like that of a military man.

"Thanks for letting us know," Xia says, gently steering Clara back. "We'll be on our way."

As we withdraw, I notice the guard's hand move to his radio. He mutters something I can't make out.

Clara sighs. "That was a bust."

I write on my notepad, *We need another approach.* I add, *Let's find a vantage point to surveil the area.*

Clara says, "The neighborhood here has some taller buildings. Maybe we can get on a rooftop somewhere."

We slip into less crowded streets, leaving behind the buzzing tourist hotspots. The area is older. Balconies are draped with potted plants and laundry fluttering in the breeze. This place is near the ancient Agora, which reminds me of the first time I visited Athens with Philip.

I remember a moment from back then. While I can't be sure, I could swear I saw Socrates debating a merchant over the nature of fairness. His voice rose above the din of the marketplace, drawing a small crowd of curious adolescents.

Modern cafés now line the streets, neon signs bellowing against the centuries-old stone walls. Things have changed considerably over the centuries, with the vibrant pulse of ancient life replaced by a different kind of hum, one less alive with purpose but equally restless.

Under the cover of twilight, we circle to the back of the Athens University History Museum. A service ladder clings to the stone wall, offering discreet access. We climb while the distant murmur of the city dampens.

On the rooftop, our efforts pay off. We have an unobstructed view of the Acropolis's north side from here. Spotlights shine up the cliff like children pointing flashlights at their faces to tell ghost stories. I bring my attention to the area beneath the Erechtheion.

I point toward the concealed gateway, hidden in a narrow, weathered rut in the cliff. We can't see the entrance here, only the worn groove carved into the stone by centuries of erosion. Behind that façade of rock is the portal into the Sanctum.

Figures move in and out of the entrance. Typically, no one except a Phylax returning from a mission would be near this place. The entrance itself demands scaling a treacherous rock. Tonight, though, an intricate network of scaffolding has been erected. It supports a flow of people far exceeding what is expected. Some wear the same faux police uniforms we saw before. Others dress in work clothes, blending into the background. They are coordinating something significant.

Workers haul enormous pieces of machinery up the cliffside. The scaffolding creaks with protest. The Phylax are risking visibility, something they typically avoid at all costs. Whatever they're up to is incredibly important.

"We need a better view," Clara whispers, lifting a pair of binoculars she fetched from her bag. "It has become too dark to see anything."

I try to answer with words. Nothing comes out. Instead, I pull out my notepad. *We'll approach from the north-east side. Fewer guards there. Getting inside is impossible, but maybe we can find clues.*

We slip through narrow alleyways, sidestepping the guards and floodlit barriers that keep the primary approach sealed off. Eventually, we find refuge behind a cluster of olive trees on a hillside. From here, we have a direct line of sight to the entrance without exposing ourselves.

We wait. Hours pass. Around midnight, a low rumble alerts us to a new development. A convoy of unmarked vehicles winds up the restricted roads to the Acropolis. We watch as they stop below the Sanctum's entryway.

Phylax agents spill out, their boots crunching against gravel as they work with haste. The crates are enormous. Most are the size of large refrigerators. One looms larger, nearly the size of a small car. A crane groans under the strain as it lifts the heaviest load, chains jangling with every movement.

From the seams of the largest crate,

an ominous hum vibrates through the air, accompanied by the crackle of static. Blue light spills from within, painting the agents in an unnatural glow. The vibration from the crate feels alive, a pulsing energy that prickles my senses.

"What is that?" Xia whispers. I can see the eerie glow reflected in her eyes.

A subtle electric charge stirs the air, raising the hairs on my arms. Clara shifts uneasily. "Do you feel that?" she asks.

I nod. Whatever these crates contain is powerful—and dangerous.

I scribble, *I need to get closer. Wait here. It's too dangerous for all of us.*

Clara's frown deepens. She doesn't care for it but knows I'm best suited for this. Shadows have protected me before; they will protect me now.

Keeping low, I leave Clara and Xia behind. I slip along the ridge's edge. The stone is cold beneath my feet. Closer now, I see the steady flow of workers hauling equipment. I move beneath the scaffolding. Dust coats my tongue. It is difficult to keep steady against the steep cliff. I do my best to remain still, listening for a clue.

Most of the people moving equipment are Phylax. They work in perfect unison, periodically communicating with their sign language. They haul crates and metal devices into the Sanctum. Not all of them, however, are Phylax.

I spot a few contractors scattered among

the group. Their clothing is unkempt, and they fumble as they work. They complain to each other in hushed voices. Unlike the Phylax, these outsiders move without a sense of purpose, oblivious to the true nature of this operation. I wonder how many of the agents know what is being built.

A contractor struggles to unload a large metallic box, his arms shaking. "What is this place?" he mutters to another man. "We've built bunkers before, but this? What is this? Who are these people?"

His colleague shrugs, shifting uneasily. "They're paying us well. Keep your head down and do your job."

A supervisor barks from near a parked truck, "That's right. Now keep it moving."

I notice their vehicle has a tented cargo bed. Behind the wheel, a woman sits, working on a stack of paperwork.

Above the Acropolis, the sky crackles with energy. Arcs of lightning dance all around. The atmosphere grows more oppressive. Time is slipping away. We need to act now.

I hurry back to where Clara and Xia are waiting. Before I reach them, I'm already scribbling on a notepad. *We need to get onto one of those trucks. We might get information from the crew.*

Clara's doubt is evident. Before she can voice it, Xia says, "Yes. That might work."

I press my pencil against the paper. *We should go up the street. One of us flags down the truck while the others hop into the back.*

Clara's shoulders tense. After some hesitation, she agrees. Together, we slip deeper into the night, positioning ourselves along the truck's path.

The engines grow louder as they approach. When the first truck draws near, Xia steps out, waving her arms frantically. The truck stops. She spins a story about a car accident and how she needs their help.

Clara and I scramble onto the tented truck bed, covered among the crates. Adrenaline courses through me. The cabin door opens, then closes. It sounds like they let Xia inside.

Soon, the truck pulls away from the main road. When it does, we edge forward, knocking on the back window. The driver slows, confused. The man sitting in the middle turns to Xia for an explanation. She smiles, then punches him. His hands fly to his nose in pain. Blood pours steadily from his nostrils.

In a state of panic, the driver slams on the brakes, bringing the truck to an abrupt stop. My face slams into the back window. She throws her door open and jumps down, stumbling as her feet hit the ground. Without looking back, she sprints frantically down the street.

Xia's voice rises urgently. "Hurry, catch her! I

can handle this guy," she declares. She directs her attention to the bleeding passenger.

We take off after the fleeing driver. She is fast, but we have more stamina and close the gap. Clara reaches out, grabbing the woman's arm. "You're coming back to the truck," she asserts.

The woman hesitates, then surrenders, raising her hands in submission. "Okay," she says. Her gaze darts nervously between us.

When we return, I rummage through the back of the truck and find a coil of rope. I hand it to Xia, who sets to work tying up the man. Clara binds the woman and forces her to sit on the back bumper. They shiver with fear.

It's nearly one a.m. on July 1st. We have less than two hours left before we must shift back in time.

Clara speaks first. "What did you deliver?" she demands, arms folded.

The woman hesitates, lips trembling. I step closer, raising my hand as if to strike. She flinches and blurts out, "Okay, okay. Don't hit me. I'm a physicist." Her voice is shaky. She glances at my fist and swallows hard. "It—um—utilizes a rotational mass-energy tensor akin to Gödel's rotating universe solution, effectively enabling clo—"

Clara rolls her eyes. "In English, please. I'm not a physicist. Spell it out so we can understand you."

The woman exhales shakily, glancing

between Clara, Xia, and me. "Alright," she begins again, trying to steady herself. "Gödel once theorized that, under the right conditions, you could *twist* spacetime so it loops back on itself. Imagine rewriting a few pages in the middle of a book. The device I worked on helps create a miniature version of that twist. When the rotation is stable, history in that localized region can be edited, so to speak."

Xia's lips press into a thin line. "Edited? As in removing events that already happened?"

"Or inserting new ones," the physicist says, casting her gaze at the ground. "I overheard one of them say it was for something called the Convergence of Dominion. I—I don't know the details. My role was to develop a system that keeps the loop from collapsing. If it's too unstable, the rotation breaks, and you can't overwrite anything."

Clara looks ready to unleash hell. "So, you've basically allowed them to rewrite history."

The physicist nods. "Yes, essentially. It's what Gödel predicted could be done if you rotate spacetime fast enough. It's dangerous, but they don't seem to care."

Scribbling over old text to change reality? That should never have been conceived, let alone attempted.

Clara echoes my sentiment. "You realize how insane this is, right?"

The woman's eyes brim with regret. "They

paid us too well. I never thought they'd actually —"

Clara interrupts, "How do we stop it?"

The physicist swallows hard, her voice faltering. "I don't know. The part I worked on—what I saw—it was just one small component. With all of the equipment in that fortress, I don't know how it all works together. Whatever they're building—it's beyond anything I've ever seen. I wouldn't even know where to begin."

Xia cuts her off with a curt nod. "That's enough," she says, stepping away. "At least we know what it is. Now we need to figure out how to stop it."

The physicist exhales, relief and dread mingling as she stares at us. Clara ushers her toward the truck, where she and her companion remain bound. We don't have time for more. If rewriting history is genuinely on the table, every minute counts.

My knife feels good in my hand. Part of me wants to finish this, to tie up loose ends for good. They are part of the Phylax's deception. They deserve it. I lift the blade, weighing my options.

Clara steps between me and the prisoners, her tone unwavering. "That's not the best option, Adam. We don't need more blood."

I hate that she's right. I roll my eyes, then slide the knife away. We leave them alive, bound in the back of the truck.

Another flash arcs over the Acropolis as we

move away, followed by a deep, unsettling hum. It scrapes at my nerves, reminding me that time is running short.

Clara says, "It seems this machine is at the center of our problems. Is the Sigma Event the same as the Convergence of Domion?"

Xia replies, "I suspect it is. There's one way to find out. We stay to see what happens."

I do my best to write with the notepad resting in my hand. *That's a terrible idea. It isn't even a real plan. It's just a guess.*

Clara shrugs. "Sometimes we have to take chances."

Xia adds, "True. It's risky, but our options are limited."

Taking this plunge is no different than stepping into a storm blindfolded. The Phylax has resources, while we barely know anything about the Sigma Event. I shake away the fear that gnaws at me. I can't let it win—not now.

I've spent my life under their control, their lies shaping my every step. If I hesitate, I'm no better than the broken child they created. If we fail, we lose more than our lives. We lose the future.

After a long pause, I decide to take the chance with them. It is a little after two in the morning. In less than an hour, the world as we know it will end before our eyes.

TWENTY-TWO

It is ten minutes before 3 AM on July 1st, 2051. Everything is unnaturally serene. I wait for something —anything— to break the silence. Nothing comes. Even the distant hum of city life has faded into nothing. Maybe it won't happen at all. The idea plagues me as the seconds crawl by. Wasn't this supposed to be when everything changed? The day that time travel ended? Yet, here we are, surrounded by calm.

"Maybe it's not the Phylax," Clara mutters, arms crossed against the night's chill. Uncertainty creeps into her tone. "Maybe it's something else. Something we never considered."

I don't respond. Clara's words stir an uneasy question. If we are wrong, then what? The Phylax are my enemy, but what if they're pawns in a larger game? I write down, *This is our last chance, do you still want to stay?*

"Yes." Clara doesn't sound entirely convinced.

The anticipation is crushing. Time drips by,

stretching into melted wax—still, nothing.

Then the clocks are striking three. In an instant, everything changes.

The vibrant lights of Athens flicker and die. Neighborhood by neighborhood, the city plunges into a veil of night. Malaise settles like a suffocating blanket. I watch, horrified, as armed Phylax agents spread out through the streets, setting up checkpoints at every major intersection. Surveillance drones whir overhead, their cameras endlessly scanning the city. Propaganda posters bearing the Phylax emblem appear on walls and billboards as though they've always been there, rewriting the city's narrative.

Searchlights pierce the darkness, slicing through the streets. Metal footsteps echo in the distance. I catch sight of an autonomous patrol unit marching through Athens. The city has become a fortified prison, with every movement monitored, every breath controlled.

As the world transforms before my eyes, the talisman I carry goes utterly dead. I had stopped noticing its consistent thumping until now. It is a heart frozen mid-beat, its warmth gone, leaving a cold ache. I do not believe in omens, but this cannot be a good sign.

Clara's grip on my arm tightens. "They've locked it down," she whispers. "They have control over everything."

I struggle to comprehend what I'm seeing.

What kind of machine could trigger this? The Athens we arrived in hours ago has transformed into a fortified stronghold under the Phylax's command. Somewhere in the Sanctum, their machine hums—an invisible force that seems to tether the timeline to this point. If the Sigma Event is the poisoned blood that sustains this dystopian future, then the machine is its wretched heart, pumping corruption through every vein of time.

While remaining concealed, we watch the Phylax tighten their grip on the city. Agents patrol in coordinated units. Clara whispers with urgency, the fear evident when she says, "I'm not so sure this was a good idea. We should try to go back in time and devise a safer plan. No point in confronting them unprepared."

Clara inhales deeply, placing her hands on our shoulders as she tries to guide us back through time. Nothing happens. Panic creeps in. "I don't see it," she says. "I don't see anything."

Xia takes Clara's hands gently, grounding her. "You're okay," she says, her voice calm but firm. "You're just overwhelmed. Breathe with me." She presses her forehead to Clara's and speaks soft, steady words. One hand moves to Clara's back, rubbing slow circles. It takes time, but eventually Clara's breathing slows. Her shoulders ease. The panic begins to loosen its grip.

The sudden, absolute nature of the Sigma

Event makes no sense unless something fundamental about time changed instantly. If time travel is impossible beyond this point, then whatever happened at 3 AM must have altered the structure of spacetime. One possibility is a quantum bind, a mechanism that forces the timeline into a rigid, unchangeable state. If the Phylax manipulated time loops to enforce a closed system, then time might be folded in on itself. It would redirect any attempt to move forward back to the same point. Instead of an open road, we're trapped in a Möbius strip, looping endlessly in a reality they designed. If they reinforced that with something akin to quantum decoherence—a dampening field that forces time into a single state, time travel would be impossible. No cracks left to slip through and no way out.

Gödel's time loops might be the key. The physicist we interrogated described a system that could rotate spacetime, allowing the Phylax to edit history. Maybe the Sigma Event was a way to force the world into a new timeline where they hold absolute control. The moment it activated, the expected future simply ceased to exist, replaced by whatever they designed. A world sculpted by their laws with no way to escape it.

That would also explain why my talisman is silent. If time travelers leave a temporal resonance, the faint signal that marks where and when something belongs, then whatever the

Phylax did might have snuffed that out as well. If they manipulated time on such a scale, it might have created a field that suppresses or distorts resonance altogether—leaving nothing for the talisman to detect. If that's true, we're trapped inside this new reality. Until we figure out how to break the quantum bind, we're stuck.

I'm not too worried yet. If there is one thing I believe from Philip, it's that he managed to cross back through the 2051 threshold. I jot down a note. *We will be okay. We'll make the best of our time here and figure out how to leave. It is possible.*

Xia considers this. She replies, "First, we must find a more secure location to rest. There are guards everywhere. We can't stay here."

I write, *Good call. Let's move.*

We pick our way through backstreets as the Phylax patrols the city. The transformation is staggering. Everywhere we look, they've left their mark. I cannot comprehend how quickly and thoroughly they've taken control.

A rhythmic hum growls under our feet as we trek through the streets. We don't see the Phylax's machine, but its presence is unmistakable. Periodically, lightning arcs over the Acropolis. The machine seems to pull at the air, distorting the space around me as if something unseen is watching, waiting. It feels alive.

Phylax patrol drones hover nearby, their sounds growing louder. We freeze against a crumbling alley wall. The crisp snap of a Phylax agent's footsteps approach. I want to attack, but I know better. One misstep, one careless sound, and we're finished.

Spotlights sweep the alley. The light is so close I feel its heat on my skin. It is proof of the danger we're in. Clara stands beside me, holding her breath. Xia's gaze meets mine. She seems calm, focused, and patient.

The patrol stops a couple of feet away. The agent's silhouette is stark against the glow of the streetlights. His uniform is unnervingly pristine. Its black and gold design reflects a sharp, predatory elegance. The helmet's visor emits a faint blue light, giving him the appearance of something more machine than man. He taps a device on his wrist. A red beam sweeps out from a sensor on his shoulder, scanning the alley. The beam dances inches from my foot. The hiss of hydraulics accompanies each step, harmonizing with the mechanical whir of the drones above. Momentarily, he pauses, his hand hovering near his weapon. Mercifully, he moves on, disappearing into the night.

Xia whispers, "They're sweeping systematically. Every patrol will loop back to cover their tracks. If we move with their pattern instead of against it, we might find a gap to slip through."

As we move with them, the city quietens in its forgotten corners. The buildings here are older, their outlines jagged against the light of dawn. Cracked pavement gives way to patches of overgrown weeds. The air takes on a neglected stillness. This part of Athens has been forsaken.

We find an abandoned building tucked behind some crumbled stone. Perhaps it was once grand, now reduced to ruins. Broken windows line the upper floors, and shards of glass litter the ground. The brick walls are streaked with grime, giving the place a haunted air. The door hangs crooked, creaking as we push it open, the sound echoing in the empty space.

Inside, it is hollow and cold. The air smells of decay. Faded wallpaper peels in curls, revealing layers of neglect. The wooden floorboards are warped. A broken chair and a rusted lamp hint that people once lived here. It's a forgotten shell, ignored by the Phylax brigades sweeping the streets.

We settle in one of the larger rooms. The ceiling sags but holds to provide us with cover. Clara leans against the wall, lost in thought. Xia sits cross-legged, her hands resting in her lap. She is always alert, always thinking.

I remain standing, surveying the room. It is a temporary refuge that time has abandoned. We don't speak; we are trapped in our own ruminations, uncertain about what comes next. We know we'll have to move again soon.

Clara says, "We might be trapped in this hell. That also means we're closer to their operations."

Xia reaches out for Clara's hand. "We know it's in the Sanctum. If we can pinpoint its vulnerabilities, we might have a chance to disrupt it. A machine this powerful has to leave traces—energy fluctuations, signal outputs —something we can exploit."

I write, *We need more information. That's all there is to it.* Despite everything, hope stirs inside me. The Phylax have the upper hand; however, we're resourceful.

"Let's rest for now," Xia suggests. "We'll need our strength."

Xia is correct.

The floor beneath me is cold. A chill seeps into my bones. The room carries a familiar scent of dampness that I associate with hiding places. It is like many temporary havens I have found while on missions—abandoned buildings, caves carved into mountainsides, and even forgotten tunnels beneath ancient cities. Each one a brief sanctuary, a place to recover just enough before stepping back into the fight.

Something pokes me from my jacket pocket as I roll over to sleep. I pull out the Dalek toy and inspect its broken arms. The little dome swivels as I twist it between my fingers.

I don't know why I've decided to carry it —perhaps for luck, if there is such a thing. It evokes memories of my mother, though most of her features remain blurred. Yet, more fragments have begun to resurface. Impressions of her smile, the warmth of her voice, the way her hands moved as she spoke. Over time, I know I will continue to remember more details.

I can piece together one memory. "Adam, even the smallest things can protect us," she said one rainy afternoon as she handed me the Dalek. I think its paint was chipped even then.

I'd been scared of the storm outside. My mother crouched beside me, placing the toy in my hands. "The Daleks are fierce, you know. They protect themselves by moving forward, no matter what. Just like you."

It doesn't matter if the words were meant for a scared child hiding from thunder. She believed in me. At least, that's what I want to believe.

I nestle the Dalek in my palm, feeling its smooth surface. The memory is fleeting but warm, a rare sliver of kindness from a past that feels is more of a story than anything else. Maybe everyone feels that way about their distant past, though.

And Clara—Clara found me. My sister, someone I never knew existed, reached through time to pull me back from a miserable life. She has a familiar spark, something I've been unknowingly searching for. I imagine my mother had that same spark, that same ability to anchor someone to more than mere survival. Maybe that's where my sister got it from. I don't understand how Clara held onto hope after everything that happened to her. I'm glad she did. She's the one good thing in this mess, the thread connecting me to something real.

I am not alone.

This fact scares me. Being alone is easier because I don't have to care for others. Yet, being together also fills me with gratitude. I'll be damned if I lose either of them now.

I clutch the Dalek tightly while letting my head rest against the floor. The machine's hum creeps back in, but I'm too tired to care. For now, I have this moment of respite, this memory, and the undeniable truth that, against all odds, someone cared enough to find me.

TWENTY-THREE

I bolt upright from my sleep. Outside, loud shouting erupts. It shatters the uneasy stillness that had settled over our makeshift haven. I impulsively reach for my knife. Adrenaline floods my veins. A shot rings out, then another. My muscles coil in response.

I stay low, creeping toward the window. The jagged teeth of broken glass frame the opening. I flatten myself against the wall, listening. Muffled voices and more distant gunshots filter through the early morning air. After a tense pause, a drone's low hum passes. Through the fractured pane, I spot dark figures scrambling below. It's over as quickly as it began, leaving the essence of a threat.

Behind me, Clara and Xia freeze. Clara whispers, "What was that?"

I attempt to form the words with my mouth. There is little more than a squeak. I will continue to try. For now, I take out my notepad. *Not sure. It's over, though.*

We wait, listening for any sign that the chaos

might resume. The street holds its breath.

Eventually, Clara breaks the hush. "We need to get inside the Sanctum." She doesn't say it as a suggestion.

Xia frowns. "Break in? That's suicide." She shakes her head.

It is impossible to sneak into the Sanctum. Yet, if we want real answers about the Phylax's machine or how to get out of here, we may have to find a way.

Clara crosses her arms. "We find the cracks. They must have supply runs, maintenance access, or something similar. They have a weakness somewhere. We just need to find it."

Xia exhales sharply, but she doesn't argue. She's right to be skeptical. The Phylax doesn't make mistakes.

I write, *We watch tonight, look for vulnerabilities, then act.* Without a better plan, I don't want to go near the Acropolis again. Unfortunately, without more information, we can't devise a better plan.

Each of us keeps to ourselves throughout the day. The sun's slow arc drags across the sky; each minute feels like an agonizing test of our patience.

Finally, the sun dips below the horizon. Twilight descends over the city. Again, drones hum above, scanning for any sign of unrest. Phylax patrols glide through the streets, enforcing a curfew that keeps Athens in a state of fear. Perhaps foolishly, we return to the former Athens University History Museum rooftop. While a great spot to watch the Sanctum, we have no cover if a drone passes.

From our vantage point, the entrance to the Sanctum is hidden in the weathered cliff. It is the only way in or out of their lair, so we will see anyone who leaves.

We watch. My muscles ache from remaining motionless for so long; however, I know the cost of impatience. I was trained to endure long hours of vigilance. While I haven't dwelled on my missions as much since meeting Clara, this reminds me of Knossos in 1375 BCE.

The Phylax sent me to assassinate King Rhadamanthys. I remember the suffocating heat and the stale air thick with dust. The space where I hid was barely large enough to stretch out, wedged between rough stone walls that scraped my skin if I shifted even a little. My body was stiff; every muscle ached in protest with each moment of forced stasis.

Hours bled together in silence, the passage of time marked only by the distant echo of footsteps and the occasional flicker of torchlight filtering through the cracks in the stone. Sweat beaded on my skin, mixing with the fine layer of grit that formed a second layer of skin. I slowed my breathing because even a sharp exhale could unravel everything. So, I waited, hidden in the wall. Back then, I never thought to question the missions.

By comparison, this is plush.

As I stare at the Sanctum's entrance, I wonder if those missions had a pattern. Each episode of violence must have served some larger purpose. What was the real goal behind all those killings? I can't shake the feeling that I played an essential role in building the reality that now suffocates us.

Finally, the tension breaks as a small group of Phylax agents emerge from the Sanctum. I see their crisp military whites through my binoculars—a stark contrast to the Phylax I once knew. Before the Sigma Event, we operated as a scattered network of assassins and covert agents trained to remain unseen. Our numbers were small.

Now, Athens alone is swarming with thousands of soldiers patrolling the streets. It's unlikely that any of them are time travelers; however, one figure stands out. A high-ranking officer leads the group, distinguished by the intricate insignia on her arm. She carries herself with authority, someone of importance. She doesn't belong with the group of grunts, leading me to believe they may be en route to a formal gathering or gala.

Clara leans close. "They're on the move," she whispers. "We need to follow them, see where they go."

I agree. At my hand signal, we slip out of our spot, hugging the deepest shadows that stretch across the ancient stones beneath our feet.

It's not easy tracking them. Their movements are difficult to follow from a distance, forcing us to make a few course corrections. Meanwhile, we must stay alert for the ever-present sweeps of Phylax agents and drones, constantly adjusting our route to avoid detection. It's a tightrope act—close enough to keep them in sight, far enough to stay invisible.

We glide through the city, silhouettes skimming along deserted alleys. I glimpse the outlines of the Phylax agents as they pass beneath stuttering streetlights. I signal to Clara and Xia. We close in, carefully maintaining our cover.

Their path leads us deeper into Athens, through a maze of twisting narrow streets. The buildings loom overhead, their crooked forms pushing in as if herding us into some forgotten alcove of history. I notice that the windows are boarded up. Each road takes us further into obscurity.

Every so often, pairs of Phylax sentries emerge from the main thoroughfares. At the first hint of them, we melt behind dumpsters, half-collapsed fences, and rusted metal doors.

When one pair gets too close, we stop and brace ourselves against an alley wall. Only a thin shrub separates them from us. We can smell the tang of gin on their breath. They pass without speaking, their footsteps heavy on the cracked pavement.

Out here, the drones seem absent from this part of the city as if it's too remote or inconsequential for their circuits. Clara's relaxed grin has given way to a tense mask. Xia's habitual caution intensifies, her focus cutting through the gloom. I feel my own nerves tightening.

Then the figures we're tailing slow down, halting beneath a streetlight. We also stop, hopping into a pile of crumbling bricks to observe our surroundings. A subtle movement in my periphery draws my attention. To the right, figures slide into view. It's as if they have stepped out of the masonry.

A trap.

Before we have time to strategize, chaos erupts. Clara moves first, her foot lashing out with a ferocity that sends an attacker staggering backward. He clutches his midsection. She pivots, then snaps her elbow upward to catch another square in the jaw with a sickening crack.

Xia is a blur, her fists darting like vipers. One strike crushes into an attacker's throat, sending him reeling. Her other hand delivers a bone-crushing blow to the ribs of another.

I swing at the closest figure, my knuckles colliding with his chin, the impact sending a jolt up my arm. He drops.

More figures emerge, swarming us in a tidal wave. The air fills with the sound of cursing. I duck as an elbow flies toward my face, countering with a hard shove that sends my attacker sprawling over a pile of rubble.

Clara fights fiercely, but the attackers outnumber her. She ducks a swinging baton, returning with a sharp uppercut that catches her opponent off guard. A second attacker grabs her from behind. She twists violently, driving her heel into his shin, forcing him to let go with a pained cry.

Xia grabs an attacker's arm mid-swing, wrenching it behind his back with a sickening pop. She then uses his body as a shield when a taser's electrodes are discharged in her direction.

More of them close in, overwhelming us with sheer numbers. I feel rough hands grab my shoulder, yanking me backward. I twist, throwing an elbow into someone's ribs. Before I can follow through, another set of fingers clamp down on my arm. Cold metal bites into my wrists. I hear the click of restraints locking into place.

Clara snarls as someone else grabs her. Her voice cuts through the chaos, "You'll regret this!"

She twists violently, her inhalations coming in sharp bursts, but the numbers are too great. Even as they shackle her wrists, she jerks against the restraints, her glare burning with raw defiance.

I wrench against the bindings, frustration boiling over as they rip victory from our grasp. We fought hard. It wasn't enough. As they force a hood over my head, Clara calls out, "Xia, any brilliant ideas?"

Xia doesn't answer immediately. I can hear her struggle. "Not yet," she shouts. "Stay ready."

Rage surges. How could I have missed this? The Pied Piper led us, unwitting rats, into a trap. I believed myself too experienced to be so easily tricked.

I feel a sharp yank at my wrists. We're on the move. They shove us forward. We stumble blindly over uneven ground. It is impossible to guess where we're going. Every turn disorients me further, my sense of direction slipping away as we're herded through the streets. It's deliberate, I realize. They want us confused. We're at their mercy. They know it.

Eventually, we're marched inside a building and forced to a stop. Through the shroud, I catch the pungent stench of mildew, stale cigarette smoke, and something sour lurking underneath. The foul odors cling to the back of my throat.

Suddenly, they rip away my hoodwink. I blink into a dimly lit interior. The floor is bare concrete, and broken chairs are shoved haphazardly against cracked walls.

Clara speaks with a hiss, "Aren't the Phylax obnoxious about order? What kind of place is this?"

She's right. Whoever runs this place isn't interested in official procedure. They have free rein here, which means no limits to what they might do.

They march us down a narrow concrete hallway lined with doors on both sides. Through some of them, I hear faint screams that send my stomach twisting. It's a grim preview of what we might endure. Before the guards shove me into a separate room, I catch a final glimpse of them forcing Clara and Xia into their own chambers. Clara's fear is etched on her. Xia assesses everything that she can. Heavy doors slam, cutting them off from me.

A muscled enforcer holds me against an uneven table. The surface's pitted grooves scrape against my skin, pressing into my cheek and jaw as I struggle. My skin splits in a few places. Blood drips onto the table. Another memory carved into my face, where everyone can see it.

Above me, fluorescent lights buzz, flickering erratically, casting jagged outlines that crawl along the grimy walls. Rusted stains mar the bare concrete floor. From somewhere deep in the building, irregular drips of water reverberate.

Sweat trickles down my back, soaking into my shirt as the humid air presses in. My chest tightens as screams echo from the nearby rooms.

As they fasten my handcuffs to the table, something unexpected happens. At first, I think I had imagined it. The talisman tucked in my pants pocket stirs. The softest thrum pulses against my skin, a whisper of life. It grows steadier until it beats in time with my racing heart. Its sudden vitality sends a surge of defiance through my veins. I'm not beaten yet.

I focus, expecting to find my usual map of time unfurl, but I don't see the familiar catalog. Instead, it tastes like electricity. A low hum vibrates through my bones, its pitch wavering a broken melody. Beneath it, an incoherent fog of whispers drifts. Light fractures into kaleidoscopic patterns that shift unnaturally. Heat blooms then vanishes into a biting chill that sends shivers racing down my spine. A deep unease coils inside me. I can't shake the feeling that this anomaly is alive, watching me. It pokes my memories with a predatory curiosity.

I search for something that might set me free. This place fights me, dragging me deeper into my subconscious. Before I can wrest control, one memory snaps into sharp focus: Egypt when I was sixteen. No, not quite a memory.

I am an observer in my sixteen-year-old's body, back in that hot, torchlit temple, crouched behind a sandstone pillar. The firelight crackles over ancient hieroglyphs. I wait, watching Pharaoh Akhenaten approach the altar, his white and gold robes shimmering in the glow. He is serene, otherworldly, as if in communion with Aten, the sole god he imposed on his people.

Philip stands near me, clasping my shoulder. *Kill quickly and quietly, lad*, he signs a whispered command. *Make no sound, leave no trace. You are the blade; you are the silence.*

My young self is taut with fear, but beneath that fear is a desperate need to impress him. I must prove I'm worthy of his trust and the Phylax's promises. My grip on the bronze blade tightens. I creep forward, synchronized with the ceremonial chants that fill the temple. I lock my eyes on Akhenaten. His devotion to the god Aten has upended Egypt's centuries-old pantheon, threatening the traditions of the past.

As I draw closer, I remember the doubts stuttering in my mind and the hesitation with each step. Akhenaten didn't resemble the tyrant Philip had described. He looked human. I tightened my focus. The need to please Philip consumed me.

With a swift motion, I struck. My blade sliced into Akhenaten's sternum, ending his soft prayer with a breathless gasp. The remorse of what I'd done hit me, but Philip's smile of approval cut through the shame.

The pull of memory is suffocating. Its vividness threatens to trap me. I want to follow this experience to its end. I must remain in the temple to hear more of Philip's rare approval. Somehow, I muster up the knowledge that I cannot stay.

My fingers dig into the present, clinging desperately as I tear myself free from this strange sensation. I drag myself back to the stale air of the interrogation room. The world around me slips back into focus. I collapse onto the table. Every muscle in my body aches. My thoughts circle to one name that rises through the fog: Philip.

That strange experience must be the anomaly Philip spoke of to the priest. In the weird, fractured world I just visited, there has to be a way out of here, a means of moving through time.

If the Phylax used some kind of quantum bind to seal off time travel, maybe the leftover temporal resonance was squeezed into these tiny pockets, these anomalies, where reality isn't quite pinned down. They'd be fragments of what used to be an open timeline, now jammed into corners of spacetime and occasionally bleeding through.

It's only speculation, but these anomalous pockets may form in areas where decoherence breaks down. I believe the strange experiences are caused by fractured temporal energy leaking through. If the Sigma Event was meant to slam the door on time travel, these anomalies could be cracks around the door frame. In these spots, time might churn without direction.

Of course, I can't prove any of it. We're

dealing with an unknown phenomenon. I doubt even the Phylax understands it. However, if I'm right, these anomalies might be our way to break out of this wretched future. They are unpredictable windows to a reality I can't grasp, except that it is more than a mere passage for travelers. There's something about it that is untamed. It seems to hold onto fragments of the past. It's as if the anomaly has collected memories, truths, and maybe even entire lives. I sense that staying there too long would be dangerous; however, there must be a way through it. Philip found one.

TWENTY-FOUR

The door creaks open; an officer steps inside, flanked by two guards. Both keep their weapons locked on me. The officer's face is a grotesque mask of sharp angles and sunken hollows. His cheekbones jut out like blades beneath papery skin. The suspended light casts deep shadows into the recesses of his eye sockets, making the orbits seem cavernous. His lips are stretched over yellowed teeth, pulled into a cruel grimace. He stands with arms crossed, his bony fingers tapping against his sleeve. I am nothing more than defective equipment to him.

"So," he begins. "Who are you? What's your purpose in this city?" He lets the question linger. "Why were you following the Phylax soldiers?"

His lips tighten. He's clearly used to captives crumbling at the first show of force. However, I sense something in him—not a man made of stone. He wears a plastic mask of an expression. I'm not afraid of him. My concern lies elsewhere, with the talisman's pulse in my pocket, calling me to something far more significant than whatever game he's playing here.

He waits a few seconds before his patience snaps. His fist crashes into my jaw, the force jerking me to the side. Blood pours into my mouth. Still, I keep my lips sealed. Another blow follows, this time to my ribs. Pain explodes everywhere. I refuse to give him the pleasure of a reaction. He strikes again. His frustration mounts with each unanswered attack. I anchor my focus on the talisman's steady pulse.

In my peripheral vision, the room wavers. The walls warp with a convex distortion. The anomaly creeps in at the edges of my perception, threatening to yank me away. I fight the urge to dive into it.

"Interesting," the officer murmurs. He gestures for the guards to step forward. Hands claw at my shirt, tearing it away. They unhook the handcuffs from the table and shove me against the wall, then secure me to a set of chains dangling from the ceiling. A lever groans, pulling my arms upward until discomfort flares in my shoulders.

Then, the officer's vision falls on my arm, where the marred Phylax insignia stains my flesh. He freezes, shock spreading across him. He steps back. "Notify the Council immediately," he barks to the guards, his composure slipping.

As I stand shackled to the wall, the room starts to distort again. I cannot fight it this time. The cracked paint melts into brilliance. The talisman's pulse grows stronger. With the guards gone, I let the interrogation chamber dissolve into the background.

The kaleidoscope of fractured images flares to life. Swirling patterns writhe, animated with a life of their own. Light fractures into shards, colors bleed together, then dissolve into darkness. The whispers return; an incoherent fog encroaches. As suddenly as it started, the chaos stops. The kaleidoscope snaps shut, leaving me standing in the Sanctum.

Braziers line the edges of the perfectly circular chamber. Their flames cast a dancing glow across murals of triumph etched into the stone walls. At the center, a raised platform gleams with ancient carvings. The two-headed serpents coil toward infinity, embedded in gold and silver. The polished green marble floor beneath my feet seems to shimmer with a secret of its own. The setting feels impossibly real, more vivid than the grim chamber I know I occupy in another layer of reality.

A sudden, unseen force drags me forward. I'm thrust into a chamber I've never seen before. In the center of this spectral room stands a massive machine, alive with humming energy. Metal surfaces gleam as gears and wires writhe.

Six cloaked figures encircle the device, their forms wavering in the hazy glow of the room. The Archon stands at the forefront, locking his attention on the machine as its hum pulses through the air. The others are shrouded until a flash of light reveals one. Something about how he juts his face forward and tilts it at an awkward angle—the stillness in his stance—strikes me as hauntingly familiar. I think I know him. I latch onto the image, but in the next instant, the light shifts. He's swallowed back into darkness.

Someone I expect to see next to the Archon steps forward. Philip. The machine lights his skin with a sickening green glow. The Archon's words captivate him.

"The time lock is operational," the Archon declares. "All timelines have collapsed into a singularity. Travel will remain shut down except when we allow it." Pride seeps into his voice, " The Convergence of Dominion is successful. Our power is now unbreakable."

I once read about forced wavefunction collapse in quantum mechanics—how particles exist in multiple states until an external force locks them into one. If you apply that concept to entire timelines, then maybe the Phylax machine chooses a single outcome, forcing all probabilities to collapse into one fixed reality. The ultimate convergence.

The editing machine must be how the specifics of this world were created. The Phylax manipulated events, stored them somehow, and the convergence fuses it all together. If they've merged them thoroughly, then time itself has been reforged into a single trunk, with all other branches forcibly absorbed into this one unbreakable thread. No wonder the world changed so quickly. What remains is a singular narrative, sculpted by the Phylax and upheld by their machine.

The edges of the scene begin to fray as Philip signs. *What about the anomalies? Scientists warned they're scattered across Earth.* Philip's signs blur, and the scene bends like a candle in the wind. *Danger... trap someone... slip through...* His message splinters, each fragment collapsing into nothingness.

The Archon's reply begins with renewed clarity. "It doesn't matter. Everything is under our control. We will contain the anomalies."

Thankfully, they have not done that yet.

His voice dissolves into the rising hum of the machine. The sound diminishes, making it difficult to hear. The words fragment, unraveling into incoherent whispers as the scene pulls away.

"The lock... hold, Philip... obey..." The figures stutter in and out. The window I view it from splinters. I reach toward Philip, desperate to see, but my fingers pass through empty air. The vision collapses into ribbons of light, melting into the void. The machine, the Archon, Philip, the Council—all of it leaves me gasping in the suffocation of the interrogation room once more.

I blink, disoriented, my tongue dry with the

acrid taste of fear. I can't tell if I saw a vision, a memory, or some lie dredged up by the anomaly itself. The highlights stay with me: the time lock, the singularity, the Phylax seizing control over all time. It's burned into my mind.

As my senses settle, I realize that chains still bind me to the wall in the interrogation room. The talisman's pulse lessens. My eyelids flutter, struggling to distinguish reality from whatever the anomaly showed me. My vision clears; my heart lurches as I see the Archon standing in the doorway. Momentarily, I believe I am trapped in some half-world, but the Archon's voice assures me he's in the room with me.

I see pity in him before it hardens into loathing. "Such a disappointment," he spits. "You had so much potential when we picked you up. You were meant for the Council." He draws closer. "You had the skill, the focus, the loyalty. Yet, you failed. How was that possible?" His voice lowers. "The Temptation broke you. Now, you've gone rogue. I didn't believe Philip when he warned me this would happen."

He paces slowly, savoring each step. "This all started with Qin," he says. "Your failure in China set us back decades. A mission ruined because you couldn't do your job properly."

His words are a distant thunder. Loud but empty. They mean nothing. The Phylax no longer has a hold on me. His contempt fuels my resolve. I will see their empire fall.

He stands straighter, his voice cooling into something more dangerous. "No matter. We managed to build our future, even with your mistake. This little rebellion of yours ends now."

He is dismissive. "I only came down here to ensure that they captured you." he sneers, waving for the guards. "Kill this traitor."

The Archon leaves without another word. As his footsteps fade, the talisman's pulse returns. I focus inward, feeling the anomaly tug at my senses again. I know it's connected to the machine hidden in the Sanctum. It calls to me, urging me into its strange currents.

I let go, slipping back into the anomaly's embrace. The interrogation room dissolves into layers of shimmering light, each pulse revealing a lattice of energy threading through every solid object. Time flows strangely. Movement slows to a crawl as the guards enter the room, raising their guns. The world warps around me, bending to possibilities that I can only attribute to the concentration of temporal resonance.

Awe washes over me as liquid light dances along my veins. I push through the handcuffs as though they were made of smoke. The guards are frozen mid-action, their forms blurred and unreal. I step forward, passing through one of them effortlessly. In this state, I am a ghost.

I focus on the gun in one guard's possession and return to solid matter. The world snaps into focus. His weapon is heavy in my grip. Before they realize I'm free, two shots crack the silence. The guards drop to the cold floor. Their expressions forever reflect confusion.

I stand over them, the gun hot in my hand, the sharp scent of discharged gunpowder hovering in the air. They thought they had me cornered, unaware of the anomaly surrounding us. The Archon believed this would be the end of my rebellion. Instead, he's given me the weapon I need to turn the tide.

I slip into the corridor and hurry to the next room, where Xia is being held. Pressing my ear against the door, I hear muffled struggles—my pulse quickens. Gun in tow, I ease the door open to look inside.

Xia sits upright in a chair, hands bound, her visage mottled with bruises and smeared with blood. A Phylax officer stands over her, fist raised to strike again. He doesn't register my presence before I pull the trigger. The shot cracks through the room. The officer collapses. I collect his side-arm.

"I knew you'd come," Xia says. The pain etched into her posture seems to provide her with strength.

I free her wrists. She winces as she tries to stand, yet the hardness in her attitude is more potent than any wound. "Where's Clara?" she pleads.

I gesture toward the hallway, indicating that

I haven't reached her room yet. Before we leave, Xia grips my arm. "I know how to get home," her voice is urgent. "I saw it in a vision. This place showed me the way back. I don't know how, but I know it'll work."

I place my fingers on her shoulder and give a brief nod. It's enough to let her know I understand the importance of her discovery, but there is no time for details. We need to find Clara.

Xia and I race down the hallway toward the room where we believe they hold Clara. When we fling it open, the sight of her hurts me. Clara sits slumped in a chair, head tilted downward. Her face is a tapestry of bruises. She's alone, her breathing shallow, eyes half-open and distant. She is lost in another place. I rest a hand on her arm. Xia kneels, gently shaking her.

I try to call Clara's name. My voice fails me again.

"Clara," Xia begs, "Come back to us."

For a long moment, Clara remains unresponsive. Then, her eyelids flutter. The haze clears. Confusion drifts across her features.

"You're here," she murmurs, relief threading through her ragged voice. "I... I saw..." Her words fade. We silently agree the details can wait.

We stagger down the corridor together, battered but alive. Adrenaline keeps our legs moving. By the time we near the entrance, the talisman's thrum fades to nothingness. We've left the anomaly behind, returning to the harsh reality of this dystopia.

Pausing at the entryway, we hear footsteps coming down another hallway. I toss one gun to Clara and the other to Xia. I take cover around the corner, gesturing for them to do the same on the other side. We brace ourselves, drawing on our last reserves of strength.

When they come at us, I grab the first guard, slamming him into the wall, his weapon clattering away. Xia pokes from behind her corner, firing two swift shots, each finding its mark.

Another guard surprises us by running into the entry and swinging at Clara. She ducks beneath his fist, countering with a gun shot that drops him instantly. Two more fire several rounds in our direction. The bullets ricochet off the walls behind us, missing their mark. They foolishly race toward us, their guns raised. I grab a fallen weapon and fire. One guard falls; the other hesitates long enough for Xia to find her target.

Once again, there is calm at the entrance.

We burst into the early morning air at a full sprint. We weave through alleys, never daring to glance back. The city begins to stir around us, its muffled hum growing as the day awakens. Finally, we stumble into a deserted courtyard, collapsing behind a low wall, lungs burning.

We wait long enough to steady ourselves before walking back into the alleys, retracing our route toward the abandoned building we used as a hideout. The first light of day stretches across the streets. There are fewer patrol routes this early. It helps us hold onto hope.

When we are inside the safehouse, Clara drifts toward the broken window and surveys the street below. She sits with her hands clasped in her lap, fingers twitching. Her jaw stays tight, the words locked behind her teeth. Whatever she saw in the anomaly had left its mark. She holds onto something distant, shaded by fear. She rubs her temples absently.

When Xia asks, "Is everything okay?" Clara flinches.

Xia waits with concern. Clara opens her mouth, then closes it again. Again, she retreats into herself, folding deeper into sullenness. Clara isn't ready to share—not yet. She is always the voice of hope, but her words falter, leaving an unsettling void.

I sit on an old cushion and pull out my notebook. My pen scratches frantically, writing down everything I can recall from the anomaly: the scattered fragments about a time lock, the Sigma Event, and the Phylax achieving absolute dominion. The idea of a timeline singularity hovers.

Xia watches me closely while I note the details about scattered anomalies across Earth. *They're unstable pockets of reality where we slip into something beyond the ordinary.* I'm sure Clara felt it, too, though I can't guess what visions might haunt her now.

Xia sits beside me, fixed on my notes. "I saw something, too," she says. "I heard them talking about traveling to the past. I was eavesdropping on their meeting. They mentioned the next transportation period is coming in two days, at eleven AM. It lasts two minutes. We will need to be near the Sanctum. If we miss it, I think we'll be trapped here for a very long time."

My eyebrows raise as I write, *The talisman will alert us when that moment arrives. Two minutes isn't much of time. We have to be there.*

Clara remains at the window, her back to us, lost in her own turbulence. Xia moves close to her. "Clara," she asks softly, "did you experience anything in the anomaly?"

Clara's shoulders tense. I think she won't answer. Then, still facing the glass, she snaps, "I don't remember." She is brittle. This is a side of her I have not yet seen. Xia stays seated by Clara's side, doing everything she can to soothe her. Clara will talk when she is ready.

TWENTY-FIVE

Morning light filters over the city as the Phylax patrols continue. The city's tension hangs in a choking fog. Each corner is secured behind armed patrols and metal barricades, as if the Phylax have bolted the streets in place. Occasionally, a surveillance drone buzzes above.

Clara stands a short distance away, looking at the streets below us. She seems more like herself today, except there's a burden in her —a remnant of whatever she endured in the interrogation room. I don't question her. Whatever she's holding back will surface in its own time.

Xia says, "We need to move in closer. The reset window should open in about an hour. If we're too far away, we'll miss our chance."

Clara continues to watch the street. "There are guards everywhere," she says, laced with frustration. "Getting near the Sanctum without being seen seems impossible."

I pull out my notebook to quickly outline a plan. *There's a maintenance path near the*

Acropolis. It's a long shot, but we might be able to slip through. I hold up the page.

Both women are on board.

We hurry along the narrow service road; our steps quicken to meet the short countdown. Halfway there, Clara stops abruptly. A barricade stretches across the route, guarded by two Phylax agents. We're too exposed.

I scribble a message: *We're not close enough.*

"This place," Clara whispers, her voice trembling with anger, "is cursed. It's designed to break us down." Her voice falters. "Back in the anomaly, I... I saw..." She can't finish. Tears threaten to spill, and she closes off again.

Xia and I move closer to Clara, each reassuringly touching her shoulder. "It's okay," Xia says gently. "We're here. You're not alone."

Clara exhales, her shoulders dip with a flash of defeat. She seems adrift in thought. Her eyes linger on the rocky slope, then slowly trail upward, following the jagged ascent toward the Acropolis. A new idea sparks in her. "We have to go completely off-path," she says. "Straight up. Why would they guard the top of the Acropolis? Every route is blocked. We can reach the Erechtheion, right above the Sanctum, if we climb. I bet the window will be open there."

I follow her line of sight, taking in the cliff she's focused on. She's right—it's our best shot. No path will get us closer. We move toward the base of the rising rock.

Xia eyes the cliff with an exaggerated smirk. "Doesn't look too bad," she quips. Her slumped posture betrays her confidence. Although the jagged rock offers small holds, nothing about this will be easy.

I take the lead, testing each grip against the strain in my arms as the rock's sharp edges bite into my fingers. Behind me, Clara moves steadily. I notice the tension each time she shifts. Her knuckles are pale against the stone. Her shoulders stiffen before each reach, bracing for something worse than a fall. Her breathing is uneven. The climb pulls something from her that isn't only physical.

Midway, she pauses, bowed over as she grips a narrow ledge. I wonder if she's about to break.

"You okay?" Xia asks with concern.

Clara forces herself upward. "Fine," she mutters. The crack in her voice tells me otherwise. Despite whatever burden she's carrying, she keeps climbing.

A sudden gust of wind tears through the air, tugging at our clothes. Pebbles tumble down the cliff. I grit my teeth, clinging tighter as the strain in my muscles intensifies. For such a small cliff, it feels endless. Each pull upward is a test of endurance. With every inch gained, we get closer to our escape.

Loose stones scrape above us. Gravel cascades down, stinging my skin. I flatten myself against the rock, signaling Clara and Xia to do the same. The noise grows louder. I catch movement on the ledge above.

A guard steps into view, his boots raking stones as he scans the area. His line of sight sweeps dangerously close. We're nearly invisible from this angle because of the cliff's curve; however, the slightest shift could give us away. I signal Clara and Xia to stay motionless. My arms burn from holding my position. I don't dare move.

The guard stands close enough that I can make out the insignia stitched onto his jacket. He pauses, tilting, listening for signs of trouble. At last, he moves away, footsteps fading as he rounds the cliff's edge.

I exhale slowly and let the pounding in my chest subside. I signal for Clara and Xia to continue.

The ledge above gets closer, yet my talisman remains unresponsive. I hope the transport window hasn't opened. It can't—we're not close enough. I signal Clara and Xia to hurry. Urgency is a tightening noose. Moving faster might make too much noise—but we must.

At last, my fingers find the edge of the cliff. I haul myself up with one final effort, then help them over the top. The light is blinding after our shaded ascent; however, there's no time to adjust. We're exposed now.

Once on level ground, I hold up a single finger—one minute left. Clara and Xia read the message printed in my expression. We break into a sprint, feet slamming against the stone path as we race toward the Erechtheion. Every second stretches thin, each heartbeat louder, the world narrowing to our desperate race.

The talisman stirs in my pocket. Its presence is impossible to ignore. At first, it's merely warmth against my skin. It quickly builds, spreading outward like a living pulse. Once again, we are connected. Through the fabric, I feel its energy thrumming, anchoring me even as violence threatens to erupt around us. The time-travel window is open.

I don't hesitate. I reach out for Clara's and Xia's shoulders. In that instant, I glimpse the shimmering tapestry of time—past and future unfolding before me. Every possibility waits, ready to be chosen.

A deafening crack tears through the air before I can fix on a destination. The serene morning shatters, splintering into jagged fragments of chaos.

I yank time back, forcing everything to slow to a crawl. The gunshot cracks through the air with a warped echo. Motion lags around me. I spin toward Xia, dread clawing up my spine. The bullet streaks toward her in a blurred arc, inching forward with lethal intent. I grab her and pull hard—just enough to shift her off center. The bullet misses her chest by inches. Her shoulder snaps back as the round strikes, dimpling her flesh before a fine red mist bursts outward.

She stumbles, twisted in pain, her hand flying instinctively to the wound. Blood spills between her fingers, running in uneven streams down her arm, staining her clothing.

I move before I think. My hand clamps onto Xia's arm, gripping her tightly. Her blood is warm against my skin, soaking my fingers as I haul her closer. Shouts erupt behind us, guards' voices barking orders, their footsteps pounding closer. Another shot hits the ground near me, sending stone chips flying into my chin. I need to block out the chaos.

There's no time for panic. No time for fear. I concentrate, opening the gateway through time again. Clara drops to her knees to tend to Xia. I clasp her arm, linking the three of us together. The air shifts; the world dissolves.

We are sliding through time's steady current. The overwhelming haze of 2051 fades, replaced by something calmer.

The transition feels gentle when we land. The air is lighter. My first breath feels clean, a reprieve from the suffocating future where the Phylax's time lock twists everything into ruin. Finally, we're out of the nightmare.

Relief is short-lived. Clara kneels beside Xia, using a strip of fabric torn from her sleeve to create pressure on Xia's shoulder. Her hands are steady despite the crimson staining her fingers.

My lips form the word I intend to shout: *Xia!* I am unable to make a sound.

Around us, hundreds of tourists wander the Acropolis, cameras in hand, their laughter and idle chatter a jarring contrast to the chaos we left. The ancient ruins, now swarming with life, stand untouched by the horrors to come. It's hard to believe that this place will be swallowed by the Phylax's tyranny in a few short decades.

The sounds of the bustling crowd ground me, even though it is nothing more than a fragile veneer. Xia's condition is urgent. Clara's determined hands don't falter as she works to stem the bleeding. We've escaped one battle, yet the war against the Phylax's dystopia is far from over. First, we must ensure Xia lives.

TWENTY-SIX

Soon after we emerge, there's a ripple of shock at the Acropolis. Voices hush and heads turn. Xia lies on the ground, her shirt darkening as blood spreads across the fabric. Clara kneels beside her, trying to stop the bleeding while I hover close by.

The curious crowd gathers. A woman gasps while others shout for help, their voices blending into a confused chorus. Xia is conscious and agrees to move. After she gets up, we work through the throng as Xia inhales in ragged bursts. Her body sags; her legs give out. Clara and I support her as best we can, carrying her down the sloping trail that leads to the exit while pushing aside nosy tourists.

Clara's whisper reaches my ear: "What now?"

Xia forces her voice through clenched teeth. "Somewhere to rest," she manages. "Get this bullet out. Need stitches."

She almost slips away, her eyes drifting shut. I tighten my hold around her, refusing to let her collapse. Determination propels us forward, guiding us through the tight knot of onlookers.

The hotel room is small. I hurry inside, arms full of supplies: gauze, antiseptic, scissors, and a makeshift suturing kit scavenged in desperate haste. Clara clears a space on a small table beside the bed; she prepares to remove the bullet. Xia lies on the bed with the wound near her collarbone.

Clara fixes her attention on Xia's injury. She probes the area around the bullet's entry point with gentle fingers. Xia stiffens, pain etched into every line of her face. I arrange the supplies, spreading them out so Clara can grab what she needs. She hasn't been this focused since we entered the interrogation room.

"Xia, this is going to hurt," Clara apologizes.

Xia responds with a shaky, "Uh-huh."

I kneel beside Xia, laying a hand on her arm, hoping to steady her. Clara picks up the tweezers. She eases the metal tips into the wound with measured care. The bullet is lodged deep beneath the bone. I can feel Xia's agony as she tenses. A low grunt escapes her throat; sweat beads on her brow. Finally, with a careful twist, Clara extracts the bullet, dropping it into a metal dish with a sharp ping.

"Almost done," Clara mutters with a strain in her voice. She reaches for a needle and thread. Steadily, she stitches the wound closed. Each tug of the thread makes Xia flinch. Her grip on my sleeve tightens. Her nails dig in as she rides out the pain.

When Clara knots the last stitch, she wipes her forehead with a long sigh. Xia's eyelids flutter, then drift shut. Exhaustion washes over her while relaxing into something resembling calm for the first time in days.

I gather the bloodied cloth, tossing them into a pile in the corner. Clara washes her hands as if cleaning offers a shred of control amidst the chaos. The room smells of antiseptic and sweat, but the tension eases. We have momentarily won the fight for survival.

Clara and I slump onto the nearby sofa, fatigue settling into our bones. She leans against my shoulder.

Outside, the world remains uncertain. However, within these four walls, we have found a moment of peace. This silence is unlike the oppression of my past. It is a gentle quiet shared with Clara without fear or judgment. This shared interlude offers a more profound comfort than anything I've known before.

I reach into my pocket and pull out the Dalek Clara gave me. As I rotate the figure in my hand, my fingers trace the spot where one of the arms broke off long ago. A tiny glint catches my eye in the empty socket—a tiny nub of metal I hadn't noticed before. It doesn't seem to be part of the toy. I try to pull it, but the piece is too small to grip and impossible to pry loose. Holding the Dalek up for Clara, I point to the strange fragment. She shrugs, dismissing it as part of the old joint. I let the thought go, deciding she's probably right, and slip the Dalek back into my pocket.

I feel Clara tense beside me. Her lips part as if to speak, then snap shut again. Her fingers twitch against her sleeve. Briefly, I think she will let it pass. Instead, she lifts her chin.

"You'll think I'm crazy," she mutters. It takes her another minute to continue. "You should know," her lips press into a thin line. "In the anomaly, I saw our mother."

Clara's shoulders slump as though speaking the truth has drained her. "I don't know why she was there. She looked... real." Her voice wavers. It is easy to see that this truth costs her more than she wants to admit. "I didn't want to leave. I wouldn't have if it weren't for you and Xia. Whatever the vision was, it was pulling me in." Her voice shakes. "What do you think that means?"

During my first encounter with the anomaly, I saw a moment from my past. The second time, I found the time lock. Xia saw an escape from the future, while Philip claimed he could travel through the anomaly. Now, Clara says she saw our mother. I don't know what connects these experiences.

I squeeze Clara's shoulder, trying to ground her, then step over to the nightstand. From our supplies, I pull out a notebook and pen. *I don't know what it means. It might be real or a trick of the anomaly designed to lure you in.*

"I guess," Clara says, "What if mom is in there? Maybe the anomaly lured her in. I know I was. Weren't you?"

I have to agree. I wanted to stay in the anomaly, too. I reply, *Yes, I did feel that way. I don't know if someone can be trapped inside or not. She might be in there. What do you want to do?*

Clara doesn't answer right away. I can almost see her working it out. She straightens, determination set. "I want to keep going after the Phylax," she says firmly. "That's what mom wanted. If she is trapped, it's because of the Phylax. Maybe if we destroy that machine she will be freed." Clara offers a sad, half-smile. "Besides, we have no proof she's even alive, right?"

Is it possible that the anomaly could swallow someone? If so, is it possible to bring them back out? Regardless, Clara is right. We have no evidence that our mother is alive. Still, I know that if Clara had chosen to chase the phantom of our mother, I would follow.

Clara brushes a strand of hair from her mouth. "Where do we go next?"

Reaching into my jacket, I feel the talisman's warm surface and hold it up for her to see. I write, *I know exactly where to go. I believe the merchant who sold this to me was a Phylax. I believe*

I saw him in the anomaly. He was on the Council. He has answers. I know it.

Clara lights up with a genuine smile. It's the first one since our time in the future.

The day slowly passes while waiting inside our cramped hotel room. Clara loses herself in the pages of a book. I sit by the window, occasionally glancing at the city below as life continues. We have peace for once—no alarms blaring or footsteps pounding at the door.

By late afternoon, though, Xia's restless energy is impossible to ignore. She paces near the window, gingerly testing her bandages. "I can heal as well on the way to Sachu as I can here," she declares. Her tone leaves no room for argument. Wounded or not, she's ready to move.

I knew this calm would be short-lived.

We pack our few belongings before rushing to the airport. On the way, Clara maps the quickest route to Dunhuang, a historic city in Gansu Province, China. Once known as Sachu, it is where we will find the merchant. Sachu is a place woven deep into the tapestry of my past. I also hope it is the key to unlocking the Phylax's secrets.

After two long flights and a connecting train ride through the Gansu corridor, we arrive in Dunhuang. Late at night, in a tranquil corner of the city, I take Clara's and Xia's hands. I focus on ancient Sachu, looking for the day after meeting the merchant. Time begins to peel away, layers of old parchment unraveling as it draws us back.

Moments later, we stand in the descending sun of ancient Sachu's marketplace, ready to confront the merchant again. Warm air wraps around us. I enjoy the smell of ancient spices on the desert wind.

As we walk through Sachu's crowded streets, Xia lags slightly behind, her good arm resting protectively against her injured shoulder. She doesn't complain, but she struggles.

I scan the rows of stalls until I spot the one nestled between a silk trader and a dealer of bronze trinkets. The merchant's stall stands as before. He comes into view with his head jutting forward, tilted at an awkward angle.

He notices me at once, watching as we approach. Recognition sparks in his expression. "Ah-ha, back again, are we?" he quips. "So soon and yet so long, I believe." His eyes probe me. "You're different," he murmurs, almost to himself. "You've found truths that don't sit well with you."

His attention shifts to Xia and Clara. "Oh, you've brought family! I wondered when you'd find them, of course."

Clara gasps, her astonishment cutting through the merchant's odd manner of speaking. "You're the historian."

"Why, yes," he replies, his tone almost playful. "Like Adam, I knew you'd need help getting on the right path. Isn't that right, Adam?" His smile deepens. There's something about it that feels disingenuous.

Xia shifts uneasily, her weight moving from one foot to the other. "There's something off about him," she mutters to me. Her discomfort seems to exceed mine. "He's helped us, but I don't trust him. Men similar to him always have their own agenda," she adds, as if he has offended her somehow. Maybe it's the same reason he unnerves me—he sees too much, more than anyone should. Things that are better left hidden.

I hold up my notebook, showing him my first question. *Who are you?*

He gleams with mischief. "Ah, the eternal question," he says, leaning forward slightly. "Are you sure you want the answer?" A smirk forms on his lips. "I believe you already know." He looks toward the talisman in my pocket.

I tap the page, insisting on more than riddles. *Who are you?*

The merchant exhales sharply. When he straightens his posture, he almost becomes a different person. "Fine. You want answers?" A gust of wind whips through the air, kicking up dust. He takes his time to wipe grit away. "My name is not important; however, I was also once a Phylax, of course."

I knew the anomaly had shown me the truth.

"Unlike you," he continues, his tone

sharpening, "I never broke during the Temptation. I passed." His lips twist bitterly. "They welcomed me into the Sanctum. I had missions—different from yours but equally ruthless. I believed in them. Every single one."

He pauses, like he's remembering something he would rather forget. "In time, I rose to the Council. That's when I learned the truth—the Archon's true vision." Shame, perhaps regret, leaks into his demeanor. "Ah-ha, a single global government. The Phylax pulling the strings of history to forge a world he desires."

Xia shifts slightly. Her unease continues.

Clara's voice cuts in, "How?"

The merchant's voice hardens. "The time lock." He lets the words hang in the air. "It's an impossible weapon. The Archon chooses the mission outcomes that best serve the Phylax. Every assassination, every replaced leader, and every revolution that agents manipulated all compile into a single point. They call it the Convergence of Dominion."

Clara whispers, "The Sigma Event."

I helped create the travesty that will plague humankind. I never thought to question the missions, and it will lead to disaster. I didn't stop to see what I was shaping. I let them use me. When I swallow, I taste rust. I will atone. I will make it right.

He nods slowly. "Yes, people outside the Phylax call it the Sigma Event. Naturally, when we make decisions, we create branches on the tree of time."

I've heard this before. If I were to go back and stop my own abduction, I wouldn't erase my past —I would only create a version of myself who never lived it. The me that I am now would still remember everything that I experienced: the Renegades, the missions, the blood on my hands. My history wouldn't change. The only difference would be that somewhere, in another thread of time, a different version of me exists. A child who never became a weapon. My actions would force a new timeline, leaving another me to live a different fate.

The merchant shifts his weight. His tone drops lower. "The real horror lies in the collapsing of timelines. On July 1, 2051, infinity narrows into a single story. The Archon merges endless timelines together. Everything slams together into one horrible, unified reality. No escape. No diversity. Just one world—his world, selected from our missions."

I don't know how much is truth and how much is manipulation. From what we have seen, it rings too real. My mind flashes to 2051, to the broken city of Athens. I assumed I had seen the worst humanity could endure, but the harsh dystopia of the future is too painful.

The merchant lowers his chin. "I saw it happen the day they activated the lock. I watched from the Acropolis as suffering rippled outward, spreading its rot. The world decayed."

Slowly, he pulls back his sleeve, exposing his shoulder. The brand is gone—replaced by a scarred mess of disfigured flesh that looks hauntingly familiar. "That's when I knew I couldn't stay, of course. I tore my anchor free."

The sight of his ruined skin is grotesque, a reminder of the price he paid for freedom. It is a distorted mirror of the mark I carry. For a second, I see myself in him—another pawn who tore free from the lie. A weapon that refused to be wielded. The merchant and I are different men. Yet, the Phylax shaped who we are. He chose to break his chains as I did.

"Now I disguise myself in this life," he says, "waiting for you. Because when I saw you inside an anomaly, I sensed your potential. I set this in motion, knowing you would find the path with Clara's help. That is why I helped Clara find you. It is a fate you must fulfill."

Clara steps closer. "How did you know Adam would come through here?"

The merchant shifts to Clara, a smile tugging at the corners of his mouth. "The anomalies reveal unknown truths," he says. "I didn't know how to escape the Phylax until I stepped into one. That insight brought me here, to all three of you. Your roles are as vital as Adam's.

"I knew Adam would pass through here after his mission in China, that he wouldn't be able to resist General Cassianus' talisman. I knew he'd return with both of you. I've seen him stand against the world's desolation after 2051, defying it with the potential to challenge the Phylax's control over time.

"Ah-ha, every choice we make echoes through history," he continues. "I knew Adam would find a path that could fracture the Phylax's iron grip. He might offer freedom from the suffering I helped create."

"Then tell us," Clara demands, "how we destroy the time lock and end the Phylax's control."

The merchant's smirk fades. "I know two things. First, you'll need an anchor. I'd give you mine, but it's long gone. Perhaps Adam has his."

My thoughts jump to Clara burying the anchor in Merv's past. Retrieving it should be easy.

The merchant continues, "Beyond that, only the Archon knows how to disable the lock. He keeps that knowledge to himself. Even Philip, his right hand, doesn't know."

Philip now serves as the Archon's vizier. The realization ignites a surge of disgust. His role is infuriating; of course, Philip stands close to the heart of the Phylax's tyranny.

Clara snaps, "How do we find the Archon?" her voice is tempered steel.

The merchant hesitates, scanning the market's periphery as though wary of unwanted listeners. When he speaks, his voice is little more than a murmur. "The Archon is adept at concealing himself in time. He wields an artifact that erases any trace of his presence when he travels. Once he leaves, it's as if he were never there. It has one limitation—it doesn't protect him when he remains in his own era."

Clara leans in closer.

"The chance to find him is during his quarterly ritual," the merchant continues. "It must be completed in his natural timeline, in his era. His next ritual is on September 6, 2025. He will visit a sacred temple in the desert beyond Merv that day. He travels with a small escort who remains stationed outside during the ritual. Inside the temple, he will be alone. There's a side passage that could allow you to enter unnoticed.

"It comes with great risk," the merchant warns. "The Archon is prepared for every contingency. He is a master of manipulation. Facing him will be dangerous."

"We have to try," Clara says. "If we can get information from him, maybe we can shatter the lock." Determination radiates from her.

The merchant says, "Let me come with you. I have my own score to settle. I know that temple, including some of its secret passages. I can stop the Archon from escaping through time, at least briefly. Your talisman, if used correctly, can help. I know how."

The merchant's offer is too casual. Has he been waiting for this opportunity all along?

His words carry enough conviction to make me wonder if he genuinely wants to help us or has another agenda.

His hand brushes the edge of his scarred arm, a fleeting, unconscious gesture that catches me. The bitterness in his voice when he speaks of the Archon feels genuine. However, bitterness toward the Archon doesn't mean loyalty to us.

Clara watches him with guarded curiosity, while Xia seems warmer to the man. I don't trust him, but he knows things we don't. His knowledge outweighs my doubts. I signal Clara and Xia to step back so we can speak privately.

Huddled together, Clara disagrees. "Bring him along? We've met him before. I've always thought he was shady," she whispers. "I don't trust him. What if it's a trap?"

Xia says, "I don't know. He did help us find Adam and gave us information about the Sigma Event. He was on the Council. He could probably help us."

I take my time writing. *I agree with Xia. He has good reason to turn against them. When I saw him in the anomaly, he looked haunted, not loyal. He gave me the talisman. He told us about the Archon and the anchor. Besides, I can't use the talisman against the Archon without him. The Archon could easily slip away.*

Clara sighs, "If you're sure."

Even with Xia's injuries, she's ready for a fight. She takes Clara's hand. "No, none of us are sure. But if he tries something, I'll kill him myself," she smiles.

The merchant raises an eyebrow as I reluctantly nod. Apparently, he is coming with us.

"Great," he says, "let's get going." He steps away from the stall without even glancing back. I would ask why he doesn't pack up first, but I doubt his answer would make much sense.

Before leaving, Xia tries to adjust the strap on her bag. Her injured arm falters halfway. She curses under her breath, irritation flashing across her face before she lets Clara help.

"I'll take us there," Xia says, demonstrating her strength. She grips Clara's arm, then mine. I place a hand on the merchant's shoulder, feeling him tense. The air warps. A surge of light pulls us through time again, depositing us back into 2025.

While the ancient city of Sachu is busy, it doesn't compare to the assault of modern Dunhuang. Car horns blare, people shout in Mandarin, and the buzz of passing motorbikes makes the old market nothing more than a whisper. I blink against the neon glow of shop signs, their lights gleaming off the polished lenses of tourist cameras. Laughter and idle chatter drift through the air, a surreal contrast to the severity of our mission.

Dunhuang is no sanctuary. It is a fleeting pause before the storm. Soon, we'll leave this fragile pocket of peace. The journey will take us across the sands near Merv to recover the anchor. Beyond that lies the Archon—the inevitable confrontation that will decide more than our fate. It will determine the future of billions of people. And time itself.

TWENTY-SEVEN

We take turns driving for the next two days. I can't shake the unease. The merchant's presence throws off the hard-earned rhythm Clara, Xia, and I have established. We've learned to trust one another to move in unison. Now, there's an unpredictable element added to our fragile balance. I tell myself this is temporary—a necessary step. Soon, it will only be us again.

I tighten my grip on the steering wheel, fixed on the dusty ribbon of road stretching through the empty plains.

"Next stop," Clara says, "the ruins of Merv. We should pick up the anchor first since it's on the way to the Arhcon's temple."

I try to respond verbally. Of course, the words won't leave my throat. It is frustrating, but I must continue to try.

"Isn't it interesting," the merchant asks, "how the anchor restricts the Phylax from traveling freely? The Archon uses it to control his guardians, limiting their power, of course. At the same time, he relies on it to feed key historical events into the machine. That's why agents must return to the Sanctum after each mission—the anchors need to be near the machine to sync data. It serves as his tool of oppression and a source of power. The Archon goes out of his way to recover the anchors because they can open the time lock, too."

Is that meant as a warning? We already know that we must get to the anchor before the Phylax does.

The landscape shifts as we travel. Rocky outcrops give way to cracked plains that show no sign of life. When the sun dips low on the horizon, casting a golden light across the barren land, we arrive at what remains of Merv. Half-buried city walls stand as faded monuments to a city long gone.

This is where I first met Clara. After she cut the Anchor out of me, we shifted forward in time and arrived in this same parking lot, where a car had been waiting for us. Now, after cutting the engine, we step out of the car.

I take out my notepad. *Stay here.* I hold the note up for the merchant to read.

"Stay here?" he repeats, his voice edged with irritation. "You need my help. I know things about this place you—"

Xia steps closer, cutting him off. "You're here for the Archon, nothing else. If you can't follow a simple instruction, then start walking." She points toward the endless desert. The sun begins to hide behind the horizon, promising to extinguish the day's heat with a bitterly cold night. As Xia's injury heals, she becomes more brash.

The merchant's eyes dart between Xia and the empty plains. After some hesitation, he sighs, shoving his hands into his pockets. "Fine," he mutters, trudging back to the car. He slumps into the passenger seat.

Clara, Xia, and I walk toward the edge of the ruins. We pass through what was once the mighty gate, moving toward the old safe house. The city's broken walls jut upward, tombstones etched against the deepening sky. Clara takes our arms.

The shattered stones rise, forging themselves into towering walls. Crumbling archways reform. The streets come alive with the rhythmic clatter of wooden wheels while Pahlavi's nearly forgotten language echoes around me. Clara has brought us back to ancient Merv when these walls stood firm. It surprises me—this isn't when she buried the anchor. At least, I didn't think so.

A warmth settles over me as I appreciate this place. It's here where I truly began to break from the Phylax, where Clara and I first met. My fingers brush the scar on my arm. I remember how she removed the anchor, leaving me incapacitated. She proved that she was more intelligent than I gave her credit for. If I could laugh, I would. A smile will have to suffice.

Clara's voice is gentle. "This place will always be important to me. It's where we finally found each other after years of planning and searching."

I approach the door, feeling a strange familiarity in its rough grain. Within these walls, I started to learn who I was beneath the Phylax's lies.

Before I enter, Clara says, "The anchor isn't inside. I wanted to see this place one more time." She smiles, then gestures ahead. "It's a little way down the road."

Xia and I follow, anticipation simmering between us. Clara focuses as she leads us to a small, unmarked patch of ground near a crumbling wall. Kneeling, she brushes dirt aside, dust rising in thin clouds around her hands.

I reach into my pocket for the talisman. Its steady rhythm tells me that nothing is out of time here. The anchor cannot be near. I scrawl in my notebook, *I don't think it's here.* Xia passes the message to Clara.

"Yes, it is," Clara insists, voice taut with certainty. She keeps digging, fingers scraping through layers of packed dirt. Xia and I join in, dust billowing around us as we work.

Minutes pass. We find nothing.

Clara's hands slow until they're motionless. She stares at the ground. "I know I buried it here," she whispers.

"They must have found it. The Phylax got here first," Xia says. "They can track the anchors."

Truth settles with the dust. Of course, the Phylax anticipates this move. They probably retrieved the anchor long ago.

Clara's nails dig into her palms. She's staring at the ground, her lips zipped tightly together to hold back a scream.

I write, *Didn't you go way back in time to bury it?* I show it to Clara.

"Long before this," she replies. "I went to the Triassic Period."

It seems obvious what we should do. I scribble, *Then let's go back to the moment you buried it. We can get it before the Phylax.*

A grin washes over her. "Right," she says, "We should have gone there first."

She steps forward, gripping our arms firmly. "Hold on," Clara warns with a note of adrenaline.

Before we can move, a shadow falls across us. My muscles tense, preparing for a fight. The Phylax must have been waiting for us. Footsteps echo softly against the worn stone. Light catches the edge of a familiar silhouette. Stepping out from the narrow alley, the merchant emerges. "Ah-ha, I couldn't let you have all the fun without me," he says, pretending to brush dust from his sleeve.

First, a sigh of relief. Second, I want to punch him.

Xia stiffens. "Stay here," she mutters, striding toward him.

I take out the notebook. *How did he follow us through time?*

Clara crosses her arms; her distrust is evident. "He always seems to know too much. What's his angle? I don't buy this sudden allegiance to our cause."

I don't either, I admit. We watch as they exchange words. I can't hear what they're saying; however, there's something odd in Xia's posture. It's not hostility, exactly.

"None of us should," Clara says while watching Xia.

When Xia returns, the merchant lingers at a distance. He peers at me, tilting his head slightly, raising a hand in a slow, deliberate wave. There is something familiar about it that wants my attention. Unfortunately, he vanishes through time before I can place it.

Xia says, "There, I got him to go back to the car." She reaches out for our arms. "Let's go," she says abruptly, deciding not to share any of their conversation.

The world that emerges is alien. Soaring ferns loom overhead, their trunks thick with tangled vines. The air is hot and humid—alive with the hum of a vast prehistoric wilderness. Strange calls echo through the thick canopy. Massive dragonflies skim through the dense, moist air. Light filters softly through layers of vegetation, giving everything an otherworldly glow.

I briefly forget our mission. I feel the raw, unspoiled force of nature at its peak. Endless life surrounds us, reminding me how small we are in the grand sweep of existence. Here, I'm not a time traveler or a soldier. I'm a witness to a world that existed long before humanity.

The serenity is short-lived. The undergrowth rustles too forcefully to be the wind. I catch a glimpse of something. Scales reflect sunlight before vanishing into the jungle. The hum of insects fades. Clara freezes beside me. I unsheath my knife.

"What was that?" Clara whispers.

"Something we don't want to meet," Xia answers, scanning the dense foliage for any sign of movement. The rumble of a low growl vibrates through the ground.

With the excitement, each inhalation feels shallow, never fully satisfying. Clara must sense my discomfort because she explains before I ask, "Oxygen levels are lower here. We have to move slowly. You'll feel breathless."

She is correct. It is challenging to get enough air. Something else isn't right. I fish the talisman out of my pocket, frowning when it remains unchanged in my hand. If the anchor were here, shouldn't it react? At least a little?

Clara steps toward a mossy rock, kneels, and

brushes dirt aside. Her posture sags as her hand finds empty space in a hollow of soil. The anchor is gone.

I hold up a finger, signaling Clara and Xia to stay put.

The present peels away while movements of the ancient forest rewind. Then I see what happened. Clara kneels on the forest floor. There is urgency as she digs a hole. Sweat streaks her brow. She places the anchor inside the hole and smooths the dirt as best she can. She rises. Seconds later, she disappears.

She wasn't alone.

They emerge from nowhere. Dozens of Phylax agents step into the clearing, their cloaks blending into the foliage. One kneels, uncovering the anchor, while another opens a sleek metallic case. They handle the sacred anchor, locking it away for safety.

The leader pauses, his watch sweeping the forest. He gestures, and the agents follow his cue, vanishing into the gloom, leaving no trace of their presence behind.

I pull myself back to Clara. The forest snaps to its present state, alive with sound. I scribble furiously, *They were waiting for you. They knew exactly where you buried it.*

I pass the note to Clara, watching as she skims the words. Her jaw tightens. I see the anger flare. She grips the paper like it's her enemy.

Xia examines the empty hollow. "We go back and fight for it," she suggests.

I scribble more words. *Too many. Dozens of agents. We don't have a chance against that many.*

Clara exhales sharply. "Then we'll have to find another way," she says.

I tap my pen against the notebook in deep contemplation. A possibility comes to mind. I write, *Someone at the Renegade compound might have one—perhaps the priest.* Taking it from him would be justice after everything he has done. *That means going back to America. We must confront the Archon first.*

Clara reads my note. Her resolve mirrors the fire burning inside me. Xia adjusts her pack. She scans the trees, expecting the Phylax to reappear.

"Let's get going," Clara says.

I tuck the notebook back into my satchel. This anchor is gone, but there are many more out there. However, there is only one Archon. If any fairness exists in this world, we will learn how to stop the time lock from him.

TWENTY-EIGHT

The jeep rattles along the uneven road, kicking up clouds of dust that swirl in the dry air. The horizon stretches endlessly. Thankfully, the temple should be near.

In the back seat, the merchant leans casually against the door, his posture at ease, though he gleams with a mischievous spark. "If you'd brought me along," his voice drips with mockery, "we'd already have the anchor in hand. But no, you had to do things your way."

Clara glares at him in the rear-view mirror, her knuckles white on the steering wheel. "Thanks. Do you have anything useful to say?" she snaps.

The merchant chuckles, unbothered by her irritation. "You would have needed an army to take that anchor. I told you they work hard to recover them." He leans forward with a widening smirk. "I'm sure you made a valiant attempt."

Xia, seated beside him, shifts uneasily. "You talk a lot for someone who wasn't there."

"Ah-ha, because you forced me to stay behind

like a sad puppy."

I sit, listening to the merchant. His tone grates against my nerves.

Clara snorts, "You're nothing more than a stray who can't take a hint."

The merchant grins. "Yet, here I am, still with you, of course."

Yeah, this is fun.

We park our vehicle behind a dune nearly a mile from the temple, ensuring no one sees it. Time has half-buried the edifice. Its weathered walls are cracked and barely visible against the rising dunes. A crumbling archway frames the entrance, which centuries of decay have nearly swallowed.

I had never heard of this temple during my years with the Phylax. When the merchant first mentioned it, I doubted its existence. I am proven wrong—the temple's massive stone exterior juts out of the sand. A twist of relief and suspicion coils in my gut. The merchant's knowledge has proven accurate so far. That doesn't make him trustworthy.

"The Archon will be here soon," he says. "If we hurry, we can keep our advantage."

He leads us into a narrow passage that spirals downward. It is barely wide enough for us to pass in single file. With each step, the air cools. Damp stone replaces the desert's dry heat. The thin beams of our flashlights stretch across the walls, and our footsteps echo in the stillness.

"Stay close," he whispers, his voice nearly lost in a series of echoes. "This temple was once dedicated to Zurvan, the ancient Zoroastrian god of infinite time. The Archon chose it for its history and isolation, of course.

Zurvan was a god of time, but he was also infinite time itself. His followers believed that from Zurvan sprang light and dark, order and chaos—twin forces destined to fight for eternity. Under that belief, past, present, and future were ticking toward an outcome no one could escape. The devout thought everything served at time's mercy. True fatalists.

It's ironic, really. A temple devoted to a faith that saw time as an unstoppable river is now being used by someone who bends and twists time to suit his will. I wonder why this place.

"The Archon comes here every four months to perform a ritual—a binding ceremony he believes reinforces the time lock across all timelines. He calls it the Rite of Convergence. It's practically time-worship," the merchant says. "The Archon reveres the power of time. He believes this place gives him a cosmic edge. I doubt this voodoo does much of anything."

The merchant continues, "He comes in alone, believing solitude is crucial to this ancient ritual. He'll be unguarded inside but fully attuned to the forces around him. Stopping him will be dangerous. It's also a rare moment when he's truly vulnerable."

We descend the narrow steps into the temple's lower passage. The stone beneath our feet is worn smooth by centuries of tread. The walls catch the glow of our flashlights, revealing murals painted in astonishing detail despite the ravages of time. Colossal figures with elongated limbs loom over kneeling worshippers. The figures' outstretched hands offer blessings and domination. Spirals intertwine in flowing patterns, suggesting the endless cycle of existence. I recognize the spirals as being identical to the ones on my talisman. My talisman responds with a subtle thrum, as though it recognizes something about this place.

I note the repeating symbols woven into these vignettes. In one mural, a gigantic figure hunches over a city, dissolving it into dust. A visual representation of time spirals around it. In another, a lush forest scene freezes worshippers in mid-step, their expressions caught between wonder and dread. A final image shows a fractured clock tower atop a desolate hill. The clock's hands twist in impossible directions while serpents coil at its base.

All of it points to a force both revered and feared. The repetition of these motifs hints at a grand design—time as both creator and destroyer.

As we continue, I spot two words in Pahlavi beneath one of the enormous figures: دهر خدای,

Dahr-khoday. It means Master of Eternal Time. A chill prickles my skin. Is my talisman linked to the Dahr-khoday? Could it be a relic from Zurvan's period? There's a kind of thrill in that possibility. We leave the unexplored truths of the murals behind. The talisman continues to vibrate in my pocket. Whatever connections lie between Dahr-khoday, Zurvan, and my talisman will have to wait. I can't dwell on them now. We have the Archon to confront. The fate of countless lives may balance on what happens next.

Before entering a dark chamber, the merchant whispers, "We'll hide here and take the Archon by surprise. Don't say a word."

I exhale slowly, then offer the talisman to the merchant. Distrust pricks at the back of my consciousness; however, we need him for this.

The second his fingers wrap around the talisman, it glows more brightly. I am awestruck when the worn carvings on the temple walls illuminate in response to the talisman. It takes a moment for the light to die down again.

It strikes me as interesting that I met the Archon not that long ago, but he hasn't had that encounter yet. For him, it's still far into the future. It's a twisted moment outside the flow of time. The version of him walking these corridors is still on a path that leads to the Sigma Event. Will our actions here alter humanity's history? Or has this always been a part of it?

We wait until footsteps echo throughout the corridor—the Archon. Just beyond our hiding spot, he pauses. I hear the rustling of his movements. When he finally enters the room, he doesn't notice us.

I give a quick signal to Clara, Xia, and the merchant. We rush forward as one. The merchant lifts the talisman high. A blinding pulse of energy rips through the room. The Archon stumbles, and shock contorts his features. I see it dawn on him in that instant: he's trapped. The talisman severs his ability to manipulate time as the merchant promised.

Before the Archon can recover his bearings, Clara and Xia spring forward, forcing him to the ground. I secure his limbs with the rope we brought. We drag him onto a stone bench in the corner, where he glares up at us. Rage burns in his eyes.

For the first time, the Archon—the leader of the Phylax—sits powerless before me. A cold jolt of satisfaction courses through my veins. At last, he's the one at our mercy.

Despite his predicament, the Archon regards us with unsettling calm, barely registering the ropes that dig into his appendages. A smirk tugs at the corner of his mouth as he calculates how to twist our weaknesses to his advantage.

"So," he patronizes, "you believe you can force something from me?" Arrogance is a foul stench clinging to him. He's certain we're wasting our time.

Despite the satisfaction of capturing him, his smug attitude annoys me. He is the architect of my suffering. Despite losing his power, he maintains a confident air. I step closer, trying to curb my anger.

Clara's voice slices through his amusement when she says what I'm thinking. "Tell us how to destroy the time lock," she demands.

The Archon's laugh is humorless. "Why would I do that?" He oozes condescension. "Do you think you can change the Order of Time? You are nothing compared to the Phylax. We have shaped every important truth you have ever known. We control humanity's future."

Beside me, Xia's grips her dagger. She holds the blade close to his throat, her voice deadly serene. "Talk," she warns, "or this ends now."

The Archon's composure barely wavers. He gives a short, mirthless chuckle. "You wouldn't dare. Killing me won't alter a thing." His tone is ice. "You still won't know how to disable the lock, a new Archon will ascend, and the world will still belong to the Phylax."

The Archon's sneer deepens. "Oh, Silanus, I expected more from you. Yet here you are, siding with this motley rabble. Pathetic. I always knew you'd fail us when it mattered. Isn't that my talisman you are holding?"

The Archon tilts forward. His grim smile widens. "Hear that?" he asks, gloating. "My guards. Your time is up. You'll all die here."

I catch it, too—the sound of boots slamming against stone, rushing toward us. Five Phylax guards spill into the room with their weapons raised. My pulse thunders in my ears. I shift my stance, ready for the fight. Clara and Xia do the same, bracing for the onslaught.

Silanus steps back, gripping the glowing talisman tighter. Its light intensifies as he channels its power, providing enough illumination for the battle. "The Archon's not going anywhere," he says, barely audible in the surge of motion. "I'll keep him locked down. You know what you need to do."

I rush forward, adrenaline igniting me. The Archon's laughter rings out, resonating with the clash of bodies reverberating off the ancient walls like a foreboding symphony.

Metal crashes against metal, each strike echoing, the pounding of a war drum. Sparks flare, accentuating moments of chaos. A guard lunges forward. Clara deflects a blow. Xia delivers a sharp kick that sends her opponent sprawling. Our battle warps into grotesque outlines on the wall as combatants collide.

My muscles strain as I parry a strike. Boots scrape on the cracked stone, and the uneven ground adds to the unpredictability of the fight. A shout pierces through the cacophony, its echo swallowed by the relentless sounds of battle. The vibrations of each blow hum through the floor.

Xia twists out of reach as the guards strike at her. The gunshot that nearly killed her doesn't seem to faze her now. Her strikes are precise and merciless: one sharp jab to a guard's throat takes him down. In a fluid sweep, she catches the next one off balance. He collapses, shock stamped on his lips before she finishes him with a swift, lethal strike.

Fueled by white-hot rage, I charge the other two guards. They swing with brute force, but my training runs deep. I deflect the first blow, then step forward, slamming my fist into the guard's ribs. The impact reverberates up my arm. He staggers; I don't give him time to recover before driving my knuckles into his cheek. He crashes to the ground.

The second guard rushes me with desperate aggression. I sidestep, then bring my elbow down hard on his neck. When he stumbles, I seize his collar, slamming him down with finality. As he collapses, the room falls into tense silence.

Clara struggles with a hulking guard—she's quick, but he's an unrelenting monster. She ducks a swing while landing a fierce jab to his midsection. He barely flinches. Rushing forward, he grabs Clara's arm, twists it, and hammers a punch into her stomach. She gasps, doubling over, fighting for balance as he advances.

His weapon glints, catching the light as if suspended in midair. Everything around me slows to an excruciating crawl—the falling bodies, the sounds, even the talisman's pulsing energy. I push against time, forcing it to drag further, bending it to my will. Each step I take is wading through quicksand. My limbs are heavy; my movements are agonizingly slow. The guard's blade inches forward, sinking into Clara with cruel precision. I lurch toward her, my outstretched hand barely making progress, every heartbeat pounding louder in my ears as the world holds its breath. Time won't bend far enough.

The guard nearly freezes, oblivious to my approach. My hand finds its mark as I twist sharply. The sickening crack of his neck rips through the suspended air. He crumbles like a puppet with its strings severed.

It is a hollow victory.

I turn to Clara, my movements still trapped in the heavy drag of time. Her blood blooms outward in slow, creeping tendrils, staining the ground in vivid crimson. The life within her ebbs away with each agonizing second as I fall to my knees, cradling her in my arms. Time bends at my will, yet it's not enough to undo the damage. Not enough to save her.

Desperation consumes me. I reach deeper into the strands of time, yanking them backward with a ferocity I've never felt before. The scene rewinds—Clara's blood flows back into her body, the blade retracts, and the guard rises as if none of it ever happened.

I try again, rushing to throw Clara out of harm's way. My hands pass through her. The scene plays out the same—the blade plunges into her side, her cry rips through the air, and the crimson tide begins to surge again.

I snarl, pulling at the reins once more, wrenching it backward with sheer will. The scene resets with the same grim inevitability.

When I stop, Clara chokes out a ragged breath, her gaze locking on mine with pain. Her body goes limp, sliding from my grasp onto the cold floor. The light in her eyes fades as she looks at me one final time while Xia rushes to her side.

Horror settles like ice in my veins. I hover in a numbed haze, watching my sister's last moments. Clara's breathing is shallow; each gasp is a battle.

"Adam," Clara murmurs, "you've always been stronger than you think. Stronger than them. You have to finish this—for all of us. Find the truth. Don't stop fighting." Her fingers weakly tighten on my arm.

Her attention shifts to Xia. A soft smile breaks through her pain. "Xia... you were always my light. You still are. Stay with him. Finish this. Together, you'll break them."

Her voice weakens, but her determination never wavers. "Promise me, both of you," she says with a final spark of fire. I believe in you. I love you both."

Her eyes flutter, and the fire fades. She holds my gaze a beat longer, willing me to carry her strength forward. Slowly, her fingers slip away. Her body rests in my arms while she softens. She has found peace.

My knees hit the ground; my body folds over hers. From somewhere deep within, a sound erupts. A guttural, twisted cry ripped from the darkest part of my soul. Decades of silence, of bottled rage, explode from me in that one horrible wail. It's as if every buried word, every memory of betrayal and loss, has unraveled.

The sound ricochets off the walls, a hideous echo that fills the chamber with grief so potent it's unbearable. It's a sound of despair that no silence could ever contain, a piercing lament that belongs to the broken, the hopeless, and the damned. My vision blurs. My throat feels torn. The scream keeps pouring out, long past when my voice should give out. A primal, agonizing release for every wound I've carried.

My tears fall as I rock back and forth. The guilt coils tighter with every beat of my heart. I failed her. I couldn't protect her. After everything she risked, I let her down. In the hollow of that emptiness, something shatters within me. A whisper that claws its way from the deepest part of my soul.

"Clara," my voice is broken after decades of oppression. "Clara, I love you." The words spill unevenly from my lips, each syllable shattered with pain. I know I have severed my ties to silence forever. What's left is the beginning of something more menacing: rage and revenge.

Xia holds onto Clara.

The Archon's smirk lingers, but it's a ghost of what it was minutes ago. His lips twitch, betraying his struggle to maintain a mask of control. I take another step forward. His focus darts to the door behind him. I can see the cracks spreading in his confidence.

"Do you think your rage frightens me?" he says, the sneer painted on his lips, except there's tension in his voice. My fury has reached him. No amount of bravado can conceal it.

I steady myself. My voice is hoarse. "You. You did this to her."

TWENTY-NINE

I leap before I can stop myself. My hands clamp around the Archon's throat, tightening more with every second. I hear his strangled gasps as my rage explodes, fueled by the pain of Clara's death.

Venom laces my broken voice. "You took her from me! You killed her! You destroyed everything!"

His eyes bulge as he fights for air. I tighten my hold even more. The temple's walls blur at the edge of my vision. Fury and grief clog my senses until all I know is his throat beneath my fingers. His life begins to slip in my grasp.

The Archon thrashes against me to no effect. His struggles are loud in the confined chamber, amplified by the stone walls. The jagged stone wall scrapes against his back as I pin him in place. His boots scuff against the uneven floor.

"Do you think this will stop me?" He chokes, desperation seeping into his words.

"Adam!" Xia's voice pierces through the haze. Silanus and Xia try to drag me backward. I grunt while clawing for the Archon's neck.

"Let go, Adam," Silanus shouts.

My voice cracks in one last yell before their force breaks my hold. I stagger back while Silanus does his best to keep the talisman pointed at the Archon. The Archon coughs, trying to regain some composure.

Rage burns while Xia tries to soothe me. "I want to kill him, too, but we still need him." She rubs my shoulder.

"You're too close to this, Adam," Silanus says calmly. "If you go near him again, you'll end up killing him before we learn what we need."

My teeth grind together while Xia agrees, "Silanus is right. Neither of us is clear-headed enough. Let him handle it."

I don't want to leave, but Xia has an arm around me, leading me away from the Archon. Eventually, I concede.

Silanus pulls out a small device from his pocket. It is a sleek apparatus threaded with wires and glowing lights. "Don't worry," he mutters with cold satisfaction. "The Wraith will make him pay twice for what he's done."

Before exiting the room, I see Silanus step toward the Archon. The Archon recognizes the device, and fear sparks in him. Silanus wears a cold grin as he sets it against the Archon's cheek, activating the device. It casts a cold blue hue against the Archon's skin.

A piercing scream echoes throughout the

temple. He deserves this. I feel a flash of satisfaction, though it is fleeting.

"Let's go, Adam." Xia tugs me gently toward the door. I hesitate, watching the Archon convulse. Xia's voice anchors me back. "Silanus will get answers for us."

I glimpse the Archon's tightening fists. He tilts back, overcome by the agony. As we walk away, his screams chase us down the corridor. I hope it continues.

Xia and I walk through the winding stone halls. Each step away from the Archon reverberates with the hollow ache of Clara's absence. When we reach the entrance, the world feels emptier. The fresh air does nothing to dull the raw grief.

Xia folds her arms across her chest. "She should be here." Her face contorts into a mask of sorrow, lips trembling. For a moment, she looks away, blinking rapidly. When she speaks again, her voice is brittle. "She fought so hard. She believed in us. She believed in what we were doing." Tears slide down Xia's cheek.

I swallow against the raw ache in my throat. "She deserved to see it through to the end." My voice cracks with hers. "We have to finish this— for her. The Phylax must fall."

Xia places a hand on my arm. "For Clara," she echoes. "We'll do it together, no matter what it takes."

Movement catches my eye. Two figures

emerge from behind a crumbled obelisk about a hundred yards away. They meander around the ruin without much care. They have no idea that their leader is being interrogated.

"I guess there are still a few guards out here. We should go back inside. Finish up with that bastard. Both of them." I say.

Together, we step back into the temple. The quiet is foreboding. Or it could be the murals. They beckon my attention, demanding closer scrutiny.

My gaze traces the worn panels, each a dichotomy of horror and serenity. Why do they depict both? What truths do their contrasts hide?

A quiet certainty settles in me. There is something I want to learn here. When my mission is complete, I will return and give these murals the attention they deserve.

Soon, we reach the dark chamber. Silanus greets us with a grimace. I look past him to see the Archon slumped against a stone wall. He is staring into the next life.

I glare at Silanus, anger rising. "Now what?" I snap, "What good is any of this?"

"He was tougher than I expected," Silanus shrugs. "He gave up everything we need, of course."

He holds out an anchor, its metallic finish glistening with fresh blood. The talisman is in his other palm, both waiting for me to take them.

I slide the talisman into my pocket, its familiar warmth pressing against my side. I keep the anchor in my fist. The Archon's arm is a bloody mess where Silanus must have cut into him.

"Why is he dead?" I ask.

Silanus gives another careless shrug. "The Wraith," he says, tapping his pocket, "pushed him past his limit. He couldn't take the pain when I cut out the anchor."

"I didn't think the Archon had his anchor. He travels whenever he needs to."

Silanus explains, "Ah-ha, during the Archon's ascension, the Council remotely alters his while it remains in his arm. They delete the three-year limitation. They still need to track him if he goes missing. It is never removed."

Every time Silanus speaks, Xia's discomfort is evident in how her fingers curl into her palms. She steps back enough to keep her distance when he moves closer.

Silanus continues, "He explained how to destroy the time lock. It requires two people —one in the future and one in the past—and precise timing. First, the person in the future must be in the Sanctum after the Sigma Event. That's when you can open the lock. You'll insert the anchor," he gestures at the device in my hand, "into the lock's power core. When it opens, you smash it. After you break the core, there's a ten-minute window before the lock resets itself. During that brief span, one of you must detonate explosives in 455 BCE."

Tension rises in Xia's voice. "So the other person has to go back to 455 BCE?"

Silanus nods. "Exactly. The time lock was first activated right after the Sanctum's construction in 455. Its power runs through the entire building. If you place explosives near the lock and detonate them while resetting, the disruption will collapse the Sanctum across time, shattering it for good."

He pauses, allowing us time to think.

"You'll have to coordinate these actions perfectly. One person forces the lock to reset in the future; the other sets off the explosives in the past. The result is an overload it can't withstand."

Xia forms fists. I can see the toll of losing Clara in how she stands. "We only have ten minutes," she murmurs. Her attention fixes on Silanus' pocket, where the Wraith is stored, before finally breaking away.

"Exactly. It's an interesting paradox. It happens everywhere, simultaneously. From the instant the lock shuts down in the future, it's also off in 455 BCE for that same ten-minute span. Whoever is in the past must watch for the reset."

Even as Silanus explains the details, his tone is cold. He is detached from the stakes. It's hard to trust a man who seems to take nothing personally.

I tighten my grip on the anchor. "That's it?" I ask. "If we pull this off, will the Phylax's control be destroyed?"

Silanus answers, "Yes. However, there's no room for error, of course. If either of you fails, the lock resets and the Phylax keeps its hold."

I'm skeptical that the Archon gave away this much detail before his death. It doesn't fit; he was too tight-lipped. These instructions feel too convenient. Yet, how else would Silanus know so much about this closely guarded Phylax secret?

Xia is determined. "Then we have no choice but to succeed."

I agree with Xia. Our shared resolve sealed us together for this final mission. I recall Clara's smile, her last words, her pain—all of it scorches my memory like a fresh brand. The silence I once clung to is nothing more than a broken chain. I must forge it into a new weapon.

They took my family and my freedom. They can't take away this final act. This day of reckoning isn't for me and Xia. It's for Clara. For every life the Phylax stole.

THIRTY

The walk feels endless as we ascend the ancient stairway. My legs ache with exhaustion, but the murals once again capture my attention. I examine the towering figures; their hands stretched outward in gestures that still puzzle me. Once more, I see the words etched beneath one of the towering figures: دهر خدای. Dahr-khoday. The words stir something unsettling within me.

"Who are they?" I ask, gesturing toward the inscription.

Silanus pauses, looking at the mural with a grin. "The Dahr-khoday," he says with unusual solemnity, "is an ancient order of timekeepers. They were true masters of temporal power. They predate the Phylax by centuries, maybe even longer."

"What happened to them?" I ask. The emblematic spirals seem to tighten and shift in the unsteady light.

"They were destroyed," he explains, "or at least, the Phylax tried to destroy them. Most were wiped out. Perhaps some survived." he pauses while considering his next words. "There are rumors that some have returned to the old ways, seeking strength in the nearly forgotten. The Archon feared them. Perhaps rightfully." The merchant's grin deepens.

I find myself staring at the mural again. "And you?" I ask. "What do you think?"

Silanus snickers. He gleams with a cryptic light. "How would I know? Maybe there are Dahr-khoday around today. Maybe someone close to you has already embraced them, of course. Maybe one day you will." He laughs again.

Xia calls out from a couple of paces behind, "Did you know this would happen? Did you know Clara would die here?"

I turn to Silanus. It is a valid question.

"No," he says, recoiling like Xia threw a rock at him. "I swear I didn't."

Xia's shoulders tremble as she brushes past Silanus and me. "I'll meet you outside," she mumbles.

I would pursue answers on her behalf, but the merchant won't admit to knowing anything.

Guilt eats away at me. I'm not the only one suffering. Clara wasn't just my sister; she was Xia's wife. I can't begin to imagine the depth of that loss for her. For all the pain I feel, hers likely cuts even deeper.

Xia's footsteps echo down the corridor. I let her go, knowing she needs space to grieve in her way. I want to call after her to offer some reassurance. No words exist that can mend this. Instead, I stay rooted, my thoughts circling back to Silanus. "What about you? What happens next?"

His expression darkens. I think he might not answer. Then, he shrugs. "What I always do. Sell historical items. Set people on the correct path. Play my part."

"That's not a real answer."

"It's the one you're getting." He steps closer. "You always want clear answers, Adam. You must accept something: truth is rarely clean. It doesn't come tied up with a bow. It's messy. It always will be."

He is frustrating. "I don't understand. Why wouldn't you even tell me who you were? Why the theatrics?"

Silanus smirks. He seems amused. "Ah-ha, there you go again, wanting simple answers. Do you mean my name, Silanus? That's an epithet the Archon knew me as. It's not my real name, of course."

Before I press him further, he steps back. He gives that same strange slow wave that he did in Merv. Then, the air ripples around him. In an instant, he vanishes. I stand frozen, staring at the empty space. The anchor is still heavy in my grip. Dried blood clings to its surface, a painful reminder of the blood that was shed here. I can't shake my doubts. How much truth did Silanus, or whoever he is, speak? He's gone now, and I'll never know. If he lied about the time lock, all this was for nothing.

Xia and I arrive in Greece, returning to the same hotel room where we stayed after she was shot. The creaking floors bring back memories of Clara carefully laying out the suturing kit. It's Xia who now meticulously checks over her gear, organizing each item. Meanwhile, I sit on the edge of a battered wooden table, my fingers tracing the grooves etched into the Archon's anchor. This anchor is the key to our final stand.

Xia finally stops working. Neither of us is in the mood for small talk. It would feel hollow. The raw ache of Clara's absence wraps around us, forming a bond stronger than words. There's no need for explanation; we both know what's at stake.

I swallow back my fear. This is it—no more delays.

"I'll find my way into the Sanctum's construction site in 455 BCE," Xia says. "There are always workers, suppliers, and overseers coming and going. I'll figure out how to get on a work crew. The tools you need will be waiting in the tunnel, and the spot where you need to break through the wall will be marked."

My thumb traces the edges of the anchor. "When they build the ceremonial chamber, they'll line it with braziers. One will sit at the northwest side of the room, in front of a mural depicting time as a river. Connect a tunnel from that brazier to the lock's chamber," I say.

Xia says, "I will. Then, I'll plant enough explosives in the walls to bring the entire Sanctum down."

Splitting up now, despite its necessity, creates an ache. All the doubts and potential problems flood my awareness. The Phylax could catch her. One of us might miscalculate the timing. Perhaps the lock cannot be opened at all. I disregard those fears as best I can. This is the path. We both have a role, and now it's time to play.

When the lock resets, the entire timeline between 455 BCE and 2051 CE experiences one shared, overlapping window—ten minutes, everywhere, all at once. Imagine stepping outside of time and starting a stopwatch. At that moment, those outside the timeline observe ten minutes ticking away. For those inside, it begins at zero across the twenty-five centuries during which the lock has been active. Every instance between 455 BCE and 2051 CE initiates the same ten-minute countdown. This means these ten minutes unfold across all those years.

Somehow, it's both ten minutes and twenty-five hundred years. A moment and an eternity. It's an impossible paradox created by this ungodly machine.

I say, "You must be there to detonate the

explosives when the lock is down. When it happens, set a short fuse and run before the fire finds you."

Xia says, "Meanwhile, you're planning to hand yourself over? Let them think you've surrendered?"

"I have to. With my hands up, I'll demand to speak with the new Archon. After that, I'll do what needs to be done."

Her voice is strained. "What if they kill you on sight? End it right there?"

"They'll want to hear me grovel first." I force a smile. "It'll buy me enough time to reach the brazier. From there, I can race to the lock before they realize what's happening."

I imagine walking into the Sanctum unarmed. I tighten at the vision of their scrutiny. Of their laughter as they strip away the little dignity I have left. What if I'm wrong? They may choose to kill me before I get close enough to the brazier.

Xia studies me, unable to hide her worry. "This is risky, Adam. Even for you."

My lips tighten into a thin smile. "They've already taken everything from me. If I die there, so be it. At least we tried."

Xia inhales deeply, her eyes shining with unshed tears. "For Clara," she says, her voice cracking. She steps forward, pulling me into a hug.

I wrap my arms around her. "For Clara," I

echo. My voice chokes with sadness.

We cling to each other. Her heartbeat matches mine, steadying me. We hold on, grasping at that last unbroken bond—an unspoken promise to see this through. Even at the ultimate cost.

When we break apart, Xia continues to pack the gear we gathered earlier. Tools go into one bag, and she fills a second with enough explosives to flatten a town. After Xia places the detonator into the duffle, she freezes. Her fingers linger over the strap, trembling before she pulls her hand away. Her shoulders slump, as if the bag carries more than just weight. She inhales sharply, straightens, and zips the bag closed defiantly.

I watch her, memorizing the determination on her face, knowing it could be the last time I see her. A small photo tucked into her pack slips loose as she reaches for her gear. She crouches to pick it up. I glimpse Clara's familiar grin in the picture. Xia runs her thumb over the edge of the photo before slipping it back into the pocket.

"I'll find you in the next timeline," she says behind a hollow smile.

"We'll finish this," I reply. If we succeed, we'll reunite at the top of the Acropolis in 2136.

I know that Xia, in her mind's eye, concentrates on an era before the Sanctum existed. When she finds it, a surge of energy flares. She's gone, leaving the shimmer of displaced air.

The emptiness she leaves behind feels vast. I stare at the empty room. I try to imagine Xia alone in the tunnel, chiseling through rock while Phylax soldiers patrol above her. If they suspect anything, they will not hesitate to kill her. Unfortunately, there's no other way. She will dig while I walk straight into the lion's den.

I take the Dalek from my pocket, turning it over in my palm; its worn edges remind me of Clara and the family I should have. My thumb brushes the arm socket, feeling the tiny piece of metal lodged inside. I tug at it again. It doesn't budge. I remember the missing arms moving around. This metal piece doesn't.

Sliding the Dalek back into my pocket alongside the anchor, I feel a little happier about what I must do next. It's like carrying a piece of Clara with me, a way to ensure she sees our mission through to the end.

I glance around the safehouse one last time. Sunlight streams through the worn curtains, casting a warm glow over the walls. I step outside into the blinding light. The world may not know about the Sigma Event, but its fate depends on us stopping it. With Clara in my heart, the future isn't waiting. It's mine to re-write.

THIRTY-ONE

The heavy metal doors of the Sanctum groan open as two Phylax guards march me inside, my hands raised in a show of compliance. The columns towering over me are meaningless props, supporting a ceiling cluttered with mosaics exalting the Phylax's delusions of grandeur.

One guard steps forward, signing to a figure half-concealed in the shadows near the dais. *We found him attempting to breach the outer defenses. He claims to be a former Phylax and demands an audience with the Archon.*

A hush ripples through the gathered officials. The figure steps out of the shadows. I am taken aback. Of course, it's him. He hasn't aged a day— sharp eyes, an unyielding stance, and a smirk I'd recognize anywhere.

"Philip?" I ask, even though the answer is evident. Time seems to have bent itself around him.

He descends the steps with an air of leisure. Robes trail behind him in a theatrical wave. "Adam," he purrs, his voice laced with amusement. "You've certainly gone to great lengths to get here, lad."

Lad. I want to spit on him. "I need to speak with the Archon."

Philip's soft chuckle rings out. "Ah, that's the twist, you see." He gestures to himself, a lazy sweep of the arm. "I am the Archon now. I believe you had a hand in that. Killing my predecessor left his seat open."

He motions for me to follow him into the central ceremonial room. He calls out behind him, "Guards, leave us be. Adam and I must discuss his future."

Satisfaction dances in his expression. "So you finally abandoned your silence," he observes, his tone shifting to something more personal. "The vow was never meant to last forever. Breaking it is how you find your true power, your voice. Silence is a cage, Adam, not your strength. However, let me warn you—whoever led you here is playing their own game. Someone sent you on a fool's errand."

His lies fuel my fury. The audacity of this man who has twisted my life. I see he will always deal in deception.

I can't rush him here. Not yet. He commands an army of guards. I'm not ready to die before my mission is complete.

"How dare you suggest someone else is manipulating me," I shout, my voice aching.

"Every part of the Phylax is a lie. Every word, every lesson—it's all designed to control us. We fought, believing we were saving humanity when we were chaining everyone to the Phylax's tyranny."

My pulse thunders in my temples. Clara's death, the manipulations of my past, the branding, even the Temptation—everything has led me here. Philip, who once represented all I believed was good, stands now as the embodiment of all that's wrong. He hasn't aged, but I have. I've suffered, and I've grown.

"I'm telling you the truth, lad," he insists. "Someone with great power altered your mission at Qin's camp. They wanted you to take the path that led you right here, right now. You're too angry to see it."

My voice is steadier now, though fire rages behind it. "More lies. I can't trust a single word you say. You and I are not alike. I don't want this life. I want to choose my path. I'm more than what you've made me."

Philip's calm façade wavers when his jaw tightens. He's not used to being defied. My challenge surprises him.

"You're quite right," he responds, "You aren't the same as your mentor at all." He takes a step forward, his gaze drilling into mine. "Your grasp of time makes you even more capable than I am. You are formidable—a force the Phylax cannot afford to lose.

"Do you think we want control for its own sake? We've been saving humanity. We guide it. Without us, there would be chaos." His tone softens into something paternal. "You have a place high up in the Phylax, lad. A place beside me where real power lies, where we make decisions that shape history. All you have to do is accept it."

He lowers his voice. "You might think us deceptive. Sometimes we need to be. There are people out there who are far worse than we are. Without us, an unseen enemy will claim countless lives. You've seen what happens in an untamed world. Join me. You won't be just another Phylax operative. You'll sit with us, here in the Sanctum, forging history."

Stepping closer, he tries to bridge the gap by sheer presence. His voice carries that old, persuasive rhythm that used to quell my doubts. "You have proven your worth," he says softly. "You have overcome your past, fears, and even your silence." A gleam catches in his eye. Whether it's admiration or calculation, I can't tell. "Now, join me."

The offer hangs there, a promise laced with command, as though he expects the pull of power to lure me in, as it has so many others.

Years of loyalty, discipline, and sacrifice unravel in a violent recoil, the release of a spring held too long in tension. I recall the countless instances when I endured hardship, confident that every act served a noble purpose. The Phylax vow was at my core. It defined who I was, supposedly setting me apart as a protector of time. It had once given me a sense of purpose.

Now, rage boils. I fight the urge to strike. Xia is out there, far in the past, waiting for me to disengage the time lock, allowing her to complete her part of the mission. Timing is everything—she has carved out a hidden passage under the northwest brazier in 455 BCE, ensuring it will remain undetected for centuries. We planned this carefully, trusting each other across the gulf of time.

Forcing myself to move slowly, I edge toward the northwest side of the circular hall. I glance at the green marble beneath me, savoring the thought that it hides a newly created secret —one astonishingly concealed for over twenty-five hundred years. To my side, I see the mural we used as our reference point—an elaborate depiction of time as a river.

My only weapon is patience. I can't afford to waste it, not with so much depending on me. If Xia has done her part, I need to do mine. The fall of the Phylax depends on us both.

Philip steps closer, his voice echoing in the vast Sanctum. "You've already felt how time bends and obeys you. Only a handful have such power. You've learned to move within it. With more practice, you will be able to master and shape it. Even fewer can do that. Time has made you stronger than I ever imagined. With that strength, we could do more than wander through history," he says pointedly. "We can control it."

He gestures around the grand hall, inviting the ancient stones to witness his words. "Together, we can bend all of history to our will. Think about it, Adam. We've always existed to protect time, to protect humanity from itself. We can stop the disasters you've seen before they ever begin."

I step back from him, moving toward the secret brazier.

I run my hand over the branding scar; the skin never fully healed. The memory of the device buried beneath it burns in the background. "The Phylax have always sought to dominate, seizing power wherever they find an opportunity," I say. "Those missions they sent me on were about eliminating threats to their control. Even worse, the Phylax kills anyone they can't recruit. Anyone able to time travel on their own."

I pause, anger sparking again as I recall Clara's death. Her blood is on their hands. It's the second time they've taken my family.

I turn my back on him, taking another step. I see the slightest gap in the stone at the corner of the brazier's base. This is it—I'm sure of it.

Philip's mood darkens. He lets out a resigned sigh. "I'm disappointed, lad," he says. "I can't say I'm surprised. You've always been difficult. Even after everything I've done for you, all the chances I've given, you can't see the bigger picture."

I can't stand listening to his patter.

"I hoped you'd rise above your anger. If you won't join us, you leave me no choice." Philip calls to the guards at the entrance. "Guards, ki—"

Before he finishes, I cut in. "Did you ever care for me, Philip?" The words escape before I can stop them. My voice is steady, threaded with something I'm unsure I want to admit.

A flash of regret crosses Philip, but it is instantly gone. "Maybe once," he says. "That time has long since passed." He takes a step closer. "What now, lad? Because I don't love you like a son, you think you can kill me? You think this ends with a simple act of violence?"

"Not a simple act, no."

Before he can react, I slam my fist into his throat. My movement is sudden and fierce. He staggers, gasping, hands raised to protect his neck. That moment is all I need.

I lunge for the brazier, shoving it with all my strength. This reveals the passage beneath. I drop into the hidden tunnel without reservation.

Behind me, Philip tries to shout for his guards. His voice is hoarse.

If everything moving forward goes smoothly, I might pull this off. However, after only a few steps, the oppressive darkness becomes disorienting. Panic scratches at my soul. Without light, I'll never make it through.

I look back at the entrance, where a faint beam spills in. There, on the ground, a gift from the past is waiting. Xia left a torch and a box of matches. Of course, she knew how dark this passage was.

I strike a match and light the torch. Flame flares to life, washing the ancient stone walls in a flickering orange hue. Though I can't see far, it's enough.

I press on; there is no room for doubt. I have prepared for this.

Before long, I reach the tunnel's end. My hand runs along the stone wall. I spot the painted X. An old sledgehammer is leaning against the wall beneath it, exactly where Xia said it would be.

I set the torch aside and grip the sledgehammer, swinging with all my strength. The impact reverberates through the corridor. The thin wall crumbles faster than expected. Before long, it gives way, revealing the chamber beyond. Sledgehammer in hand, I push through the debris.

The time lock stands at the center of the room, exactly as I remember it from the anomaly. The sight halts me. It's a marvel—ancient and impossibly advanced at once. The massive device rests on a raised platform, glowing with blues and gold. Lines of shimmering energy pulse through it as though it's alive. I can practically feel time itself concentrated here, pouring from the device in relentless waves.

This machine is the key to the Phylax's hold. As long as it runs, it anchors itself to a single historical point—a day in 455 BCE. Everything within these walls resets back to that date, repairing even the hole I smashed as if my entry never happened.

Beyond that, every event the Phylax deemed critical—every assassination, every manipulation—feeds into the time lock, culminating in the Sigma Event. The scale of their deception is terrifying.

I study the lock's exterior, scanning for the tiny pinhole where I need to insert the anchor. My fingers graze a minuscule indentation near the base where the merchant said it would be. A chill races down my spine. This is it. Carefully, I take the Archon's anchor out of my pocket. The Dalek comes out with it and falls to the ground.

With a measured breath, I slide the anchor into the slot. I wait. Nothing happens.

Still nothing.

My frustration slips out as I slam my hand against the time lock. The metallic surface reverberates with a clang. I pause, trying to piece together what might be wrong.

While I think, my hand instinctively moves for the Dalek on the ground. Before my fingers can close around it, agony erupts in my shoulder. The pain sears through, forcing the sledgehammer to slip from my grasp. It crashes to the floor with a resounding thud.

Biting back a howl, I spin around. My vision swims. There he is again. Philip stands at the entrance with a smirk plastered across his face. He glints with satisfaction as he surveys my struggle.

With a grunt, I reach behind me, yanking the knife from my back, fire igniting through every nerve.

Philip chuckles. "I always said we should keep guns in here before installing the time lock. If they had listened, this would already be over. Tradition and grandeur first, I suppose." He gestures at the room with mock reverence. "I wanted to be practical."

He circles the chamber, his voice dripping with amusement. "I wonder," he says, "what did you put in the time lock just now? We took your anchor after your sister buried it."

"It's the Archon's," I tell him. There is no reason to lie about it.

"That's impossible," Philip scoffs. "When an Archon is crowned, the anchor is removed. It's part of the ceremony." He clears his throat.

"That's not true. Silanus took it from the former Archon. He gave it to me."

"As you can see, whatever he gave you isn't an anchor." Philip laughs.

I look at the unopened time lock and

must agree. The merchant's deception does not surprise me, although I am unsure what to do next.

Philip's smirk fades into bitterness. "Silanus, or Lei, or whatever name he goes by now, is a traitor. He stole a talisman from the Archon. It is a sacred item. The Archon discovered his treachery and immediately ordered his execution.

"Silanus was always clever. When he heard the Archon wanted his head, Silanus used an anomaly created by the Convergence of Dominion to slip away. We haven't been able to find him since, though I have heard rumblings about his involvement with the Dahr-khoday."

I have many questions about Silanus, but they are less important than my mission.

"Anyway, even if you could smash the lock with that sledgehammer, it'll shut down, then reset itself. A few minutes later, everything will be back to normal. You can't win."

Philip circles closer, his confidence evident in each step. The knife in my hand is slick with my blood. I didn't want it to end like this.

But it must.

I rush forward, driving the knife toward Philip's chest. He grabs my wrist at the last second, brutally twisting. Agony shoots through my arm. I stagger but don't fall. We lock into a savage struggle.

"Adam, don't be an idiot!" Philip growls,

twisting harder to disarm me. "We could've done great things together!"

"Great things?" I manage, wrenching my arm free. "Do you mean kidnapping more children or controlling the world? You never cared about anyone except yourself!"

We clash again—fists, blades, bodies colliding. A flash of memories sting: Philip teaching me how to survive, showing me the ropes of time travel, our grueling training sessions together. Even times of relaxation were survival training—fishing, hunting, and late nights playing cards. In those moments, I pretended he was the father I never had. Even on our trips to Athens and Egypt, I imagined us as a family. I really do wish this could have ended differently. I want him to be the man I once thought he was.

Fury surging, I slam Philip backward with all my strength. He falls against the wall. I spot my opening. I swing the knife low, slicing across his side. He contorts away with pain.

"You've lost, Adam!" Philip hisses, blood seeping from the wound. He staggers forward. His movements are slower now. I see the fear beginning to rise in him.

"No," I say, stepping toward him. "I've been lost my whole life. Now I know where I am going."

I launch myself at him again, going all in. We grapple, smashing into the ancient walls, debris raining around us. Finally, I drive my elbow into his jaw with everything I have, sending him sprawling.

He stumbles, stepping on the Dalek and cracking it open. Yet another piece of my childhood ruined by this man. I must finish my mission. I spin, delivering a fierce kick. The impact knocks him off balance. He teeters, then tumbles onto a low-hanging piece of the time lock.

When his body collides with a glowing branch of the time lock, the machine crackles with violent energy. I step back, breathless, watching as the man who once guided me lies unconscious on the device he sought to protect.

I'm frozen, unsure what to do next. Desperation tightens around me. My eyes dart around, searching for answers. With nothing else to cling to, I crouch down. My hands tremble as I sift through the shattered remains of the Dalek. My fingers pause when I spot something metallic amid the bits of plastic. I pick it up to take a closer look. It's a sliver of metal, unmistakably the piece lodged in the hole where the missing arm once was. The grooves along its edge, the weight in my palm—it's an anchor. Is it possible that my mother left this because she knew I would need an anchor?

Clutching the metal piece, I step toward the time lock. I remove the fake anchor and guide this one into the pinhole. Again, nothing happens. Perhaps I was wrong to hope.

Then the lock hums to life. Ancient gears grind as hidden panels shift, revealing the glowing core within. I exhale. The heaviness of the moment lifts.

Enough is enough.

I grab the hammer and heft it high over my head. My muscles tremble with the effort. As I stare down at Philip, a torrent of emotion floods me: anger, betrayal, and even regret. I cared for this man once, far more than I should have. None of that matters anymore. The Phylax must end. I must break the chains that have kept me bound to the Phylax. I will end their manipulation—the force that turned my life into a lie.

The hammer reaches its apex. Time seems to stretch itself thin. With a single, decisive swing, I bring the sledgehammer crashing down.

It lands dead center on the time lock's glowing core. There's a crack, followed by a blinding surge of darkness. An impossible void ripples out from the machine, swallowing the light in the chamber. I feel the air shift like time is knocked off its axis.

A sound follows—a low, erratic ticking that reverberates throughout the Sanctum. It gradually slows, each echo lingering in the silence. The pitch sinks lower, filling the room with a somber bell tolling doom. The final tick fades, leaving a deep, suffocating stillness in its wake.

Oh shit.

I bolt toward the front entrance, pushing my legs harder than ever. A deep rumble from within the Sanctum vibrates through the walls, urging me to run faster. As I burst through the doors, guards sprint for their lives. They sense that something horrible is coming.

I want to jump through time to vanish from this chaos. I cannot. Even if I could travel here, this destruction extends beyond the present, reverberating across every epoch of the Sanctum. My only hope is to outrun it.

Panting, I race down the path leading away. Behind me, ancient stone walls crumble, the air quaking with the roar of collapse. A quick look over my shoulder reveals an eerie gloom spiraling from the time lock, twisting everything in its wake.

I burst through the doors, my lungs burning as I gulp in the cool air. The rumble of impending destruction pushes me forward. Without thinking, I scramble to the cliff edge. Heart pounding, I begin scaling down the jagged rock. My hands grip tightly while loose stones slip beneath my feet.

I manage to descend a few feet when the explosion erupts behind me, a deafening roar that shakes the ground. The force of the blast sends a wave of heat and debris shooting outward. I press myself against the rocks, clinging for dear life. Fragments rain down. The aftershock trembles through the cliff in a pulse of fury. I shield my head with one arm while the other keeps me anchored to the rock.

When the chaos finally subsides, the silence is more peaceful than I have ever experienced. My limbs tremble, my body aching from the strain. I hope that Xia found her way out as well.

Summoning the last of my strength, I finish descending to safer ground. Exhaustion washes over me in waves, threatening to pull me under.

As I collapse against the cool earth, Clara's face rises in my awareness. Her smile, her unshakable belief in me, and every step I've taken feels like it was a part of hers, too.

"This is for you, Clara," I whisper. My body aches, my mind reels with grief, but something feels lighter. The Phylax had confiscated so much from me, except they couldn't take this. They didn't take my choice. For the first time, the path ahead feels like my own. With that thought, the familiar sensation of slipping through time takes hold. Everything fades away.

THIRTY-TWO

The year is 2136. Xia and I sit on a bench overlooking the sweeping skyline of Athens. Skyscrapers shimmer in the evening sun. Neatly trimmed trees line the streets far below. It is a beautiful contrast to the world we explored after the Sigma Event.

As the sun sets, a warm glow lights up the horizon. Birds chirp softly over the hum of distant traffic. It's peaceful, almost dreamlike. I lean back, resting my arms on the bench, gazing at the golden skyline. Xia, beside me, takes in the relatively untouched beauty of the Acropolis. It is filled with tourists. We're both silent, letting the serenity of this future sink in.

"It really is something," Xia says, a hint of wonder in her voice. "Incredible."

I nod, a smile curling my lips. "Spectacular," I agree. A group of children walk by, laughing.

I think about the 2020s, which is much more straightforward than this polished era. The future has its marvels, but there's a raw, authentic quality to our own time that I miss.

Xia sighs, elbows on her knees. "Honestly, I've always enjoyed the '80s best. Before everything went digital yet advanced enough to feel modern." She smiles softly. "The comforts of this age are pretty nice, though."

I chuckle. "True," My fingers graze my chin. "It's good to know this place exists—that we made it possible." My smile fades, replaced by the familiar ache of missing Clara.

Despite the noise, we are content in each other's presence. Eventually, Xia speaks again with solemnity. "We should get together again soon. You know, to celebrate Clara's life. Properly honor her this time."

"Yes. It is long overdue." Memories of my sister surface—the sound of her laughter, the determination in her eyes, the sacrifices she made. My lips curl into a bittersweet smile.

Xia rests a hand on my shoulder, giving it a light squeeze. "She'd be proud of what we've done," she says with quiet conviction.

I draw a shaky breath, letting all we've accomplished settle in. "We couldn't have done it without each other," I reply. "Clara believed in this future. In us."

We start walking away from the bench. I pause, an idea already forming. "There's something I need to do."

Xia asks, "What's that?"

"I'm going to look for my mother," I say. "Clara asked me to, and I intend to keep that promise. She believed our mother is out there somewhere. I'm going to find out."

"I see," she murmurs.

"I'd appreciate your help. You've been with me through all of this."

She sighs. "Adam, as much as I'd want to help, it doesn't make sense for me to go."

My brow furrows. "What do you mean?"

She turns to me. "I was only on this mission because of Clara," she admits. "Now that we've done what we set out to do, I need to find my own way."

I lower my gaze. "I understand," I mutter. Xia's right; I can't expect her to follow me. She has a life to live.

We continue walking. The world is filled with new possibilities. However, before I can move on, I drift back to something that happened at the Sanctum. "Philip mentioned that the Archon doesn't have an anchor," I say. "The one that the merchant gave us didn't work."

Xia replies, "That doesn't surprise me. Lei never seemed trustworthy. How did you get the lock to open?"

"There was an anchor in the Dalek that Clara gave me," I say. "I think my mother put it there."

Xia considers this. "That's odd. How did she know?"

"I have no idea," I admit. Even though we have destroyed the Phylax, many unanswered questions remain. "If she's out there, hopefully, she can explain."

Xia is distant. "Maybe she can."

"Maybe," I echo. I consider mentioning some of Philip's other comments but decide this is a conversation for another time. "Are you sure you won't come with me?"

A sad smile touches her lips. "Our journeys are separate now. I have to figure out my own stuff. Besides, you've got this."

"Everything we've encountered, I couldn't have done it without you," I say. "You kept me grounded."

Xia smiles. "You gave me a purpose when I felt lost. Clara believed in us. I'm glad we proved her right."

She steps back, her hand resting briefly on my shoulder. "Maybe this is how it was meant to be," she says. "We've made it through so much, Adam. Now it's time for each of us to figure out what comes next."

I force a smile. "Thank you, Xia. For everything."

Her smile widens, full of impossible warmth. "Stay safe, Adam. Find her."

The city swirls around us like a distant chorus. Then, just before she slips away, I realize the name she uttered. The merchant's name: Lei. A chill travels the length of my spine. There's no way she should know that name. I never told her. I only heard that through Philip. Yet she spoke it with such familiarity. How can she possibly know?

"Xia, wait!" I shout. My voice vanishes into the currents of time. She's already gone, disappearing as mysteriously as she first appeared. She leaves behind the same uncanny unease that followed her arrival.

I am grateful for everything she has done for me. I feel a pang of loss at her departure. Now, I also have this unsettling concern. Somehow, I know we'll cross paths again. I will ask how she learned the merchant's name when we do.

I won't linger on that mystery today. My new mission is more urgent.

I face the horizon, the future spreading out before me. Clara believed in the impossible. She believed in me. With every step forward, a piece of her is with me. If I'm going to save our mother, I'll need Clara's strength.

"I will find you, mother," I whisper, letting the wind carry my vow.

PLEASE REVIEW

Thank you for reading! Reviews are an author's lifeblood. If you enjoyed The Silent Guardian, please consider leaving an honest review on Amazon. Even a line or two helps immensely! Click here to leave a review.

ACKNOWLEDGEME NT

Writing The Silent Guardian has been an incredible journey, one made possible by the unwavering support and belief of many individuals who stood beside me from the very beginning. First and foremost, I want to express my deepest gratitude to my wife, Kim, and the boys, Isaak and Caleb, who inspired me to explore every wild idea and gave me the confidence to chase those ideas onto the page. I also owe immense thanks to the friends and fellow writers who read early drafts, offered thoughtful critiques, and cheered me on through every revision. Your keen eyes, honest feedback, and boundless enthusiasm fueled my motivation at each stage of writing. You all helped shape The Silent Guardian into the story it was meant to be, and I'll forever be grateful for the generosity you showed me along the way.

ABOUT THE AUTHOR

Dylan Callens

Dylan has always been fascinated by the intersection of science fiction, philosophy, and storytelling. As a lifelong lover of speculative fiction, he enjoys exploring themes of time, destiny, and the human condition in gripping, action-packed narratives.

When not writing, Dylan can be found reading classic sci-fi, pondering time travel paradoxes, drinking way too much coffee, or researching obscure historical events.

The Silent Guardian is his first attempt at writing a complete time-traveling series, with more books on the way. If you'd like exclusive content, behind-the-scenes looks, or updates on upcoming releases, visit https://silentguardianbooks.com

Find me on social media:

Instagram: silentguardianbooks
Facebook: silentguardianbooks
X: @Dylan_Callens